The Mysterious DANCE of VINTAGE FOLLIES

HEMA SAVITHRI

Book Cover Painting: *Diwiya Dhillan*
Editor: *Tanmay Dubey*

Title : The Mysterious Dance of Vintage Follies
Author : Hema Savithri
Copyright © Hema Savithri 2022
All rights reserved

First published in 2021
Second Edition 2022

'This is a story so heartwarming and deep, a story spun with wondrous threads of ideas and words.'

—*Nikhil Prasanna Jayan, IRS (IT)*
Deputy Commissioner,
New Delhi.

~ ~ ~

'This is one of those books that is rooted in realism and deserves to be read.'

—*Harsha Pareek*
A Delhi based journalist,
Currently working with NDTV convergence

~ ~ ~

'A pulsating work of fiction with commendable characters written in a bold way.'

—*Naufa Yahiya*
Author of "Risen from her Ashes"
(Best-selling local Author by the Times of India
for "The Unmarried Widow" (2019)

~ ~ ~

'A pivotal theme constructed in an aesthetic backdrop of the iconic native art. The emotions of the tale alongside a rustic, Malayalam fragrance, lingers after the read.'

—*Anirudh Sreenath*
Author of the Book "Death to Womb", Blogger

~ ~ ~

'Myths, traditions, taboos, and customs that seep into the lives of ordinary people in a seemingly harmless way in a sleepy town in Kerala is penned masterfully by Hema Savithri in her book, The Mysterious Dance of Vintage Follies, until it explodes into pain and persecution of many nameless, faceless and powerless individuals.'

—*Feby Imthias*
Author of Children of the Sun, Sand and Seas

For Saju and Sri Dathan
two glorious companions in whom
every story begins and ends…

Contents

PART THREE

Acknowledgements

My profound thanks to all those who extended help and support throughout this fabulous journey:

Theyyam artist Vinu Panicker, Mulavannur, Kanhangad, Kasargod for opening the doors to Theyyam, the unique, splendid, and vibrant ritual form of dance worship of northern Kerala. Having taken initiation at an early age of five, Vinu Panicker led me through the enchanting world of mythological stories of gods, goddesses, heroes, and demons, the power of hypnotic chants, and rhythmic drumbeats, and the spectacular fire rituals. I am grateful to him for sharing his experiences and knowledge that helped me to write this
novel.

Abhinand C.K., Sanskrit teacher, S.R.S.S.V.M., Nellithara, Kanhangad, Kasargod, for sharing his invaluable knowledge and expertise in folklore. He was granted a Diamond Jubilee Fellowship from the Department of Cultural Affairs, Government of Kerala for the folk art Poorakkali & Maruthukali. I am thankful to him for helping me with the minutest detail of the art form and for clarifying my doubts with utmost patience. The precision and accuracy with which he replied are highly appreciable.

Vijayan T.V., Physical Education Teacher, Nallanam GHS, Kozhikode for introducing me to Vinu Panicker and for sharing his knowledge in Theyyam.

Author Tanmay Dubey, my book writing coach and

editor for instilling in me the courage and self-confidence to craft this dream book. Immense gratitude to him for being a great mentor, counselor, and guide throughout the journey and for helping me steer clear of all self-doubt. The most appreciable part is that he never edited the freedom of my thoughts but made me think from different perspectives.

Dr. Candace Jessin Graceta, Assistant Professor in English, for being my first reader. I thank her for her willingness to read my work and for her words of encouragement.

Dr. Josepheena John, Assistant Professor, poet and writer for her immense support, encouragement and love.

My love to my artist friend Divya Dhillan for her willingness and enthusiasm to paint this brilliant piece of artwork for the book cover.

Profound thanks to my publisher The Great Indian Book Tour.

In numerous ways to my brothers Rajiv Sharma, Sreejith Viswam and my cousin Adarsh T R for their invaluable support.

Heartfelt thanks to all my friends, students and family members who stood by me throughout my journey. I extend my deep appreciation to all those who believed in me. Special thanks to all my readers without whom this journey towards the second edition of my book would've been impossible.

My sincere gratitude to all my bookstagrammer friends who supported me and still support me throughout this journey.

My journey would have been incomplete without the love and support of my bookstagrammer friends Ishwinder Sialy, IT Head at Alexarya Group, Ankita Narayan and Dhanu K.V., Research Analyst. No words are sufficient to thank them. I thank each one of you for being special in your own way, for coming out of your way to support me.

PART ONE

*"Naankale Kothiyalum Choralle Chovvare-
Neenkale Kothiyalum Choralle Chovvare..."*

*"It is blood –red blood that flows out of you and
me when cutting open! And this blood is the same
in colour- isn't it master?"*

—Theyyam Folklore

CHAPTER 1

Kesu

12*th* April, 6:30 p.m.

Streaks of orange and the red lines of the evening sky dolefully watched the birds fly to their homes. Indolence painted the little non-decrepit village with a light grey. The mid-April sweltering sun had snatched the green from the fields and trees, leaving them parched. It seemed that every year, they withstood the fiery rage with a solemn endurance. It was twilight, the dreadful and mystical hour of the day. The tired trees stood with their heads drooped down in silent prayer.

I was walking past the dry, empty fields when I saw a commotion of bats hovering above the huge banyan tree. As I neared the tree, I felt I saw a coiled heap lay bundled in the barren field beside the main road. I moved a few steps forward and saw a woman lying in a pool of blood under the banyan tree. I stood there transfixed and in a state of indecisiveness. Suddenly, I heard a few angst-filled voices approaching from the narrow road. I listened. They moved closer, and they spoke about an accident. I did not wait. I darted through the fields. I disappeared.

You have never seen me. I am sure, and you will never see me. I see everyone, though. I am that invisible 'everyman' in every village and small town. I do not have a particular name. You can call me Kesu.

On some days, I am Kesu, the performer. I metamorphose into a deity on special days. I am a Theyyam performer. Do you know what Theyyam is? It is a form of ritual dance worship in northern Kerala. I am a proud inheritor of several thousand-year-old traditions. This art form is the only wealth I have inherited from my ancestors. When I perform, people call me koladari, the performer. Theyyam is a channel to god and people seek blessings from the performer. It is a seasonal dance performance and we have several performances from January to April. They are the peak seasons. There were times when I performed in several shrines in a year. The ceremonies might continue for days. As I grew older, I restricted the performance to my village. Upon insistence, I perform in the nearby villages.

On all the other days, when I do not have a performance, I work as a gardener in Saket school the only English medium school in our village, Kavampuzha. I am also a painter and sometimes a driver. On some other days, you can see me perched high on coconut trees and palm trees. I am not a clawed animal. I am not maricha, the shape-shifting demon. I am made of flesh and blood like everyone else. Unlike you, I do not see; I do not speak; I do not hear. I am the carcass of the living. I am an outcast. Fate elevates me to the rank of a god and then drops me down to live as the lowest, meanest being on the earth. I dwell between this duality.

The day after tomorrow (14th April) is Vishu, the New Year Day of the people of Kerala. It falls on the Medam month. Mid-April or Medam is the ninth month in the Malayalam calendar. I like this festival for its solemnity and its general lack of pomp. I think every penniless beggar like me would.

Tonight, I will become the holy performer in the sacred grove Kakotikavu. I will be dressed up and decorated uniquely. I will then invoke the blessings of the god and dance like a god. The Chilambu, the oval-shaped brass anklets with tiny beads around my ankles, will jingle rhythmically to the unsung tunes of my heart.

The *kavu*, connects the lives of the villagers of Kavampuzha. *Kavu* means the grove and *puzha* means the river. A wall separates the river Sindoori and the *kavu*. The river and the land are never allowed to meet each other, but they are inseparable. They have been like this for centuries. Hence, the village acquired the name Kavampuzha. You need not touch and feel, you need not hug and kiss, but the silent existence is also a testimony of true love like the river and the land. When two giant forces meet, the inevitable happens. It happened one rainy season. Love exploded, it destroyed and annihilated a large area of the village. It wiped out trivial lives from the face of the earth forever. Therefore, they mend the wall every year. The wall that separates also saves.

~ ~ ~

7:30 p.m.

The crescent moon hung low in the clear starlit sky. Kesu sat on the glistening stone steps that overlooked the river Sindoori.

He watched the mighty *Sindoori* flow mellifluously. He could not believe that the same river swallowed his father Kolavan twenty summers back. He had entered it to purify himself and seek her blessings before he prepared to transform into the sacred goddess of the grove. He never returned.

When he was a little boy, it was always been bliss for Kesu to watch his father perform the roles of gods and goddesses in the sacred grove. His heart swelled with pride as that was the day when his father transformed into a deity. He watched his father dressed in an elaborate costume made from palm leaves. His dark kohled eyes that shot from his red-painted face transformed him into an unknown entity, but that granted him the power to bless those upper castes whose faces were otherwise marked with sneers and ridicule.

"*Acha*, (father) shall I watch them paint your face?" Kesu once asked his father.

Kolavan smiled and lifted his five-year-old on his shoulders as he walked back home from the river after the regular evening bath. The empty rice field after harvest glistened in the setting sun. Kolavan held the two little dangling legs that were still wet and replied,

"Why not, but you should not touch me after my bath. I will be holy. You can watch from a distance."

Golden rays sieved in through the swaying dark green leaves and disappeared with a playful smile as little Kesu tried to swallow some. Kesu gripped his father's head tight and shouted a loud "YES" that echoed back from the tall blue mountains that encapsulated the little village Kavampuzha.

~ ~ ~

"Kesu! Didn't you take a bath yet? The entire village is waiting there at the Kavu". It was the drummer Narayanan. His thunderous roar caught him off guard. Kesu stood up with a sigh and got down the ten remaining steps, took a dip in the river, and chanted a prayer his father had taught. He climbed up the steps as water dripped from the single *mundu*, the white, thin loincloth that covered the lower part of his body, revealing his sturdy deep chestnut knees and legs. His thin frame did not shudder as the cold wind slapped his almost aging body. Years of hard labour had toughened his arms and legs and it seemed that his chest could brave more pain and suffering.

~ ~ ~

7:30 p.m

Kakotikavu, the holy grove, was getting ready for god's arrival. A few villagers were seen gathered around the small sandy ring. Sreedhara Menon, the rice mill owner stood in the front row with his wife and youngest daughter, Ammu. The shadow of his tall, round frame absorbed the frail images of his wife Parukutty and daughter Ammu. A thick gold chain peeped from the golden brocaded shawl that covered his upper body and the golden brocaded *mundu* clasped his waist in crisp obedience.

He had contributed ten thousand rupees to the temple. The gold rings on the fair, right-hand fingers tapped rhythmically on the rings on his left. His five-year-old daughter Ammu tugged at his gold brocaded cream shawl. He angrily pushed her aside and warned her with a menacing shriek,

"Ammu!" and turned behind with the same fiery anger and looked at his wife Parukutty. Parukutty hurriedly hushed little Ammu with soft warning as the little girl hid behind her mother's tender, brocaded end of the *saree*. Parukutty's defiant and intense eyes stared at her husband before it mellowed down to seek apology from the people who stood nearby. **Sreedhara Menon always believed that he should enforce authority on his family.**

A few weeks back, when Sreedhara Menon was supervising the workers in his field, he saw a *Theyyam* pass by through his field. He stopped the group and chided them for trespass. The workers who witnessed this warned him of the possible wrath of the god. The fear of curse upset him. That evening he saw a snake in his garden. He dreamt that snakes crawled all over his huge body and he spit blood. Later, he narrated this dream to everyone. He also said that the goddess appeared in his dream and told him to contribute some money for the next *Theyyam*.

"Does money redeem you from all curses you incur for your wrongdoings?" Parukutty asked him.

"What do you know about these things? All you do is question anything and everything. Your place is in the kitchen and I don't want your opinion on such serious matters. If you wish, you come with me to the *kavu*, or else you remain at home with your daughter," Sreedhara Menon scoffed at his wife.

Parukutty's eyes blazed with resentment but she spoke nothing.

~ ~ ~

8 p.m.

Ravi, the *Theyyam* face-painting artist, was waiting for Kesu in the small, shed-like room behind the temple. The thatched roof weaved with coconut palm fronds sighed in the gentle breeze.

Art like writing is latent in the human mind. It cannot be taught to everyone and it cannot be learned by all. Art illuminates life and the intricate patterns of absurdity and completeness can be felt only by those who can see and feel with their inner eyes. A whole world of wonder and joy waits beyond art's intriguing windows.

Ravi had spent twenty-five years painting the faces of Theyyam performers. He learned the art of creating costumes and ornaments from his father and grandfather He took a two-day face painting class in the city twice a week. The relatively meager amount that was paid as fees did not deter him from pursuing his passion. Ravi could paint around 400 types of Theyyam faces that represented Hindu mythological characters.

He stood there tearing a piece of coconut leaf when his friend Mani bellowed from behind, "*Changai* (friend), when did you come from France?"

A sudden freezing gust of wind blew lifting each tiny strand of hair on Ravi's muscular frame.

Mani, '*pot-bellied Lilliputian*' as Ravi nicknamed him, was his friend and they studied together until class five in the same dilapidated Government school, which was the only school in the village. It was a Lower Primary school, and it taught only until class five. After which, the affluent would send their children to the English Medium schools in the town which was 20 Kilometers from the village.

The only private bus owned by Suresh Chandran was the only notable development that Kavampuzha witnessed over several decades. The people named the bus *Pratheeksha*, Hope. There was no hospital nearby and the people had to walk several kilometers before they could hire a jeep that was the only means of transport before the arrival of *Pratheeksha*. The first trip run by *Pratheeksha* was at 7:15 a.m. The office goers, students, and labourers dashed and squeezed into the small bus. Sometimes the sick and the expecting mothers held on to the bars with a prayer as the bus moved to leave behind the groves and fields.

Suresh Chandran was Sreedhara Menon's cousin. Suresh was a wealthy and influential person in the village as well as the town. The villagers looked upon him with great respect, as he was wise and knowledgeable. A winning smile glowed on his pale ivory face as he savoured their praise as coveted trophies.

Ravi's father was a farmer while Mani's father ran a small teashop in the village. When their parents felt that school and education were meaningless, they stopped sending them to school. Ravi and Mani learned the art of painting faces of *Theyyam* performers. They grew up together. Mani helped his father in the teashop on busy days. Ravi often felt that people thronged the teashop to sip politics and gossip rather than the watery liquid Mani's father sold.

As children, they learned to swim and climb trees. As they grew, they lunged into the wavy curves of the beautiful Sindoori and felt her warm embrace caress their skin. They plunged deeper and deeper until the water swallowed them and embraced them to her loving bosom.

They knew that there was no fear underwater. They felt her heave and sigh each time they dived into the river as they searched for pretty Oyster shells. On some moonlit nights, they joined their friends on the riverbank. They sat in a circle with a few earthen pots of fresh toddy and sipped through their joys, sorrows, and memories as they drank from the woven palm fronds. These simple pleasures wove in through their lives.

Ravi, forty-seven-year-old bachelor, tall, handsome who dazzled everyone with a friendly smile and moved gracefully like a leopard, sans family, sans relatives, always carried a hollow within, a sense of incompleteness. An earthly scent swirled around him and the villagers called him a hermit who devoted his life to serving his fellow humans. Ravi sometimes sat on the banks of the Sindoori and wondered at her youthful glow that reflected his greying, receding hairline in her shimmering mirror.

Ravi had visited the U.S, France, and Korea, but he always returned to his little village's lap.

"Ah, I came last week. Didn't see you anywhere," he replied.

"Heard some *madama* has come with you," Mani winked and chuckled with a burst of laughter that shook his huge, round tummy that protruded above his white *dhoti*. He was comfortable walking around the village without wearing a shirt like many other villagers. According to him a woman and a man can't just be friends. Mani stared at the green-eyed foreigner who casually brushed aside the strands of blonde hair that fell on her face. She was jotting down some terms and definitions about *Theyyam* in a small notebook. The cropped lace-trimmed floral print blouse and deep blue Denim jeans fitted well on her slender frame.

"Romance is the only factor that connects a male and a female. True friendship is impossible as sex always comes between men and women," Mani roared with laughter as he told Ravi.

Ravi smiled, as that was not the first time he heard such comments from his friend Mani and other villagers. He had met Evelyn, a research scholar in France where he went to conduct a workshop on *Theyyam*. *Madama* was the word used to refer to foreign women. He had learned the world's ways and tried to make more friends from different walks of life.

Evelyn, the elegant-looking 25-year-old French woman had come to India to do research work on the dying art form *Theyyam*. Her sea-green eyes, accentuated with both the eyelashes and makeup, captured every movement of the little village. Nothing was overpowering about her lips that looked natural and smooth with enough colour. A messy ponytail jived with enthusiastic zest as she walked. The element of carelessness in the dressing was the only thing that connected her to the rustic village of Kavampuzha.

Though Ravi insisted that he would find a good stay in the town, Evelyn disagreed. She wished to stay in the village and feel and know the village by living there, by experiencing it. Sreedhara Menon had a house in his backyard. It was fully furnished with a living and two bedrooms. There was sufficient light and air. The prospect of earning a considerable amount as rent from the foreigner made him take a quick decision. Even though she would be there only for two or three months, it meant a handsome earning for him compared to the money he would otherwise get from the local people in the town. He did not bother to sign a rental agreement that he usually was very particular about, as he knew he could trust her.

Evelyn asked Ravi about the *Theyyam* performance that Kesu would perform that night. Ravi narrated:

"Today, you will watch *Pottan Theyyam*. *Pottan* means idiot. In this *Theyyam*, the *koladari* (performer) portrays godliness with a weird, funny, and intense playfulness. According to the legends, *Pottan Daivam* is the manifestation of Lord Shiva. The performer performs unplanned playfulness and entertainment. This should not be misunderstood as a comic act since it in a way imparts the idea of secularism and justice to the downtrodden.

Unlike the other temples, people worship the Scythe here. It denotes the harvest season and weapon of Lord Shiva," Evelyn's eyes widened in amusement.

Ravi continued, "The barks of the Chamba tree or tamarind tree are piled and burnt to make pyre. They are burned at night. By early morning, they would have burned into embers. They then separate it into two pyres: one with dying embers and the other flaring flames of fire. The *pottan Theyyam* would then sit on both the pyres -the dying embers as well as the rising flames.

During ancient times, the dagger of caste tore apart the land of Kerala. People belonging to the lower caste were never seen as human beings. They worked in the fields of the upper caste men and were paid very little. They should never see, never hear, and never speak against the injustice meted out to them. If ever they did, the upper caste would squeeze out their eyes from the socket, cut their ears, and chop off their tongue. As years passed by, the voices of dissent began to emerge from the silenced people. *Pottan Theyyam* is also a medium of communication of the caste system and injustice meted out to the downtrodden." Evelyn nodded her head as she listened and recorded his words in her digital voice recorder that accompanied her wherever she went. The black, mini, portable recorder faithfully captured voices and its eidetic memory retained every word of the conversation.

CHAPTER 2

The Fire Ritual

12th April, 8:30 p.m

Kesu walked in through the side gate of the *kavu* and the bells chimed from the temple. People stretched their heads to look at the goddess and held their palms together in prayer. Silence reigned at intermittent intervals with the sound of the bell or conch reminding them of the holy presence.

Older priests in a crisp white *lungi (South Indian sarong)* moved around busily. The drummers tested the rhythm and sound of their drums standing in a corner near the small temple. The goddess statue was decorated in red silk adorned with gold and silver chains, and stone studded earrings and nose rings. Her huge bright red *bindi* seemed to smile contentedly from the sanctum sanctorum. The smell of incense sticks and jasmine flowers filled the air with an unearthly aroma. A few raised their hands in prayer while a few others lay prostrate on the ground in absolute submission to the holy deity.

The crowd then moved to the adjacent tiled hut-like structure that held no deity but a Scythe. People prayed to the *Kathi* (scythe) and waited for Kesu. The ground was cleared and smeared with cow dung mixed with water.

Kesu entered the shed-like room that stood on the rear side of the temple. Water dripped down the single loincloth that covered the lower part of his body. He saw Ravi waiting there with a foreigner.

"Have you been waiting for long?" Kesu asked Ravi darting a sudden, curious eye at Evelyn as he squeezed out excess water that dripped down from his *mundu.*

"I reached here by 6:00 p.m. Meet Evelyn. She is from France. She is here to learn about *Theyyam,*" Ravi told Kesu.

Kesu brought his palms together as a sign of greeting and Evelyn reciprocated with, "Hello, nice meeting you."

Kesu's almond eyes expanded wide as he smiled in acknowledgement. That was not the first time Ravi was accompanied by a foreigner and Kesu understood what she said.

~ ~ ~

The *Pottan Daivam* did not require any elaborate painting on the face like the other *Theyyams.* The face was painted with primary colours and was decorated with coconut fronds. The naked upper part of the body was painted with diluted rice powder. The lower part was covered with red attire that was worn like a semi *dhothi.* The *dhothi* was then layered with tender coconut leaves that hung from the hip. The *Chilambu* jingled as he walked.

Ravi showed him a mirror, and Kesu looked at his image in it. "Tonight, I am *Pottan Daivam.*" He peered into the mirror and saw an unfamiliar image in it. He closed his eyes and returned the mirror. He was now the *koladari,* the performer. He had transformed into the divine God.

Kesu, dressed in strands of tender coconut leaves, moved towards the temple. The anklets jingled in a frantic rhythm as he walked. He bowed before the goddess as the people bowed to him because he was no more Kesu. He was the God Himself. He then walked towards the temple of the Scythe. He recited the legend of *"Pottan Daivam."* Primary and secondary colors on his face that contrasted with one another revealed Ravi's artistic skill. Kesu gradually metamorphosed into the deity. After the rituals were observed, the priests placed the headgear on his head.

Four drummers standing on the ground began to beat their drums and Kesu, the *koladari* circumambulated the temple of the Scythe and ran playfully. His feet danced to the rhythm of the drums as he murmured and recited a few godly lines. The pyre was getting ready. There were two pyres: one burnt embers and the other burning bright. The flames danced in rage.

The *Pottan Theyyam* began with the *Thottam,* (invocation) to the god. The people watched in awe and silence. It seemed that the trees and the sky watched the spectacular event with great respect.

The barks were still burning bright. It was almost midnight. Some people returned to their homes while the others stayed. Parukutty and her daughter went home while Sreedhara Menon said that he would go home only the next day after the *Theyyam*. Fear had gripped him so tight that he felt he choked.

~ ~ ~

13*th* *April 12:00 a.m*

Darkness crept in through the dark trees and shadowed the winding pathways of the village. The clock in Sreedhara Menon's huge house struck twelve times and the village was already asleep except for the *kavu*. A towering dark image walked down the stone pathway that led to Sreedhara Menon's backyard. The strong legs carried him with familiar ease and his eyes shone in the dark. He held an unlit steel torch that moved along with his long strides. The lower corners of his *dhothi* were folded halfway up, bunched, and fastened together at the waist. The dangling sixth finger on his right hand shivered as he lit the cigar from a small matchbox. The thick grown Mexican lilac fences lined as a fortress, demarcating the property lines, breathed in the smoke and the leaves coughed in the gentle breeze. His thick, dark, and coarse lips pursed in thoughtful silence. He puffed a lung full as he walked ahead. He walked for half an hour before reaching the curve that led to the backyard and put down the almost burned cigar butt and with his sandals put out the burning end. He opened the thorny gate that overlooked thick tall Mahogany, bamboo trees, mango trees, and cashew trees and crept inside to merge with the dark.

~ ~ ~

13*th* *April, 3:30 a.m*

The *koladari* ran to the pyre and lay on it shouting,

"*Enikku kulirunne...,*" (I am shivering...)

People tried to lift him but he casually sat on the pyre. He jumped and enthralled the people with sudden jiving movements that gathered speed with the rhythmic beat of the drums.

He sat on a stool in front of the deity as if in conversation with the god and then jumped up and as the music lilted, he swaggered in a rhythmic dance. His anklets flared loudly as he jumped and ran. Kesu, the *koladari*, the skilled dancer, knew how to tame the fire.

Fire is anger. Fire is desire. When untamed it could destroy the whole world. It could destroy oneself.

Pottan Daivam called forth a few people from the crowd and kneeled on the floor. He nodded his head in frenzy and blessed each of them by touching their head with the coconut leaves he held in his hand. He blessed Sreedhara Menon first.

He moved around and then asked loudly, "Don't you offer the flowers and fruits that grow in our wasteland to your gods in huge temples? Those flowers and fruits are not untouchables. They are pure and sacred. Then, how can the hardworking labourer become so low and undignified?" The *Pottan Theyyam* ran into the crowd, sang and chanted a prayer, cut a rooster, and offered the hot red blood to the *bhutas*, the spooks and spirits who accompanied Lord Shiva.

People gathered near the pyre as a few removed the unburned logs from it and got the pyre ready for the god performer. A few people covered the performer with coconut palm leaves. He lay down on the pyre heaped up like a hillock. The fire did not burn him. He prophesied and predicted the future of the village and the villagers. He was the god. He was the all-knowing, the potent almighty.

~ ~ ~

5:00 a.m

Night endured the heat of the holy pyre and dawn cracked open with the gentle light of the day. Several people left for their homes. The god still possessed Kesu as he slept and sat on the pyre. He spoke the language of the god. He joked and laughed. He blessed and chanted. A few villagers still gathered around and prayed. It seemed that the goddess deity in the temple too was awake and that she witnessed the entire ritual. The fire died to ashes. After the last rituals, everyone began to leave. The priest closed the door of the temple with a loud creak. The koladari turned behind to look at the goddess before his powers were removed from him before he would be the untouchable Kesu once again.

~ ~ ~

That night Kesu sat on the stone bench in the dark grove. Until that morning he was the God. He was the powerful deity whom everyone worshipped. His black kohled eyes peered from his darker face. He sank into his thoughts.

"Shiva manifested himself as Chandala, the untouchable, to test the integrity of Sree Sankaracharya, the renowned saint, and scholar. But who am I, Kesu, who is neither God nor human? I possess no knowledge, no wisdom. I am a simpleton, a pottan, an untouchable. I will remain untouchable throughout

my life and so will my children and their children and their progeny. He looked at the dark, peeled skin on his arms and legs and ran his fingers through the blisters and scars. These can be healed but not the wounds within," he thought as his thin lips parted.

He stood up, bathed, and walked back home. "Did Malu catch the last bus to Bangalore from the town?" he asked himself as he walked past the narrow bridge. Malu, his elder daughter was his hope. She had completed her Bachelor's degree and was insistent to join a college in Bangalore. She said all her friends were there and since she passed with excellent marks, he couldn't deny it.

Kesu knew that he will never be able to pay her fees and meet other expenses. He was worried about the youngest daughter. He should educate her and provide for her. So, he borrowed some money from Kannapan, the loan shark in town. His interest rate was higher than the bank but since no bank would lend him money, he had to resort to borrowings like every other villager in his place and nearby villages. Kesu felt a cold shiver when he watched Kannapan's weathered skin and piercing eyes sneer at him. He smiled with his tobacco-stained teeth and asked, "What brings you here to this nasty place Kesu?"

Kesu's eyes caught two huge gold chains that glittered from his dark neck. Everyone in the village was afraid of him. He was the owner of the toddy shop and ran a butcher's shop in the village.

Kesu had never borrowed money from anyone previously and he was hesitant to approach Kannapan. Kesu shuddered when Kannapan's hawkish nose and Spartan shoulders scoffed at his frail, stooping image.

"I shouldn't have listened to her…my wife…I am here only because she insisted…but wouldn't I become an inefficient father?... a father who couldn't help his daughter to realize her dream!" Thoughts flocked around him relentlessly.

Kannapan ran his fingers through his unruly hair and asked Kesu, "Won't you pay the interest every month without fail?"

Kesu shuddered as he watched Kannapan's concrete jaws munch the words.

"Yes… I certainly will," Kesu stammered as he groped for a reply in the affirmative.

"How much do you want?" Kannapan asked as his narrow eyes penetrated deep into Kesu's pale, sunken eyes.

"Well… if possible 10,000 rupees…," Kesu wiped his sweating forehead with the towel that rested on his bare shoulders.

Kannapan opened a small, wooden box as he lit a cigar, put it in his mouth, and inhaled lightly. He ran his fingers through the crisp bundle of money in the box. Kesu watched him take a few notes from it and smell each of the valuable pieces of paper.

Kannapan counted the money twice before handing it over to Kesu and got Kesu's thumb impression in a blank document. He took a few long, slow draws from the cigar and slowly blew the smoke out of mouth and nose.

When Kesu turned to leave, Kannapan added with a sinister smile that slightly revealed his golden tooth, "Don't you have two daughters? So, you wouldn't like me to visit your house every month to collect the interest."

Fear crept into Kesu's eyes as he watched Kannapan stroke his devil's fork beard with his hefty fingers. Kesu hurried home with the money. He did not dare turn behind to look the beast in its face.

CHAPTER 3

Zacharias Thomas

A baby squirrel fell from the nest on the tall Mahogany tree that guarded the Saket Higher Secondary school's rear gate, the only English medium school in the village founded twenty years back. A few good-willed men initiated in planning and building the school. The school had a humble beginning with just a few classrooms and one staff room. The Principal and Vice-Principal were also teachers, and they did not occupy special chairs in big rooms. Everyone was a teacher then, and they imparted values and knowledge with love and dedication.

The school managing committee consisted of a few eminent, educated men who knew the importance of education. They wished to raise educated men and women who could transform the villagers' lives, society, and the country. They even hired teachers from distant places and gave them accommodation and remuneration. Gradually the school became a High school, and eventually, it was upgraded to a Higher Secondary school. Students from town too preferred to study in this school in Kavampuzha. The school opened job vacancies for the educated and uneducated alike. The teachers were mainly women. Kesu's wife Latha joined as a sweeper in the school.

The managing committee people appointed new members as they began to grow old and felt that they couldn't work efficiently anymore. They wanted young and energetic people to take over and continue the school's legacy. They appointed Sreedhara Menon, Suresh Chandran, and Krishnakumar as the chief functioning members. They were influential men of Kavampuzha and the former committee members believed that they could quickly get things done for the school.

~ ~ ~

Two fair, plump hands picked the baby squirrel from the ground, and the round fingers gently moved down its spine. The baby squirrel cuddled under the warmth of the safe hands.

"Sir, what is it?" Kesu came running on seeing the new Principal bent down. He was afraid that the Principal had spotted some plastic bottle or dry leaves on the ground.

"Cleanliness" was the new Principal Zacharias Thomas' motto. Kesu felt that adherence to anything in excess led to obsession and a compulsive disorder. He remembered his grandmother who had an obsession for cleanliness. She dusted, cleaned and washed, and repeated it until night. Later as years passed by, his grandfather had to call the temple priest who was also a psychic healer who could pull the ghosts out of every human body.

"She is possessed. Make arrangements for the ritual on a full moon day," the priest told Kesu's grandfather after observing and analyzing the possessed grandmother for half an hour.

Kesu's grandfather faithfully obeyed and made arrangements for the ritual the following full moon night. On an auspicious night, the priest beckoned the gods and spirits by chanting and drumming. He made Kesu's grandmother sit on the lines drawn using turmeric and rice powder. After chanting a prayer, the priest brought down a drumstick tree bark mercilessly on his grandmother's back. That was quite unexpected and the grandmother howled and screamed.

"Spirits of the dark, ghosts that haunt the old hag, leave the body," the priest's hands hit the grandmother's back furiously again and again.

When the priest felt that the old woman was still possessed, he took an iron rod to the burning fire. That was when the spirits decided to leave and grandmother lay prostrate at the priest's feet lamenting, "I shall leave her... I shall leave..."

After so much begging and pleading, the priest aborted the final rod therapy. He threw a fistful of holy ash on grandmother's face and she fell unconscious on the floor. Grandfather sprinkled water on her face and the priest declared that the ghosts that haunted her had left. Grandfather washed the priest's feet and bowed in reverence. Grandmother never touched water after the incident and grandfather felt relieved that the ghosts were driven out of his dear wife.

Each time Kesu watched the new Principal, a smile escaped his dark, frail lips as he reminded him of his late grandmother.

A pair of calm, beady mercury-grey eyes gleamed and peered through Kesu's sunken almond eyes. The Principal smiled as his small, pale pink lips expanded over his clean-shaven face. The cleft on his chin glistened in the warm sun.

"It would've fallen in yesterday's wind," he said, still caressing the little animal.

Sweat trickled down Kesu's forehead and the loose shirt hugged his aging skin, sundried like rasin. Kesu smiled and moved to the garden. There was some more work left. He was in a hurry as he had a *Theyyam* performance that evening. He thought that he would leave for home after an hour.

The Principal walked past the playground and school auditorium leaving behind tall trees and neatly cut shrubs lined with acquired obedience. The Principal's room occupied an area within the main office building that stood at the school's center.

A small dark corridor from the main office led to the Vice Principal's office and an immediate right ill-lit passage led to the Principal's office. It was a tinted glass-covered room on one side with a huge door that bore a heavy steel handle that matched the magnificent carving. The other sides of the room were covered with concrete walls that bore huge windows on each. The room stood as a perfect square, and the walls carried pictures and phrases of eminent personalities. The wall spoke about equality, truth, and justice. Some inbuilt cupboards and shelves contained important files and books.

On one wall stood a majestic collection of rolling trophies and framed certificates in which were engraved the listless achievements of students. An excellence award for Best Principal was proudly displayed on the center wall. The first Principal, Mrs. Diya Naren received the award for her excellent service from the Ministry of Education before she retired from the post.

The school had closed for summer holidays but the office functioned on all days except weekends and public holidays. It had been only two weeks since Zacharias Thomas joined Saket as its new Principal, and he began to receive accolades from the staff and parents who met him. He sat on the huge cushioned chair and wheeled to the left and right for a while, cuddling the little wonder in his hand.

He kissed the baby squirrel on its little head and gently placed the frightened animal on his thighs. He switched on the computer that was placed on the long glass table in front of him. He had a doctorate in Animal and Poultry Science from a reputed University in America, Masters in Psychology and child and adolescent counseling. He pressed the little animal that now rested on his lap and gently ran his fingers through its frail body, and closed his eyes. It had been long since he felt such warm comfort spread across and spill over and between his thighs.

CHAPTER 4

Mayukhi

The summer showers bathed the tired trees and plants with a brief solace. 35-year-old Mayukhi hopped down the auto, careful not to step on some muddy puddle of water. She felt that Trivandrum Central Railway station still recognized her despite the changes it underwent over the years. She looked much younger in her faded blue jeans and grey T-shirt. Shouldering a backpack, she paced ahead to the inquiry. The train had just arrived at the first platform, and she got in without further delay.

The smell of murky air stirred with the rising fumes from the steaming coffee reached her nostrils as it brushed against the rusted window bars of the Nethravathi Express. It was a joy to watch people cautiously hold the paper cups with coffee filled to the brim and their eager mouths trying to take a sip while the train rattled and jerked in a zigzag. Droplets of rain hesitantly dripped down each window bar clearing the dust accumulated with continuous travel while the rust clung to the bars like memories.

As the train left the outskirts, Mayukhi peeped out through the window to take a look at the University College where she joined after graduation. The huge building was built during the British era and stood majestically amidst tall green trees. She had never wanted to pursue an MBA. She was always in love with words and wished to live in a world of books. Being a writer was her first love. She often found herself scribbling verses and stories and either tore them or burnt them later. Being a girl in a male-dominated orthodox Brahmin family was tough. It was hard to fight for her dreams.

Friday evenings were her only favorite time when she waited at the railway station for some passenger train that was never in a hurry to reach Vadakarai, a small town on the way to the land's end Kanyakumari. From there, she used to take a local bus to her village just a few kilometers away. She enjoyed the unhurried lull of the dusty train that carried the woes and joys of ordinary people. There were working women, potter women, farmers, sweepers, and children smiling with chocolate-smeared mouths.

Mayukhi smiled whenever some women asked her, "*Enga pore amma?*" "Where are you going dear?"

This was a question that Mayukhi asked herself every day: *Where am I going? What is my destination?*

On certain days, the train was filled with the smell of baked clay, and on some other days, it carried the fragrance of jasmine and lotus. It carried with it the simple life full of little wonders. Mayukhi loved to cup this brimming life and splash them across the pages of her book as pencil strokes or verses.

Kanyakumari reminded her of beaches, shells, and the salty sea. Like a child, once again she wished to chase the endless waves and rush into the blue sea. She longed to press the seashell hard against her ear and listen to the stories of the sea. The sea was her first storyteller and she loved the way he lied to her with his gentle roars. There was truth in every lie he uttered. He healed her wounds and stitched her scars into beautiful pearls.

Sometimes a worthy lie is necessary in a world, which is constantly in conflict with itself. The world will lose the truthful tellers of lies in the process of trying to discern between truth and falsity, good and bad, right and wrong.

Mayukhi loved the rough wind that tangled her long, black, curly hair and hugged her slender frame vigorously. She saw eternity in every sunset that left the gentle moon to shimmer alone on the placid sea. Nothing else was more joyous than watching the moon spread its silver on the deep grey sea.

The train screeched to a halt at some station, jerking the trove of memories. Mayukhi saw men, women, and children jostle for the seats. A young woman was trying to hush a baby crying for milk. Her fair chubby cheeks turned pink as blood rushed to her coy face that helplessly looked around at the crowd. She looked tired and her wide eyes drooped down with exhaustion. The heavy brocaded red sari and the enormous gold jewelry on her arms and neck intensified the heat. An older man seemingly her husband tried to console the baby by lifting it in his heavy, bronzed arms, and he even tried to pull funny faces with his voice soaring above that of the baby's. Mayukhi could feel the woman's embarrassment and remembered how difficult it was to feed her daughter on a crowded train when she, too, was a young mother. While the public places had a niche for such young mothers, the trains and buses had no provision. Some curious eyes always hovered around such young mothers.

"You may sit here in this corner if you feel that's convenient." Mayukhi stood up and the young mother occupied the window seat with gratitude in her eyes.

Mayukhi sensed that she had seen the woman somewhere but couldn't recollect from memory. As the baby suckled from its mother's breast the life and warmth, Mayukhi saw a sense of joy on the mother's face. She watched the baby playfully move its head in and out of the yellow shawl that the mother had used to cover her breast and the baby's head. The baby's smile and laughter enveloped the entire compartment. It burped, cooed, and made some quite contended sound before it fell asleep with drops of milk trickling down the lips.

The mother seemed to hold her breath, afraid that the slightest movement might wake her baby. The crimson rabbit ears from the baby's dress peeped out with eager eyes. It was obvious that the mother's tender hug could even put those rabbit ears to sleep. She would have sat in the same position for another half an hour. When the train halted at the next station, a few people got down. The seats were gradually getting vacant. The husband spread a blanket on the seat and gently laid the baby down between two small supporting pillows. A whole world of peace slept in those little eyes.

Rain began to pour down heavily, and Mayukhi watched the mother pull down the heavy, dusty window shutter, which fell with a thud and the baby shuddered. She patted her child back to sleep and the baby closed its eyes once again with the quiet assurance of its mother by its side.

Mayukhi moved to the single window seat and felt the rain beating hard against the tall trees and leaves and relished the rain embrace light green fields and muddy little streams. She watched the young mother stand up and stretch like a cat as her husband's eyes grazed through her curves. She tried to hide the embarrassment and walked past Mayukhi with a fleeting smile to the washroom.

She returned and sat in the seat opposite to that of Mayukhi.

"I am Kaveri. Don't you remember me?" she smiled and asked.

"Hmm… I am sorry… well … er…," Mayukhi looked at her dark kohled eyes trying to recollect her name before which the woman introduced herself.

"Aren't you Mayukhi, teacher at Saket school, Kamvampuzha? You had taught my son Raghav when he was in class 1," Kaveri's huge gold earrings dangled as she spoke nodding her head.

"Oh, yes… I remember now…Raghav, a timid, silent boy who never mingled with any of his classmates. I resigned from the job a few months back. But you changed his school after two years, didn't you?" Mayukhi asked looking at the woman's face that was as round as a moon. She was not young as she had thought but had a charm that glowed in new mothers. Her golden bangles, the gleaming long, heavy gold chain and sindoor on her forehead that burned like a headlight, were markers that showed that she was married only a couple of years back. Mayukhi knew her as a widow when her son studied in Saket.

"How is Raghav? I assume he might be in class IX now?" Mayukhi asked curiously

"Oh, yes. You remember well. He is fine," Kaveri stretched her head forward, leaned closer to Mayukhi, and continued in a whisper, "You know that he is my son from the first marriage. My parents insisted and got me married to Pankajakshan. He is also a widower. I have two children from him. At the time of my second marriage, Raghav was only eight. I was afraid that he wouldn't be able to accept a new person as his father. So, I left him with my parents. I changed his school to avoid unnecessary questions. Initially, he was sad and didn't fare well at school. He isolated himself and kept himself away from other children. My Raghav suffered a lot. But now he is happy. Pankajakshan takes good care of him. He has begun to call him '*acha*' (father), which Pankajakshan and I enjoy listening to."

Mayukhi listened patiently as she used to earlier to every parent who approached her. She told Kaveri that she quit the job to pursue higher studies.

"How many months old is the baby?" Mayukhi asked her to divert the conversation.

"He is only four months old. Ayansh, that's his name. He chose this name…," she pointed her finger shyly at her husband and smiled. Pankajakshan nodded with pride and smiled with the contentment of possessing two beautiful gifts.

"So, are you going to Kasargode?" Kaveri asked.

"Yes, I was here at Trivandrum to collect some data for the research work."

"Oh, you know my husband hails from Kasargode too," There was a sense of pride and sudden warmth in her voice when she spoke about her husband's place. She called her husband in her shrill voice, "Etta… see she is from Kasargode. She was Raghav's teacher"

Mayukhi smiled on hearing the amount of respect Kaveri showered to her husband in her '*etta*' as a mark of respect. It was always confusing for Mayukhi as the natives used the same word '*etta*' to address the elder brothers and any male elder to them. It was even more surprising as the women addressed their husbands too using the same word.

Kaveri's husband moved to the edge of the seat careful that he didn't wake up the sleeping child.

"Where is your house?" he enquired with eager eyes.

"Kavampuzha. That's my husband's place."

"My house is in the next village, Kayyoor. I was in the Gulf for many years and so I don't know many of them," he nodded and scratched his chin as his gold bracelet slipped down to the forearm from the wrist.

Mayukhi watched him glance impatiently at his gold-strapped watch. The watch reminded her of her father's fair hand. Time ticked back to the long-forgotten years. She closed her eyes and rattled in the gentle rhapsody of time.

~ ~ ~

30 years ago

I was a little girl, maybe five or six. I do not remember well but I remember my father's soft, fair hands; hands that never worked. They were pink and glowed like his cheek. He has never lifted me in his arms. Maybe he was afraid that the golden rings in his hands might hurt me. I do not remember him telling me stories or kissing me good night but he was my father. I have never seen him go for any job. I didn't know that it was necessary to work to earn a living. I heard from my friends that their fathers worked. Some worked in banks, some in office, a few others were officials of dignified ranks. My little brain couldn't comprehend what work was and why was it so necessary to work.

Once when the teacher asked, "What is your father?" I replied, "He does nothing."

The entire class burst into laughter and my teacher too joined them. I didn't know why they laughed.

The teacher then asked, "How does your father pay for your dresses? How does he pay the driver who drops you at school and takes you back home?" I had no answer. I didn't know whom to ask. I had never asked anything to my father. He bought me everything; all the fine things because he hated the ordinary. Maybe that is why I like the ordinary. Maybe that is why I find joy in the little things. When I wished to see the world, my father rolled up the windows of his car. It was always his car. Father never smelled of sweat. He always looked fresh. While he filled the rooms with imported things, amma (mother) always stood amidst them in stark contrast. She was not fair neither was she dark. She was good-looking but not as fair as my father. Amma was a good woman who obeyed her husband and always asked what had to be done and never left his side when he was at home.

Amma stood beside him always ready to serve every time he ate. She turned on the radio whenever he *was tired of sitting doing nothing. Amma would then run with her cracked heels to the kitchen, crossing two lengthy corridors and six rooms to prepare sweetened coffee for her husband. Father would then leave with his trusted assistants. Nobody asked where he went and he never told.*

I never told anybody about my father. I didn't know what to tell. I have heard that he was an astrologer and temple priest. After several years, my father died and that was when I saw amma cry. Maybe she thought that she had no work left. Father was her entire world. He left her and that was what she knew. She was always the good woman and so she did not know what she had to do with all the wealth he left behind.

I met my husband in a bank where I worked earlier. I was at the assets section and he had an account in the bank. We met frequently and gradually became friends. Both of us shared our likes and dislikes, discussed books, sports, and politics, and enjoyed our long walks together. After two years of building trust and love, we decided to marry and live together. Love is not in confinement but in the freedom and simple trust, each one shared. I learned that money is not everything. Money and beauty cannot buy love and happiness. Happiness and joy are in being with someone who embraces you as you are. I also learned that life doesn't stop with me. Now, I see my daughter who always seeks the best. She hates the ordinary unlike me.

~ ~ ~

The train moved ahead, leaving behind trees, rivers, people, towns, and villages. Mayukhi felt little worlds disappearing in the blink of an eye. Journeys always ushered in new worlds, and she loved the novelty that temporarily erased the past.

It had stopped raining. The leaves and flowers embraced the heat, as it knew it had no escape. Mayukhi saw little streams flow in muddy pathways as the train pulled to a halt at some village.

"The repair work never ends", Pankajakshan peeped out and muttered angrily. The heat increased and the huge iron fans moved hesitantly, sending down hotter air. The air at times carried the smell of sweat and urine along with it. A thick liquid arose from the stomach and reached the throat suffocating the pleasure of journeying. The baby woke up at frequent intervals and cried loudly. Kaveri wiped the baby's arms and legs with a wet cloth. After twenty long minutes, the train began to drag forward. It screeched and jostled with the railway tracks.

The train sped across dark trees, villages, and towns. More darkness blanketed the sky. The wind swirled and touched Mayukhi's face with its wet hands.

Mayukhi was running fast, faster as a few faceless beings chased her. When she turned behind, she noticed that the creatures multiplied in number with each step they took and behind her, a woman was sinking into the swampy ground. The frantic cry for help reached Mayukhi's ears like a thunderbolt and she turned behind one last time. With a disoriented yelp, she stood frozen to the ground when she realized that it was none other than her mother. The black beings with their painted red faces and angry, opaque eyes inched closer and closer...

The phone beeped a message. Mayukhi opened her eyes. She was sweating and breathing heavily. The train was still moving. Kaveri slept huddled beside her baby and her husband was flipping through a magazine. Mayukhi drank some water and checked the message on her mobile.

Had been trying to contact you since evening.
Principal Vasudara met with an accident today.
No one knows how. She is serious and is admitted
to the City Hospital.

Mayukhi went pale on reading the message sent by one of her friends. She maintained a good relation with Mrs. Vasudara. Mayukhi quit the job a few months back, and Mrs. Vasudara was the only person who contacted her since the day she left the school. The previous day before the incident, she spoke to Principal Vasudara, and she felt an unusual tension in her voice. She spoke about the new Principal Zacharias Thomas' immediate appointment even before her retirement when she had yet one more year of service. Before hanging up the phone, she mentioned about an important matter which was to be discussed later. The train paced ahead of time and distance. The train would reach Kasargode at 9:30 P.M. Mayukhi expected her husband outside the railway station. The late evening sky seemed to yell, holding on to the approaching night.

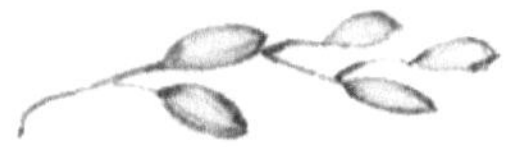

CHAPTER 5

Evelyn

Nights, they hold the secrets of the day. Mysteries gather on treetops like fireflies; fireflies, the miraculous beings of the earth. They set ablaze memories and desires as the wanton stars stare down from the sky. You don't know that what dies sometimes comes back. The night that dies every day comes back with more darkness, doesn't it?

Gently resting her body by the window, Evelyn looked out. It was an hour past midnight. Sleep evaded her sea-green eyes. The heat gradually cooled down as the wind embraced her through the thin nightdress.

The fireflies and white flowers that blossomed like swarms of nymphs, beckoned the night for an evening drink. Evelyn had never dreamt that she would be in an unknown land with unfamiliar people.

The night brought memories of her past. She could hear the voices of her father and mother quarreling and shouting at each other almost every night. As a child, she watched them helplessly, and her little green eyes bore crystallized tears that stuck her fears to her. Nights became the most fearful time for her, and when the whole world slept, she fought with her fears. The day her father left was the most dreadful in her life. She saw her mother gulp bottles of Cognac, and this time she did not mix it with Schweppes. She then saw her inhale some powder with great zest while little Eve lay hungry, blanketed with tears. Alone.

The bright stars reminded her of the warmth in her father's eyes and the tough hands that carefully lifted her when she was hardly five. They played and danced together. She even remembered her mother, a beautiful, petite woman with a charm of her own. They all had so much fun every weekend when her father returned home after business tours. She did not know when exactly her mother began to change but everything began after her mother started going for a job. On certain evenings, Evelyn saw a stranger drop her home and her mother kissing him goodbye. Evelyn would forget everything when her mother got her chocolates and macrons.

One late evening, Evelyn saw this other man in her mother's room. It was her father's room too. Evelyn felt that the stranger did not smell her father's cologne. He smelt dirty, and he sneered as he smiled at her. He patted her mother on her cheek as he made her sit on his lap. Evelyn watched her mother's face brighten.

The stranger gave Evelyn more chocolates and toys. Then her mother told Eve, "Don't tell daddy about my friend. *L'oncle est un homme gentil,*" "Uncle is a nice man," her mother's words echoed in her ears every night after that.

Then one day, her father left home leaving her with her mother. Evelyn knew that her father fought hard for her, but her mother won. Her father kissed her one last time before he left. He tried to meet her at school, but her mother changed her school. Then this other man came to live with them. He got toys and chocolates for a few weeks, but that stopped after some time. Every day he went out with her mother. Evelyn was left alone at home. She was only ten.

"I am your father. Don't call me 'uncle'. Am I a stranger?" Evelyn's new father once tried to convince her as he forcefully lifted Evelyn and made her sit on his lap.

Evelyn felt dizzy and she coughed for breath as his hands tightened the grip around her waist. She began to despise him more and more.

One late evening, Evelyn was watching television. Her mother was too much drunk and had gone to bed early. The new father was still awake and he went and sat beside Evelyn on the sofa.

He watched the little girl from the corner of his eyes and saw her tiny skirt flutter in the wind revealing her tender thighs. He nuzzled her hair and slipped his arms around her neck and asked, "Do you know to slither like a snake?"

"No, I don't," Evelyn's eyes sparkled with innocence. She thought of her father, who used to make her sit on his back as he moved around on all fours like an elephant. She felt sudden warmth towards this stranger, and she nodded her head happily.

"Then I'll teach you how," he told as he pushed her small figure down on the floor and crawled over her.

He pulled her by her frail legs and placed them between his thick, hairy, naked thighs. He forced open her tender mouth, slid his fang-like tongue deep into her throat, and spit venom-like saliva into it. Evelyn lay there tired under his weight as he peeled her skin and cut through her innocence. Fear and pain silenced her. She didn't know that she could cry.

She watched the man smack his thick, gruesome lips before he picked up his clothes from the floor and left her fragile naked body, cold and shiver in pain.

Since then, Evelyn never spoke to anyone at school. She sulked. She hated everything and everyone.

Evelyn tried to tell her mother about the incident but her mother had no time to listen to her. Moreover, Evelyn feared that her mother trusted the new husband more than her daughter.

The new father slithered through Evelyn for many more years. She tried to hide but he hunted her down. Evelyn felt that he was like the pit viper she had come across in the Encyclopaedia of Reptiles and Amphibians. He had the sensing pit organ between the eye and the nostril on both sides of the head. He sensed the warmth of his prey wherever she tried to hide. Fangs and claws came down mercilessly on her almost every night. It was no more her home. One day when the beast of the man was too much drunk and lost his consciousness, Evelyn slid through the huge window of her room. She ran out in the cold night clutching a bag of essential things. She was 17 then. She stayed in a hostel near her college and went for part-time jobs like most other students in the evening.

~ ~ ~

Evelyn lay down on the bed as sleep gradually crept into her sea-green eyes. It was a windless night and the leaves swayed softly in the gentle breeze. She woke up hearing a sudden rustling sound and stretched her head towards the thick, tall enclosure of trees through the partially open window. In the stillness of the night, her eyes caught the image of a dark figure move through the shadows of the trees.

The rented house, in which Evelyn stayed, stood in the backyard of Sreedhara Menon's house. It was a single-storied building nestled between tall trees. Evelyn loved the Gulmohar, bamboo, and varieties of mango trees that hardly let sunlight in. She noticed a thorny fence gate on the right side of the plot. Sreedhara Menon, her house owner had told her that the gate was kept to protect the land from stray animals. Tales of rare incidents of attacks by wild elephants and boars flashed in her head. She was sure that this was not an animal. She heard a hushed cry as the figure slithered through the dark. It slithered through her fears and she shut the windows and crept into the bed. Every time fear crept into her, she dreamt of Angela; Angela who never slithered; Angela who never spit venom.

Angela was Evelyn's senior at college. Evelyn never understood why she confided her fears with Angela. It had been only a month since they met and Evelyn realized that it was a strange bond. She was sure that it was not friendship. When Evelyn met Angela for the first time, her face looked extremely familiar as if they had met in hundred lifetimes, in hundred worlds. She felt a sense of acquaintance and comfort when Angela was around and her entire soul was drawn to her. Angela never made her feel afraid or judged her when Evelyn revealed her past life.

Whenever Evelyn spoke about her fears, Angela hugged her with her huge arms and Evelyn left safe in her embrace. Angela smelled of Evelyn's father's cologne and her warmth reminded her of her father. Like every other girl, Evelyn believed that she would marry a good man when she grew up.

Once, Patrick, the most handsome guy in her college invited Evelyn for a party and she accepted it gladly. She enjoyed the envious eyes that stared at the stunning pair as they held hands and stepped amidst the crowd. Patrick rolled her to the dance floor with a swoop. They danced. Patrick looked into her sea-green eyes. All that Evelyn felt was a void though she attempted to smile. She made him hold her hip firm and that was when she realized that she felt nothing for him. She didn't feel the firework which she felt when Angela's hand brushed against hers as they walked. When Patrick bent to kiss her, she couldn't take it any longer. She pushed him aside and rushed to the wash. There she saw Angela peering into the mirror. Angela looked at her questioningly.

"I…I can't …be with him," Evelyn found it difficult to speak and felt words choke within her.

"I feel more comfortable with you…I don't understand," she continued.

Angela hugged her and Evelyn reached for her lips and they kissed.

~ ~ ~

Angela and Evelyn left the party before dinner. They walked through the countryside and neither of them spoke. It was a moonlit night and they stopped by a riverside and sat down on the bank. The water glistened and Angela pushed Evelyn into the water and waded through the cold water towards Evelyn. Angela held Evelyn's hand and asked,

"So, shall we get married, Eve?"

Evelyn blushed and coyly replied, "When?"

They hugged and made love as the moon hid behind the clouds. They decided to live together. They rented an apartment and shifted to a new beginning.

~ ~ ~

Evelyn looked at the clock on the wall. It was 1:30 a.m. and she closed her eyes wondering what Angela would be doing.

~ ~ ~

A red-headed woodpecker chirped and cackled. It drummed and tapped at the glass window, waking up Evelyn. She looked at the clock that hung on the wall to her left. It was 7.30 a.m. Evelyn dressed up and opened the door and sighted a woodpecker chasing another with its high-pitched, less rolling sound. Their shrill charr-charr notes tickled the tender green leaves. Parukkutty was insistent that a wind chime be set up outside the window. She even made Sreedhara Menon hung one there, after months of pleading.

"The wind would keep the object moving, and this would fool the bird into thinking that a predator was near. The bird would be afraid and would keep away from the object," Parukutty explained to her husband who nodded carelessly. He got the job done afraid of further lectures from his wife.

When Evelyn stayed there, she was afraid of the bells that chimed at odd hours, and she removed them. Her father had once told her that woodpeckers are spirits from a happy world so she never wished to scare and chase them away.

Her father died two years back. She used to visit him in his rented apartment. When she saw him after twenty years, he was a broken man. After he left the house he was no more the same person. He failed to concentrate on his work and he took to drinking alcohol. His business partner cheated on him and he lost all his money. It was during those days that he met a young woman named Adele.

~ ~ ~

Adele was a twenty-year-old call girl and a bar dancer. She never remembered how she reached the wretched place. Adele was fond of Evelyn's father as he was the only man who was kind to her.

Once Adele told him, "You don't pounce on me like other men. You are kind and gentle. There are days when my body aches and I am afraid to cry. Some men tear my skin.

They bite and scratch as if I were not alive. They have been doing this to me for years. I was only 13 when I was raped and beaten. I cried. They did not give me food for two weeks. They locked me in a room. When I learned that I had no escape, I obeyed. Now, I am dead. I just exist because I am afraid to commit suicide."

Evelyn's father listened to her as tears dripped down his eyes. He hugged and kissed her gently on her forehead. He fed her with courage and love: love that was not enforced but gained. Adele gained the strength to think about the cruelty meted out to her day after day and began to build hope about her future.

When Evelyn visited her father in his apartment, he told her about Adele. "She loved me, the brave young woman. She loved me when everybody else left me when I was a loser. When I left you both, I was determined that I will never return. But, later I wished to see you. I secretly watched you several times from a distance. I thought you both might be living happily until one day I met that beast, your mother's new husband in the bar. He pulled Adele to him so cruelly that she slapped him across his face. Adele had changed so much by then. She learned that her body was her right and that nobody could own her without her permission. She attended classes on sex education and the possible health hazards. I helped Adele enroll in a college and she was planning to quit being the bar dancer and whore. I helped her with the necessary paperwork. The classes taught her that she had the right to file a complaint at the police station when she was abused. It was the last day in the bar when the beast attacked her."

Evelyn hugged and kissed her father gently. She wished to tell him how much she missed him during her younger years but she simply smiled when she felt that his aging body was gradually losing the strength of body and mind.

He continued, "I was worried, and I came to see you both. I peeped through the window. I saw no lights but heard screams. I watched him every day. From the neighbours I got to know that you left. They said you quarreled often. Then one day when the beast was out, I tried to enter our house. I tried the front door but it was locked from the outside. So, I tried the windows and the window in your room was open. I slid in and hid behind the cupboards. I didn't find your mother anywhere. The flower pots were broken and the cupboards were all messed up. That night the beast brought two men with him. With tears in her eyes, your mother too followed them to her room, Our room"

Evelyn's father paused and gasped for breath and sipped hot water to wet his dry throat.

"We will talk later if you feel tired," Evelyn told her father.

"No, I should speak. Allow me to speak lest I might die without telling you the truth. I saw the two men enter your mother's room and they ran out screaming. I felt dizzy ... I choked at my helplessness. The beast, your mother's new husband was drunk and unconscious. I walked to your mother's room and found her dead...," he paused and breathed heavily. Evelyn felt that his heart would weigh a thousand tons. She pressed his shoulder hard with her fingers as tears dripped down her eyes. "…and I saw a blood-stained knife beside her bleeding body. I knew she had killed herself… I took the same knife and stabbed the beast in his heart. How many times I do not know…His eyes popped open before they shut forever… I hid the knife and left no fingerprints." Evelyn watched her father laugh like a maniac. When the hysterical laughter turned to heavy sobs, Evelyn helped him lay down his fragile body on the bed.

"Do you think that I was a coward…, a faint-hearted, spineless fool who did not have the strength to fight the beast? I lost you both in the battle. It was my huge ego. I could have saved you and me from everything but I didn't. My darling girl, will you remember to keep at least a few wildflowers at my grave? Can you ever forgive me?" Tears rolled down the corners of his wrinkled eyes.

Evelyn kissed him on his forehead and held his palm in hers and sat beside him in absolute silence. Sometimes silence is the loudest emotion. Later that day, he insisted that she send a message to the priest for the Last Rites. The priest arrived and after a series of rituals, he confessed his sins to the priest. The next morning Evelyn found her father lay down on the floor cold and numb. The doctor told that he would have died the previous night. His fragile heart gave up. Evelyn believed that her father died peacefully.

~ ~ ~

Evelyn felt the presence of the spirit of her father in the little bird. Her father taught her lessons in resilience, wisdom, and strength. He made her look at the value in the most hopeless things and showed her how great good came out of it. Though broken and tattered, she built her life with the lessons he taught through his life.

Evelyn saw Kesu's wife Latha sitting on a raised stone and pull out something from the sole of her feet. She rushed to her side and touched her shoulder. Latha smiled and showed her a piece of glass bangle.

Evelyn made friends with Latha within a week of her arrival. They spoke sign language. Usually, no one talked to Latha as she belonged to the lower caste. Evelyn often visited their shack and even ate food with them. Latha's daughters translated the language to both Evelyn and Latha. On some days, Evelyn went there to listen to *Theyyam* stories from Kesu.

Once in a while, Sreedhara Menon called Latha to weed and pull out grass from his plot. He paid her 300 rupees when she worked from morning till evening. Parukutty also would assign some odd jobs like washing or cleaning.

"When you pay someone, squeeze out all the strength left with them," Sreedhara Menon once told his wife.

Latha cleaned the house in which Evelyn stayed, and Evelyn paid her well.

Latha told Evelyn, "*Thambran ariyanda*". "Master need not know", Evelyn's Google translator translated the words.

Evelyn understood what she said from the elaborate gestures she made. She had gradually begun to understand Latha's language.

She once told Angela, "When the hearts begin to know better, it can speak any language, understand any language".

Latha pulled Evelyn's hand and led her towards the enclosure of trees. She then pointed her index finger at the numerous pieces of glass bangles that lay there. A cold shiver ran through Evelyn. She did not tell Latha about the sounds she heard the previous night. Evelyn smiled and did not reply. She watched Latha collect the broken pieces in a piece of paper and carefully place them on the thorny edge of the fence.

Evelyn looked closer and saw droplets of blood on the leaves. She guessed that since Latha was short, the droplets of blood wouldn't have caught her attention, and she was busy doing a lot of work.

Latha stored secrets like the night but Evelyn did not want to tell Latha about the droplets of blood. Evelyn was a foreigner and she was very particular that she did not get involved in such matters.

She remembered Angela's words, "Always remember that you are in a foreign land amidst unfamiliar people. Watch out and don't put yourself into trouble by getting involved in things that don't matter to you."

~ ~ ~

Evelyn had breakfast, locked the door, and went for a walk. She walked into Mani's tea shop and waited for tea. The villagers smiled and stared at her golden face that glistened in the morning sun. Her blonde hair was tied up casually.

She felt relieved in the grey shorts and white sleeveless shirt as the blazing sun baked the entire village.

In the tea shop she saw two men reading from one newspaper and two others debating and discussing politics. Evelyn noticed that in the village, women gathered around the well or pond while men frequented the tea shop and toddy shop. She sat on a creaky wooden bench beside the stove and she smiled in acknowledgment as Mani served her hot tea.

"Mao- Mani, one tea," Tailor Pushpan ordered Mani in his shrill voice as he exchanged a smile with Evelyn and sat beside her on the bench that squeaked and moaned. Mani got the nickname as he spoke endlessly about his utopian ideal of Marxist China.

"So, madam, you like my village?" Pushpan asked beamingly. He believed that he was the only one other than Ravi who knew to speak in English in the village.

"Yeah," Evelyn smiled as she sipped the hot tea.

As she sat sipping tea, she saw Mani's assistant Kannan, a short, thin and wiry young man, more bones than skin that braved the heat of the sun, running through the fields waving the white towel he usually puts on his shoulder to wipe his hands and face.

He stopped near the tea shop and gasped for breath.

"*Entha Kanna, naaya vallathum ninne odicho?*" Pushpan, the tailor asked him.

Evelyn laughed when she heard the translation, "Kannan, did any dog chase you?"

Kannan breathed heavily and the bones peeped out of his narrow jawline as he sat down to drink some water. There was fear, shock, and surprise in his eyes as he said, "*Nammade Sulocha akkade molu thungi chathu.*"

Mani translated to Evelyn that Sulochana's daughter Remya committed suicide by hanging.

Evelyn watched everyone stare at Kannan in disbelief. Evelyn had never met Sulochana but realized the seriousness of the matter.

~ ~ ~

That evening when Evelyn reached home, she heard loud cries from the neighborhood. She saw Parukutty in her crisp cream coloured *set mundu* talking to her neighbor Saru over the stone wall that separated both the houses.

Evelyn noticed Saru, a plump woman with a huge round face and two curious eyes that stuck out of it like two onion bulbs. The cotton nighties she wore throughout the day were stained on the sides as she constantly wiped her hands on them. While Parukutty looked fresh and smelled of jasmine flowers, Saru smelled of dish wash bar and soap powder. Evelyn could not understand why most of the women in Kavampuzha considered it not necessary to stay fit and look good.

"Parukutty, what's this noise?" Evelyn asked.

"That's from Remya's house, the girl who committed suicide. Sulochana's daughter," Parukutty replied.

Evelyn stared at Parukutty trying to connect the people and the direction from where she heard the wailing sound.

"That house beside the fence to your left. You can see it from your house. You wouldn't have noticed it. There are many tall trees. I always tell Paru to cut a few trees and build a modern house like the ones in town. She never listens," Saru spoke in a single breath as her eyes widened.

Evelyn's green eyes widened with shock and fear. Her fair face turned pale and she sat down on the veranda of Parukutty's house.

"Ah! She might not be used to such hot weather," Saru said

Parukutty ran to get some water, and Evelyn emptied two large glasses of water. When she felt better, she walked to her house wondering why she had never seen the fence on the left side of the plot in which she lived. It was only the previous night she heard the rustling sound and the creak of the fence on the left side of the plot. Little did she think that there was an exit at the farther left end of the plot in which she stayed.

Vasudara

Mayukhi parked her car outside the huge palace. Principal Vasudara's son Varun, a tall young man, showed her the way to his mother's room with a friendly smile. Mayukhi saw Mrs. Vasudara looking out through the huge window beside her bed. She turned around when she heard the hinges of the huge wooden door squeak.

"Ah, Mayukhi, come …sit here…," Vasudara waved her tired hand and invited her to sit on the chair opposite to hers. She had a faint smile on her face and her eyes sagged with exhaustion. Varun excused himself and left the room as he had some urgent work to do.

"How are you ma'am?" Mayukhi asked Vasudara whose wrinkles seemed to hold more sorrow than her eyes.

Vasudara held Mayukhi's hands in hers as tears dripped down her eyes. Mayukhi thought that it was better to let her cry. After a while, she wiped her tears and spoke.

"I don't remember what happened on that fateful evening. That evening, there was a meeting with the parents of class 12 students. It was almost 5.30 in the evening when the meeting got over. I stayed over till 5.45 p.m. as I had to send a few urgent e-mails. The office staff had left by then. My husband had come to pick me. He prefers his old scooter to the car. We did not go home. We were on our way to visit my husband's brother who lived in the town. It was 6.30 by then and we had travelled only half the way. We almost reached the town when a speeding vehicle hit our scooter from the rear. I was thrown away from the rear seat. I don't remember anything else. But what puzzles us is that my husband usually rides very slowly and on that day he rode through the extreme edge, on the sand down the main road," Vasudara narrated as Mayukhi listened to her in disbelief.

They spoke for another half an hour. Since the doctor had asked Vasudara to take rest and had warned her not to talk much, Mayukhi left, assuring her that she would visit her the following week.

On the way back, Mayukhi checked her mobile, and her daughter's class group was flooded with condolence messages. She scrolled up and read the teacher's message: *It is with immense grief that we share the sad demise of our student Remya of class IX.*

Mayukhi peered into the screen as the girl's face flashed across her mind. She was Remya's English teacher and had taught her until class 7 and had met the girl a couple of weeks back. Remya was a quiet but determined girl. Mayukhi remembered what she said the last time they met, "I will become a doctor when I grow up. I will set up a small clinic in our village and treat the people of our village. Gradually I will build a hospital, and that will be the first hospital in our Kaavampuzha. My friend, Theertha's little sister, died of fever. They said that they couldn't save her life as they could not reach the hospital on time".

Mayukhi took a deep breath and headed straight to Remya's house.

Parukutty

The burning sun coiled itself into a glowing red ball, immersing the fields in radiant joy. Parukutty walked up the stone steps of the huge pond on the northern side of their yard. Her silver anklets that hugged onto her fair, beautiful ankles shivered as they shook off the droplets of water with gentle chimes. Sreedhara Menon never allowed her to go to the river. Most of the upper caste people in the village never allowed their women to bathe in the river. Some of their women too despised bathing in public.

Parukutty was always reminiscent of her childhood days. She thought about those happier days when she used to bathe in the pond with her cousins. The numerous games they played while bathing rippled in her thoughts. Among the games, she loved the underwater adventures the most. In this game, each one would hold their breath and remain hidden underwater for several minutes.

The one who remains underwater for the longest period would be declared the winner. Then they would dive into the water from the huge wall built on the sides of the pond.

Splash! They would all fall like huge boulders scaring the fishes and frogs. Sometimes, they hid steel soapboxes deep underwater, and the rest would go searching for them.

Parukutty climbed the steps holding on to the rails of memories as water dripped from the wet dresses she hung on her arm.

Paramu, 'Sreedhara Menon's obedient adjutant' as her sister Kaveri nicknamed him, had pulled down two huge jackfruits and kept them outside the kitchen.

"When will they reach?" Paramu asked Parukutty, as he stood at a distance with folded hands.

"They will reach tomorrow morning," she replied with a smile.

"Why don't you pull down two more jackfruits and take them home?" Parukutty asked.

"No, no…," Paramu nodded with a hesitant smile and walked away.

Parukutty knew that no one would dare touch even a fallen fruit from Sreedhara Menon's plot. "Birds or rats wouldn't dare touch even the rotten fruits," Parukutty always told her sister Kaveri.

Kaveri's husband Pankajakshan was leaving for Dubai that day. He worked as an accountant there. Sreedhara Menon's daughter Ammu liked uncle Pankajakshan as he threw her high up in the air and his strong arms unfailingly caught her tender frame. It was fun to watch Pankaj uncle pluck mangoes with his hands from the tall branches of the mango trees. His hands reached a few high branches unlike her father Sreedhara Menon.

Sreedhara Menon was always proud of Pankajakshan as he brought him watches, perfumes, and several other gifts each time he visited. Kaveri preferred to stay with her sister when her husband went abroad. She never stayed with his parents in Kayyor.

~ ~ ~

Parukutty sat on the lone stone bench outside the kitchen that overlooked the pond and the fields. She loved to watch the setting sun in the twilight skies as the huge blue, mountains stood as a lame witness. She saw a cuckoo perched on a lone, dry tree.

She asked the bird, *"I see you perched on this dying tree every day. What makes you so confident? Ah, maybe it is your tiny, black wings that you trust. I still sit here because my wings are cut and feathers are stolen. Don't you wish to fly high and explore newer realms? I have heard that you birds migrate. Don't you fall under that category?*

Migration is not limited to you winged wonders. People of our kind migrate. Do you know that there is a constant, silent migration among we women? It happens when a woman is given in marriage, and she leaves her house and moves on to an unfamiliar place. After living a greater part of her life with her parents and siblings, she is plucked from that familiar soil and planted in unfamiliar terrain and is expected to have firm roots though growth is the least expected. She has to embrace her husband's house, parents, his sisters, brothers, relatives,

*and even the servants and every little thing in the house as her
own. The displaced are always displaced."*

The clock struck six and Parukutty stood up and moved
to light the twilight lamp in the huge room set aside for the
numerous gods and goddesses. She held a silver bowl like a
lamp filled with sesame oil and thin strips of white thread
swam in it. She walked towards the *sarpa kaavu*, the holy
abode of the snake god that was built under the *Pala tree*.
The *Pala tree* or the Devil's tree was in full bloom. Beautiful
pink flowers lay strewn everywhere. Lime-like heady scent
filled the air and seeped into her memories.

"Do you know why the Pala is so special?" Ravi once
asked her as they sat under the huge tree.

"No… Why?" Parukutty asked with eager eyes.

Ravi picked up a Pala leaf and drew imaginary lines
with it on her palms and said," look, the leaves come out in
whorls of seven. The wind carried the spoken and unspoken
words as the honeybees and butterflies sucked nectar from
the numerous fallen flowers.

"Parukutty…where has she disappeared? For how long
should I call you?" Sreedhara Menon's coarse sound no more
scared her. She was neither angry nor shocked. Numbness,
that was all she felt.

~ ~ ~

A grey Ford plowed across the still village, swirling the dust
and sand like a whirlwind. The stray dogs barked and chased
the vehicle. It screeched to a halt outside Sreedhara Menon's

house and honked loudly. Paramu rushed to open the iron gates that guarded the entrance and let the car in. Sreedhara Menon was surprised and shocked to see his friend and cousin Suresh Chandran get out of the car.

"Suresh! What a surprise!" he expressed his disbelief at seeing him late in the evening.

Suresh Chandran sold his house in the village and moved to the town. He owned a villa and two other houses there. He was Sreedhara Menon's first cousin and best friend. While Sreedhara Menon had just a degree from some private institution, Suresh did MBA from Bangalore and worked as a senior consultant in a reputed company. Post-retirement he was referred by Sreedhara Menon and joined the management committee of Saket School.

There was a brief silence and Sreedhara Menon saw an unusual tension in his cousin's face.

"Sreedhara, did you know that Mrs. Vasudara met with an accident and she is hospitalized?" Suresh asked his cousin as he sat down beside him.

"I heard," he replied.

"Parukutty get some coffee. Suresh has come," Sreedhara Menon's voice rang through all the ten rooms in the house.

He saw her eavesdropping and wanted to keep her away.

Parukutty moved towards the kitchen while the cousins continued their discussion.

~ ~ ~

Parukutty brushed a strand of hair from her face that was lined with wrinkles at the age of forty-five. Her shoulders sometimes sagged in defeat. Her eyes, which once twinkled like Neruda's 'two black pools' were now puffy and drooped. She sat on the windowsill of the kitchen that overlooked a small vegetable garden. Her garden had tomatoes, bitter guards, green chilies, and ladies' fingers. She planted them all by herself and watched them grow like her children.

Sreedhara Menon's eldest son was twenty-five. He worked in a bank as a clerk and visited them once a month. Their second son was twenty-two. He studied in a college in Delhi. He visited them once in six months. The youngest was only five, and Parukutty was always afraid whether she would have to leave her daughter alone before she knew to live independently.

Parukutty got married to Sreedhara Menon at the early age of 18. Her house was in Kannur, the district adjacent to Kasargode. It was nearly eight hours travel from Kaavampuzha. Sreedhara Menon was her maternal uncle's son and they used to visit Kombath House during summer holidays. That was how she met Ravi. Ravi used to do odd jobs in her uncle's field. In the afternoons when the other workers slept, Ravi sat under a tree, holding a book.

Parukutty made friends with him as he got her beautiful white and pink lilies from the temple pond. He told her stories from the books he read, about the art of face painting and the mythological stories of *Theyyam*. She spoke about her school and friends. They walked through the fields and played in the little streams. Their friendship blossomed into love, and it was forever Spring in their lives. Then one day, her mother caught them talking near the far end of the backyard as they stood hidden amidst the thick, tall trees. Ravi was holding her hand as they spoke. Her mother dragged Parukutty by her hand to her brother and cried aloud,

"Look what my daughter has done! She will spoil the family name..."

Parukutty's uncle was a stern man. He never encouraged such inter-caste relationships.

"Do you want to see another corpse in the river? Ask your cousin Shalini. She'll explain it to you" uncle warned her in a controlled, measured voice that caused a sudden fear in her.

Shalini was Sreedhara Menon's only sister. She fell in love with a man who belonged to the lower caste. They studied together at college. His father was a daily wages labourer. When uncle came to know of their relation, he warned his daughter. She did not heed to it. The next week her lover was found floating on the river Sindoori.

After Parukutty's father's death, her mother forced her to marry Sreedhara Menon.

~ ~ ~

Paarukutty went to the porch with two cups of coffee but Suresh Chandran had already left.

Sreedhara Menon closed the huge iron gates and went into the house silently. Parukutty stared at his thoughtful face. It was 9 o'clock and he did not have dinner yet. He usually created a ruckus if dinner was not served at eight-thirty.

On certain days when Parukutty would be busy shelling areca nuts or collecting firewood from the backyard, the dinner would be ready only by 9 p.m. Then, the entire household would tremble with Sreedhara Menon's roar "Don't you know that I cannot stay hungry? How long do you take to cook?" or he would ask mockingly at Parukutty," There are only three members in this house and you say there is so much work. Is this what you call work? Bah!"

He sometimes asked, "Do you know that my mother used to do all the work in the house by herself. She had never served food late."

Parukutty then replied, "Maybe your mother had eighteen hands like *Bhadrakali*."

Before Sreedhara Menon could reply, she would disappear into the dark kitchen. Sreedhara Menon abhorred the kitchen as he thought that it was a women's area in the house. Parukutty named the kitchen as the forest of *Tadaga* where men feared to enter.

Parukkuty wished she could scream and push him hard and run far away each time he tried to straddle over the fence of her independence and self-respect. Parukutty never dismissed his remarks as a mark of respect for her spouse. She brooded over every insult and harsh word her husband uttered and stored them to sharpen her anger towards him.

~ ~ ~

She had called Kesu's wife Latha to help her in the kitchen the next day since Kaveri and her family arrived. But Latha excused herself as her daughter had come home after a few weeks.

~ ~ ~

Latha looked beyond the dark fields through the small window in their shack. There was a faint light in the room. She had prepared Malu's favourite chicken biriyani and some sweets. The house saw such rich delicacies only when Malu came home. It was a celebration for all. Kesu got the best meat and costly rice from the town. They usually got the rice from the nearby ration shop. They never complained about the poor quality of rice given away by the government. They were happy that they got it free of cost. His younger daughter Mira too waited for that day when her sister arrived.

She always said, "I too will go to study in Bangalore. Only then will you get me good food."

Kesu smiled and nodded his head each time he heard her daughter dream big. Kesu never went to school. His wife Latha passed third grade. He was always proud of his wife. They made their children study in the small school nearby. It was not as reputable as Saket. Kesu had requested the management members for a seat for his elder daughter. They laughed at him and asked, "Can you afford the fees?" Kesu walked away with a bent head as the laughter continued.

He had been working as a gardener in the school for the past 15 years, and he expected them to do some favour in return. He was paid a meager amount as salary, but he never questioned it as it was a regular income for him. The work hours included morning to evenings and even sometimes on holidays as well.

"What happened to Malu? She did not speak anything since the time she reached," Latha asked her husband worriedly.

Kesu sat on the wooden stool kept outside their little shack. Sweat streamed down his bare neck as he wiped it with the towel he put on his shoulder.

"Maybe she is not well. She is not a village girl now. She lives in a city. Maybe she does not like the pungent smell of cow dung and the heaped waste beside our house," Kesu replied.

There was a narrow stream behind their shack. It once had clear water. Kesu used to bathe in it and catch fish when he was a small boy. There were a few other shacks near theirs and everyone used the water for drinking and cooking. Gradually, the stream got clogged with plastic waste and garbage. People thoughtlessly dropped the garbage in it, and the smell was awful on certain days. Mira often fell sick, and so did the young children in the neighborhood. Nobody spoke about it or complained about it. It continued.

When Kesu's mother was alive, she used to blame the invention of plastic. The small school was also not far from the stream of garbage. The people in the slum sent their children to that school, as they served the students yellow *upma* for breakfast and boiled rice for lunch. The children too loved to go as the school satiated their hunger.

The people of the slum never owned any field or huge plots of land where they could plant trees or other plants. They worked in others' fields and lived with meager earning. The school asked for a small amount as fees even though some NGOs ran it. The people in charge of the administration pocketed a small amount through this.

Latha could not reason out with what Kesu said.

"Did she speak to you on the way home?" Latha asked Kesu.

"Yes, she spoke to me. Don't worry, she is fine," Kesu consoled her.

Kesu had changed a lot over the years. He who used to shout at her for silly matters had turned into a wise, caring, and soft-spoken man.

Latha was relieved, and she went inside. Kesu often slept outside on the creaky coir cot. Tears swelled in his eyes as he lay down and looked above at the numerous stars that seemed to peer down and shot arrows of guile and mockery.

CHAPTER 8

Sreedhara Menon

Kaveri and Pankajakshan reached Sreedhara Menon's house by noon. Sreedhara Menon liked Pankajakshan. He always said that Pankajakshan was soft-spoken and respected Sreedhara Menon.

Kaveri's eldest son Raghav hated Sreedhara Menon as he always mocked him. Raghav was born to Kaveri's first husband. After his death, she remarried Pankajakshan who was Sreedhara Menon's distant relative.

~ ~ ~

Pankajakshan and Sreedhara Menon sat on the veranda near the porch. The veranda stood beneath the extended roof of the main building. The cracks in the low walls still bore the weight of the finely carved wooden benches fixed to them. Sreedhara Menon yearned to hear stories about foreign lands, travel, and food. Pankajakshan narrated with such precision that Sreedhara Menon listened with awe. When he described the cuisine and savories, Sreedhara Menon's mouth watered. One would feel that he relished the taste of the food he had never seen before.

~ ~ ~

Kaveri put her baby to sleep in the room on the northern side of the house. It was a huge room with two windows. A vast wooden cot made of teak occupied a large area at the center of the room. It had delicate carvings on the headrest. Radha and Krishna's mural painting, the symbol of eternal love, stood etched on the wall. Kaveri felt that they were eternally in love with each other and stood beyond time and change. She felt contented that she had captured an eternal moment in which Krishna would never leave Radha alone.

She ran her fingers through the mural art and scratched at the unfinished edges with her long, polished nails. She gazed at her painting on the wall and wondered why she left every painting unfinished. She stroked Radha's long, black hair with her hands and leaned her head on the image of Krishna.

Her Krishna was fair and clean-shaven and did not have long, overgrown hair. His receding hairline revealed his high forehead and did not wear a crown. He was not in the company of other women. Only his beloved Radha was beside him. Her Krishna had a cleft on his chin and his eyes shone like diamonds. She ran her fingers through the asymmetric, well-defined, and sunken philtrum above his upper lip and stood there glued to the image until she heard a loud thud and turned around.

Kaveri looked out through the window that faced the pond and guessed that it might be the sound of mangoes falling from tall mango trees. The fields and trees embraced the heat of the burning sun. They withstood the changes of season, as they had no escape. They were all rooted to the soil like the people of Kavampuzha, who believed they were puppets in the hands of fate. They never tried an alternative to their problems. They trusted in the land they lived in and the goddess in the *kavu*. It was difficult to decipher these simple lives.

Kaveri barged into the huge soot-stained kitchen. She saw a huge pot of water mounted on a mud stove. The flames had died down, and the firewood was almost burnt. She walked towards the low wall near the stove and peeped into the well. The well was almost full to the brim despite the scorching heat. Kaveri wiped her forehead with her saree *pallu* and walked out through the rear door that led to a small extension.

Parukutty was sitting down on the floor. She looked weaker and older in the cream *set mundu*. Her frail hands cut open a huge ripe jackfruit into two halves with a knife and wiped clean the white sap. She chopped it further into halves and mechanically cleaned the sticky sap, chopped off the excess center and ridge portions, and removed the jackfruit pods off its compartments with her fingers. Kaveri watched her sister's fingers plunge into the juicy pods as her long nails tore through the juicy skin vehemently.

"So, when is Pankajakshan leaving?" Parukutty asked her sister.

"After tea. He has arranged a taxi to the airport," Kaveri told her.

"Take these jackfruits to them. They are sitting on the veranda," Parukutty handed over a plate full of jackfruit pods to Kaveri.

Parukutty did not separate the seed from the pod. She never did. She knew that her husband would fuss, but she never listened. She thought to let him work for his hands, at least on separating the seed from the sap. On some days, she cut two whole jackfruits, removed the pods, and placed them in a huge vessel. She would then keep the vessel on the wooden bench in the veranda beside her husband's armchair. She loved to watch him separate the seeds from all the pods and push the flesh into his huge, clumsy mouth. The more he ate, the more she rejoiced. He sometimes spit the seeds around him in a semicircle as if to take revenge on his wife. Parukutty never stopped giving him jackfruits. When he ate too much, his stomach would rumble and he would groan in pain. When the pain increased, he would scream her name. She would have by then sneaked out into the backyard and disappeared into the tall, thick shadow of trees.

~ ~ ~

Pankajakshan left after tea. He waved his hands at everybody and disappeared as the car turned the corner of the street. Kaveri stared at the muddy road that unevenly stretched ahead. Her two children ran to play with Parukutty's daughter Ammu. Ammu was obedient and always silent, unlike Kaveri's children. Kaveri had to wait for two years to meet Pankajakshan again.

~ ~ ~

Sreedhara Menon sank into the big, cushioned armchair that faithfully held his huge body. He rested his flabby arms, which hung like two bat wings on the wooden support on each side of the chair. He ran his fingers through the polished wood.

"Sreedhara, this is made of fine teak," his father once told him.

He was proud of his family and the huge ancestral house in which he lived. Parukutty always insisted that they shifted to the building in the backyard. Her husband never agreed. Sreedhara Menon gave the new house for rent and earned a considerable amount every month. Parukutty thought that greed blinded him.

Sreedhara Menon sat gazing languidly at the mango and jackfruit trees. Ripe mangoes blanketed the ground. He took a deep breath as his huge nostrils flared in satisfaction. He took a few betel nuts and some tobacco from a bronze box and wrapped them in lime-coated betel leaves. A deep red smile glared from his teeth when he saw Parukutty collect the fallen nutmegs from the ground. He chewed his thoughts in silent retrospection.

~ ~ ~

I know Parukutty finds it very difficult to live in this old, dilapidated house. The tiled roof gives up every monsoon season. When it rains heavily, water drenches the tiles and oozes in through the openings. The white walls turn green when moss and ferns find it adaptable to grow. Small banyan plants often find it ideal to grow in the corridors and cracks in the walls. I am worried that it would damage the foundation of the building. She doesn't understand that I cannot live anywhere else. This is my home. I was born and brought up here. This is not my father's house. This is my mother's house. When father married her, he moved to this house. That was the custom those days. We followed the matrilineal system of marriage.

During our childhood days, the summer holidays were the most awaited time of the year. My father had five sisters. Two of them died a few years back. My mother did not have any siblings. I have twelve cousins. Five of them are elder to me. We were four boys and the rest were all girls. It was so much fun.

I was not a brilliant boy. I never used to study well. I took time to think while everyone else laughed at some joke. I used to feel left out. They never included me in some of the games they played. I had to stand alone and watch them enjoy. Once my cousins told me to hide and I thought that we were playing hide and seek. I hid for more than half an hour. I was happy that no one found me until then. After some time, I came out of my hiding place and found no one there. I went inside and asked my mother,

"Amma, where have they all disappeared?"

"Sreedhara, didn't you go with them to the river?" Amma was surprised to see me there.

Only then, I realized the prank played on me. They had intentionally left me behind. I was 15 then. I walked through the fields all alone. I heard some voices echo from the dark tunnel that led to the river. I tiptoed cautiously. I was shocked to see my cousin Parukutty hold our servant boy Ravi's hand and play in the little water stream. She was twelve. Ravi was a year elder to me. I cried a lot on that day. She was my Paru. How much I loved her!

"Parukutty!" I screamed angrily.

Ravi got scared and let go of her tender hand, but Paru did not budge. She stared at me angrily and sneered. She later stomped to the river. Before Ravi could run, I rushed to him and hit him on his face and chest. I pushed him down and kicked him hard on his stomach as he shrieked in pain. I ran home leaving him there.

As years passed by, their friendship grew into love. When Ravi tried to avoid Paru, she met him and compelled him to speak. Ravi was intelligent and smart. He drew everybody's attention by his handsome features. His untamed mane seemed to suck in my pretty Paru. His dark eyes sparkled as he spoke and I was jealous of the black mustache that sprouted and lined his upper jaw. I was fair. I was educated. I went to college. Ravi was not educated. I once asked Paru,

"Why are you so interested in that uneducated, dark fool?"

"Ravi is wise. He reads a lot. He is brilliant. As you say, he studied only until class five; but he never stopped learning. He is a self-learner. Do you think that a person becomes intelligent by going to an educational institution and swallowing every word printed in the textbook? Are teachers the ultimate source of knowledge? Ravi reads a lot. You don't know how much he knows. He is sensible, unlike you. You will never know," Parukutty replied with a contemptuous little laugh and walked away. As she walked she turned behind and asked, "Don't you know, 'Beauty lies in the eyes of the beholder? I love him and his dark form. He is handsome."

She never understood that there were people like me in this world. It was very difficult for me to learn even the simplest thing. My teachers used to scold and punish me if I failed to answer the questions they asked. I made no friends at college. I thought that my brain would burst off someday.

I had to win over her. I loved her. I could never imagine her being with Ravi. I decided to marry her. I waited for the right time. Then one day, when I was sitting in my room upstairs, I saw the two of them behind the tall trees in our backyard. I strained my eyes through the wooden bars of the window to get a better view. As I had doubted it was Paru and Ravi. I ran to the kitchen and saw Paru's mother cooking. I pulled her hand and led her to the backyard. I told her,

"Ammayi (aunt), look someone's hiding behind the trees. I think it is some thief. Don't shout. You tell Paramu to find out".

Ammayi was scared and she told Paramu to go and check if it were a thief. Paramu returned hurriedly with bent head.

"What is it Paramu? What happened? Is someone there?"

"Yes, … well…er…how will I …," Paramu fumbled as he spoke

"Should I call your master then?" Parukutty's mother asked him angrily.

"No..no…it's your daughter Paru with that servant boy Ravi," Paramu hesitantly let out the words.

Parukutty's mother flared with anger and she paced in through the thick enclosure of trees. She saw her daughter sitting beside Ravi on a small stone near the wall. He held her hands in his and they were looking into each other's eyes.

"PARU!" She roared and pulled her free hand. Paru's blue glass bangles broke and it pierced through her fair skin. Blood oozed out. Beaded drops cascaded down her glowing cheeks as she pleadingly looked at Ravi for one last time. Her eyes beseeched his pardon. It was she, who persuaded Ravi to visit her in the house while he was not willing to. Ravi stood there helplessly choosing not to run away.

I was sorry for Paru but happy that their love story ended. I saw her mother slap her and pull her indoors. She was locked in a room for a week. My father ordered Paramu to tie Ravi to a coconut tree. Strangely, Ravi did not argue. He did not fight back even though he was stronger than my father or Paramu. I watched my father lash him with a whip. He lashed him until his hands were tired. I watched Ravi's face. He stood still. He did not shed even a drop of tear. I wondered at his strength of body and mind. Maybe that was why Paru loved him so much.

Paru was eighteen. She had enrolled in a college. Her father died a few years back and my father was taking care of her family. She was not allowed to continue her graduation. I completed my graduation. I applied for a job. It was a small enterprise and there was no interview. I worked there for three years as an accountant. My father insisted that I resign from the post and take care of the house.

"Sreedhara, the coconuts in our house will fetch you more than the salary you get from the Job," Father once mocked at me.

He was right. After a few months, he fell sick and he died. I married Parukutty. I convinced her mother that no one else would marry a girl who had an affair with a lower caste man. Only a few relatives were invited to our wedding.

I do not understand why she still wears that woeful face. Her eyes didn't sparkle anymore. I didn't see her bosom heave as it did when she was beside Ravi. She looked beautiful in the traditional set-mundu. The two pieces of cotton cloth hugged her beautiful, slender frame. One covered the lower part of the body and reached her ankle while the other, she liked to wear over the left shoulder like a saree.

We had a jasmine bower in our backyard. Paru loved to watch them bloom on full moon nights and sometimes I have seen her lean on Ravi's shoulder and she shone brighter than the moon. I guessed she smelled more intense than the intoxicating flowers. It was a joy to watch her giggle when wind tickled her soft underbelly through the set-mundu as she raised her fair, soft hand to pluck the jasmine flowers. I have never seen her blossom after that. I have never felt her nerve ends open with more desire. I have seen her eyes bloom with love and lust all at once like when she hugged Ravi.

When I touched her, she sat there with cold, stony eyes. Every night, she stiffened and lay like a corpse beside me. When I ran my fingers through her fine lines, I felt like touching dead fish that floated on the polluted, clogged stream beside the slum. I longed to caress her long, black, thick hair. On the day of our marriage, I saw them all chopped off. She wore no bangles. She did not line her lotus eyes with kohl. Only the silver anklets jingled. I have heard her speak to the anklets when she was alone. I knew Ravi had gifted them. I let her wear them. I have given her every freedom a woman wants.

I take good care of her. I love her a lot. We have three children. What else does a woman require in life?

I later heard that Ravi left Kavampuzha. He is a famous face-painting artist today. I heard that he has visited several countries and his skills are widely acknowledged. I console myself by repeating my father's words that 'an untouchable is an untouchable'.

CHAPTER 9

Amy Sebastian

This is how you hunt. You tear apart the skin and allow it to bleed. You do not kill but leave it half-dead and watch it wriggle helplessly as it cannot cry. The tiny stretch of the bleeding body doesn't stink. It is too tiny for the smell of death to reach your nostrils. Agony. Pain. Suffering.

Little Amy watched her friend Rosabella tear apart a millipede. After the creature's initial stroke of luck, Rosa's blade pierced through its spiracles. She picked up the docile decomposer that lay under rotting logs piled in the corner of the garden. She then placed it on the clear ground outside the veranda. It lay motionless on its double-legged segments. The dark coil couldn't defend itself by secreting chemicals from the pores.

Rosa cut the jaw lip and pulled out the single pair of antennae with the other blunt half of the blade. The flat-lensed eyes stared blindly at the closing evening sky. It laid pleading on earth's open palms.

Amy watched with tear-filled eyes. It was her house. She loved every tiny creature that lived there.

"Why did you kill?" she asked Rosa as tears rolled down her cheeks.

Rosa sneered, "I did not kill. Look, it is still alive. Can't you see it wriggle?"

Amy kneeled beside the gentle creature and touched its dying body. She touched her right hand sequentially to the forehead, lower chest, and both shoulders as she drew a cross and muttered a prayer.

"It is the Lord who goes before you; he will be with you and will never fail you or forsake you. So do not fear or be dismayed."

Her mother had taught her that parting is not the end of a relationship but only an interruption. It is natural to grieve for losing loved ones, but the dying will go to Paradise, and they will experience lots of love and joy. Death is a journey towards a new home. It is a new beginning and not an end.

Amy wiped her tears and sat beside Rosa down on the cement floor of the veranda. Rosa felt sorry for her and touched Amy's hand. Amy smiled and hugged her friend.

"Promise that you'll never do it again," she stretched her palm and Rosa held it tight as a sign of truce.

Rosa was her neighbor. Both Amy and Rosa studied in Saket school. They both were ten years old. Rosa was a tomboy who jumped over walls and climbed trees. She was quicker than the wind when she sped down the slippery lane on rainy days and preferred trousers and shirt to skirt and glittering tight-fitting girl's dresses. Amy and Rosa were a perfect jibe: one silent and the other dazzling. Amy kept Rosa's secrets while Rosa protected Amy when boys played pranks on her on the street. Rosa's cycle had no bell. Each time her father fitted one, secretly, she threw it off. She screamed loud instead as she sped by each corner and turning.

~ ~ ~

Amy had a younger sister, while Rosa had a younger brother. Amy's father was a theatre artist, and her mother was a singer. Amy's father, Sebastian Thomas, was passionate about acting and screenwriting since childhood. His father Markose was a timber merchant and his mother took care of their five children. Sebastian was the youngest of the five. His father was constantly worried about his future. Sebastian was not regular to school and scored very low marks for exams. He watched every movie released and watched every play that was staged in the nearby villages and town hall.

His father secured him a seat in a private college in the town.

"Do you know how much I had to pay them to get a seat?" he asked Sebastian scornfully.

Sebastian stood beside his mother with his head bent down.

"They are so shameless to ask for more and more. They are selling education. Why should I be angry? When parents have useless sons like you, such thieves will rob us of our dignity and money in broad daylight," he boomed in his thunderous voice and trudged to the door.

While Rosa's father Victor became an engineer, Sebastian became a theatre artist. Like every sincere artist, he did not earn much. Nobody wanted genuine talents. On most days, he had no performance. His wife Dhanya held music classes in a temporary shed they built beside their house. Dhanya, the Hindu girl, met Sebastian at a stage show. She was impressed by his performance, and she fell in love with him. From then on, she never missed a single show in which he performed.

The performances were usually held at night, and Dhanya watched the shows with her cousins and friends. She always reached half an hour early. The viewers were usually villagers and so they did not make any elaborate seating arrangement. They sat down on the grass. Some brought towels or newspaper pages with them.

The stage for the show was set in the field or on the open ground of the *kavu*. People like Sreedhara Menon and his relatives considered it below their dignity to watch such stage shows sitting alongside the workers in their field.

The stories they enacted questioned the injustices of society. It raised poignant issues about politics, social evils, and familial problems. With the booming of Cinema halls, the art of theatre gradually dwindled. There was a shortage of talented artists as most of them moved to act in cinemas. They went even if they were given insignificant roles.

Dhanya and Sebastian met after each show. Dhanya expressed her views and Sebastian felt that she was his best critic. They couldn't hide their longing for each other any longer and they decided to marry. Since they knew that Dhanya's parents would never consent to such a marriage, they decided to legally register their marriage.

"Bah! You loafer! How dare you step into my house?" was his father's reaction on seeing him with Dhanya.

His father then turned to Dhanya and asked, "Are you blind? Do you know about him? You could have lived happily had you married someone your parents found for you. It's not late. Even now, this minute, you can change your mind. Please go back to your house."

Dhanya replied, "We love each other. I respect him for the word he has given me. I have nowhere else to go".

Sebastian's father let them in, and before he died, he gave his house and the land surrounding it to Sebastian.

Sebastian was adamant that he would not leave his profession. With his second daughter's birth, he moved a step ahead to try his luck in television shows. He did not succeed much. He was paid significantly less and was made to work for longer hours.

Sebastian's eldest brother Mathai Markose took up his father's business. He built a house near the church on the blue mountains. He had twenty acres of land there, which he converted into a rubber estate. Markose was always proud of Mathai. He said that only Mathai had inherited his business tactics. Mathai was proud of his land and success in business. He owned a car, and his house was a huge single-storied building. His wife wore the finest saree to church and their children studied in the best school in town. He visited Sebastian once in a while and helped him whenever he was in need. Sebastian had three elder sisters. They were all married. One lived in the town and the other two in the nearby village Kayyur.

Mathai did not like the toddy shop near his land. It was crowded with drunkards, and they threw empty liquor bottles into his plot. Once a piece of glass pierced through his sole and he complained it to the man, he always saw sitting in at the cash. He inquired about the owner, and he got no hint of the person. One night the noises got too loud, and so Mathai rushed to the toddy shop and shouted at them,

"Why do you make such loud noise? It's already 10 p.m and why have you not yet closed for the day? Don't you know that families are living nearby?"

A colossal frame surged in from the shop and stood at the door. He seemed to occupy the whole one acre of land in which the shop stood. A gold chain hugged his dark neck and his fingers gleamed with studded rings. The 6 feet hooligan would have weighed around 120 kilograms. His black, naked upper body heaved menacingly as his biceps curled and his chest muscles pushed up.

His golden tooth glistened with a menacing laughter as he asked, "Are we sleeping in your house?"

Roars of laughter followed.

Mathai shivered and seemed to shrink down.

"Don't you know Kannapan? He is famous here in this village. He can buy all your land and squeeze out every single penny within a single day. Don't ever come here and shout.

Do you follow?" one of the men bit his teeth and gnawed the words into Mathai's face.

Mathai turned back and walked home with a bent head.

Deceit

Mayukhi watched a creamy, yellow-throated song Thrush peck its golden brown breast. She had once spotted the bird's blue eggs in the neat, mud-lined nest on the bush in the kavu. Mayukhi's life encircled between these simple wonders. She had never seen a world outside the village and the small town and never spoken to people outside her simple life. She considered children, books, and nature trustworthy friends and often found people mocking her for her childish ways.

"You gift her diamond, and she will look at it with contempt, but you give her a muddy seashell, you'll see her cry for that. You should look at the collection of shells, red *manjadi* seeds, and peacock feathers she stores in her room. She is difficult to be tamed. I just told you because you should not be disappointed later," Mayukhi's *amma* laughed as she served coffee and sweets to the groom to be.

Mayukhi never understood why it was necessary to tame a woman.

"Why do you always tell people that I can't be tamed? Do you expect me to be chained? I don't even like animals to be chained. Do you realize what you are saying, old lady?" Mayukhi asked her mother.

It was fun to watch her mother stare angrily at her whenever Mayukhi addressed her 'old lady'.

"You always argue, and you listen to only 'you.' You do only what **you** like. Do you ever listen to any of us?" Mayukhi watched her mother's face turn red like apples as she washed the dishes aggressively.

"My dear apple, I will listen to anyone who speaks sense and remember to be soft to the dishes lady," Mayukhi pinched her mother's cheeks and playfully tugged at her long hair.

While everyone thought that Mayukhi loved the sound of silence the most, she was wedded to the myriad sounds of nature that were genuine, like fresh raindrops. After marriage, she shifted from her village in Tamil Nadu to the quaint village Kavampuzha in Kerala. Kavampuzha was greener and wild. Her friends felt that Mayukhi was wild and mysterious like the Sindoori and the *kavu*.

Mayukhi remembered that day she joined Saket school as an English teacher. The former school management members appointed her for her passion for teaching. They felt that her sincerity and trustworthiness could bring a positive change in the young minds as she always thought differently and productively. Her life revolved around students as she felt that those young, innocent minds were a reservoir of vast knowledge and great ideas.

Learning is a continuous process, and growth occurs only if you are willing to accept the mistakes and start to unlearn and relearn.

Mayukhi had no time to involve in gossips. Neither did she find time to enter into a heated discussion on politics and changing fashion. Every child she met had an inert talent, and she tried to bring it out at any cost. Not everyone can become a Scientist or Doctor. Society needs people of various capacities. Thinkers, dreamers, and doers help to stabilize life.

Sometimes it is not just a plain lecture that a student requires. If a teacher fails to know the student's familial background, it would be impossible to decide the teaching necessary for the student. Mayukhi saw that all the students she taught had books, pens, and pencils. If they couldn't afford to buy, she got it for them, and she even paid the school fees for a few students who came from poor family backgrounds. The first thing she ensured was whether all students had three meals a day.

As years passed by, there occurred drastic changes in the running of the school. New systems and new bylaws that favoured a few and disfavoured the rest of the faculty members emerged. Strong-willed teachers like Mayukhi found the going tough. The teachers who fell under the second list were given extra work during and after school hours, while the *fair* ones were exempted from the duty. Fair ones were the favorable ones who supported Suresh Chandran and his cousin for every senseless and inhuman decision they took.

"From tomorrow, the following teachers should see that discipline is maintained on the school ground during the recess hours including including lunch break and after school hours." The management's strict order fell like a bee sting on those targeted teachers one evening at a staff meeting.

The school bell resounded in the nearby fields and houses at sharp 8:15 a.m. The teachers who were assigned duties had to arrive before that and take positions like warriors at the forefront. These foot soldiers were ordinary women from very simple households who had to cook, clean, wash and feed the entire family before and after reaching home. There was not a seat offered when their tired legs could carry them no more. Mayukhi never obeyed their senseless commands that could squeeze the entire strength out of one's body.

"If a child could not flutter like a butterfly and run like a deer, then what is childhood for?" Mayukhi once reasoned when she told one of her colleagues not to punish the students running around and playing on the ground.

Pregnant teachers found it challenging to work with the long and tiring working hours. Suresh Chandran retained the favoritism attitude towards certain teachers. When a six months pregnant lady teacher complained about a male teacher's misbehavior to her, Suresh and Sreedhara Menon laughed aloud and dismissed it as a common incident.

"Sir, my colleague, is a pervert, and he behaves offensively. Could you please make arrangements for a seat in the ladies' staffroom?" Gini requested Suresh Chandran

"What did he do to you?" Suresh laughed as he asked mockingly.

"Sir, how can I explain?" The teacher asked, hugging her protruded stomach as tears filled her eyes.

"We'll warn him. **Men are like that. Women should be careful**," Suresh Chandran acted as if he was busy, and the teacher walked out of his room with a bent head.

Gini shared her experience with her friend Surekha whose father was one of the management board members. Surekha informed her father and requested him to take necessary action. When Surekha's father tried to seek justice for Gini, Suresh Chandran and Sreedhara Menon ousted him from the management committee. Thereafter, Surekha was targeted and isolated. When the fault finding and insult continued, Surekha handed over the resignation.

Suresh Chandran and Sreedhara Menon were relieved that not many people came to know of the incident.

~ ~ ~

The new management that Suresh Chandran and Sreedhara Menon headed brought about a revision in the fee amount. The fee amount was increased, adding a burden to the working-class parents of Kavampuzha. The people of Kavampuzha were either daily wage labourers or ordinary government employees. Suresh Chandran and Sreedhara Menon had no reasonable point to justify the sudden increase in fee amount.

It was the practice of the school that the respective class teachers should collect the school fee amount directly from the lower class students and hand them over to the cashier in the office. One afternoon when Mayukhi rushed to the office to hand over the fee amount to the cashier, she found someone else in the cashier's seat.

"Where is the cashier?" Mayukhi asked him.

"Madam, today I am in charge of cash," the unfamiliar face replied with a grin.

Mayukhi stared at the dark, fierce face with a snub nose and two-button eyes.

"Don't think too much madam, hand over the money. We are going to close the cash counter," the office assistant urged Mayukhi.

"**Where** is the cashier?" Mayukhi repeated her question.

"Madam, the cashier has to attend a function in his house. So, he left early. You make the payment and leave," the office assistant spoke with urgency in his tone.

Mayukhi handed over the cash without further thought and waited for the payment receipt.

"Madam we will give it later. We are in a hurry," the face answered from behind the cash counter.

Mayukhi left as she felt that she should no longer linger there. On the way to the teacher's room, she met Kesu.

"Kesu, is that man in the cash counter newly appointed staff?" She enquired.

Kesu thought for a while then replied,

"Do you mean the one who is sitting in cash right now? He is not an employee of this school. Madam, he works with Kannapan in the toddy shop."

Mayukhi stared at Kesu in disbelief.

"I just handed over the fee amount of a few students to that man at the cash. Even the office assistant assured me that he was appointed temporarily," Mayukhi felt her words choke in her throat.

"Don't worry, madam. If ever they cheat you, you can check the CCTV cameras. They were newly installed in the office," Kesu pacified Mayukhi.

After a month, the cashier sent word to Mayukhi stating that ten students of her class had not remitted the fee. Mayukhi felt a sudden coldness as she stood clutching to the teacher's table in the classroom.

She rushed to the office and met the cashier at the cash.

"Sir, I remitted the students' fees last month. There was someone else at the cash. You may ask the office assistant," Mayukhi let out her words as her stomach churned.

The cashier called the Office Assistant and verified the statement.

"No, madam Mayukhi never stepped inside the office last month," the office Assistant replied without a flicker of his eye.

Mayukhi realized the trap set for her as she stood thinking hard to recollect any witness.

"Check the visuals in the CCTV camera. I am sure that it will be there," Mayukhi remembered Kesu's words.

"Sorry madam, the CCTV cameras were under repair the whole of last month," the Office Assistant's words reached as a thunderbolt in Mayukhi's ears.

Enraged and deceived, Mayukhi stormed out of the office. The next day she flung an amount of Rs.20,000/- at the cashier's face and told him in a low grunt, "Feed the hounds around."

Mayukhi knew that the cashier was a sincere and truthful man, but he blindly trusted the people around him. She felt hurt and insulted as there was no one to listen to her. She hated sympathy and fake moans.

Mayukhi decided to talk to Suresh Chandran who was responsible for the running of the school.

"Mr. Suresh Chandran, you would have known about the unfortunate incident that happened to me in this school," Mayukhi stared deep into his eyes as she spoke in a low, harsh tone.

"Yes. It was very unfortunate," Suresh looked away from Mayukhi as he replied.

"So, do you agree that the fault was on your side, with your people?"

"Look Mayukhi, there is no proof. It shouldn't have happened but…," Suresh twisted the edges of his lips as he tried to convince her.

"I am not going to be convinced with whatever you say. I will definitely inform the incident to all the teachers and parents of the students. The whole school and entire Kavampuzha will come to know of the incident," She warned Suresh and firmly walked out of his room.

Suresh stared in disbelief at Mayukhi's words.

"She was such a soft-spoken teacher and how does she behave so boldly now?" A baffled Sreedhara Menon asked his cousin.

"Those who are calm hold the storm," Suresh replied.

Sreedhara Menon wondered what his cousin said as he could not relate storm and calm with a human being especially a woman.

~ ~ ~

Mayukhi met Kesu in the school ground. Kesu was watering a new rose plant.

"Kesu, what I feared happened," Mayukhi narrated the incident to Kesu.

Kesu listened in silence and continued to water and weed.

"We must weed out whatever threatens the growth of useful plants," Kesu replied as he weeded the parasites that grew on the bushes.

The parents and students of Saket school loved and respected Mayukhi for her sincerity and the love she showered on each student. To her, the students were the whole world. Mayukhi called for a meeting with the parents and informed them about the incident.

The following month Suresh Chandran implemented a new rule that students can make the payment through bank transfer. Since there was no bank in Kavampuzha, the school decided to talk to the bank and request them to open a branch in the school. Within a few months, all transactions were done through the bank for the great relief of teachers and parents, but Mayukhi had to face new problems from then onwards.

CHAPTER 11

Arjun

"I expect you'll get the first salary this month-end," Meera said with a glimmer of amusement in her eye as she set the teakettle on the stove to heat up for the second time that morning. It was Sunday and her husband Arjun sat down lazily on the chair on the opposite side of the table. He moved the Kissan jam bottle to the center of the table and stretched his arms lazily on it.

The low-quality wooden table bore lines, scratches, and wax pockmarks where the candle had been the previous night. They had frequent power failures, and they dined and their eight-year-old son studied by the faint flickering candlelight.

"Yes, I will get my first salary this month-end. It will be credited to my bank account," Arjun answered as he watched the wilting yellow leaves and the quivering green leaves in the gentle breeze that entered through the half-open window.

Meera smiled with the tiniest purse of her lips as she poured steaming, hot tea into Arjun's mug. Arjun was appointed as a Physical Education teacher in the government school in Kannur. Arjun had to travel for more than three hours by bus to the school. Since the only bus Pratheeksha was not dependable, he opted to rent a room near the school. He couldn't afford to take his family with him immediately. He had planned, though, to take his wife and son with him after two years. He would have by then cleared the bank loans.

"So, will you get me a few things next week?" Meera asked, edging her shrill voice with a smile.

Arjun's strong jaw and the dark skin beneath his eyes expanded in a warm smile as he watched Meera break off a piece of crumbling pumpkin. The pumpkin seeds lay scattered on the kitchen slab. Arjun felt that he was awash in joyous, warm sunlight when he talked to her. Meera dropped the knife and finger-fed their son Abhinav with hot *idli* and *sambar*.

Arjun ran his fingers through Meera's hair and watched the way it curled.

"Sure, we'll do some shopping next Sunday," he patted her cheek with his heavy, dark palm.

Arjun had decided to comb through his house, his father's house that Sunday. He wanted to sort out his father's leftovers, reminiscences, and the sordid past.

"Meera, I am climbing up the attic. I promised you that I'd clean up the mess when I am free. I will be down only after a few hours," Arjun spoke in his full-throated rough voice as he climbed up the ladder. It was a simple house made of cheap wood, and a tiled roof, and below it spread the rough cement floor stretch. The two bedrooms in the house were small but comfortable. It was a quaint little dwelling, which glowed with love and warmth of togetherness.

Abhinav saw a beehive on the giant mango tree in the garden as he sat there watching his father climb up the ladder to the attic.

He wished he could climb the ladder and accompany his father to the attic. That was a forbidden place for Abhinav as he was a small boy. Arjun was afraid that there might be insects and snakes under the unused logs and other things dumped carelessly. Abhinav kept his little right foot on the first rung of the iron ladder. Arjun's sore eyes blazed with anger and melted with love as he turned behind and looked down at his son. Abhinav put his raised foot down, sensing the danger, and gave his father a toothless smile.

He pointed his finger at the tall mango tree and asked his father, "*Acha* (father), wasn't your father a brave man? You've told me that he used to collect honey from beehives. Can you do it now?"

Arjun looked at the beehive and said, "We cannot do it now. I will tell you later how to extract honey from a beehive. Now, I have some work to do."

Arjun moved aside a few logs and picked up a red cloth that lay suffocating and torn under thick layers of dust. He dusted it and brought the cloth close to his nostrils. He smelled it and held it close to his heart. That was his father Prathapan's *Theyyam* costume. Arjun sat down on the dusty floor and looked out to the mango tree through the attic's small opening.

~ ~ ~

Thoughts sting like bees. You would never put your hands inside a honeycomb when the bees cloud the combs. They sting you on your face, neck, and everywhere. They can even kill you within a few hours.

Arjun had watched people like his father climb tall trees searching for honey when he was a boy. They light coconut fronds and drive the bees away without harming the working bees: the tireless, loyal workers who obey the queen. the hive is then moved to a location away from the other bees and insects as the flowing honey would attract them. Next, they uncap the honey by drawing a heated knife over the hard beeswax that covered the comb filled with honey. After which, they cut the comb off the frame with a spatula and collect the straining liquid in a container lined with cheesecloth for straining. It is then broken down, the cut comb is mashed until they get it as fine as possible and strain out the honey through the mesh leaving behind as much of the solid bee wax, pollen, and other parts of the hive. Finally, they collect the honey and store it in containers.

It is all in the planning, charting out ways, and finally executing it so that you enjoy sweet honey flow down through you, giving a sense of joy and gratification without being stung.

Arjun worked in Saket for four years. He trained the students in sports and gave them extra coaching in football and cricket, which would mean an extra one hour to the interested students after the official time of closure at 4 PM as per management's request. He agreed to work extra hours as the school assured him extra payment for each hour he stayed. The meager salary he earned was insufficient to take care of his family and his wife's family.

Sreedhara Menon, Suresh Chandran, and Krishnakumar were the decision-making members of the management committee. They were influential men of Kavampuzha, and people respected them.

Sreedhara Menon was tall, and his baldhead faithfully reflected the sunlight. His heavy body moved around clumsily, and the chair in his room creaked as he sank into it. He was assigned the role of the Director of the school. The Director's room was often closed as Sreedharan visited the school only twice a week to dust off the excess dust that got accumulated in the chair. Each time, the parents and teachers raised doubts and complaints about the school, he tapped at his golden watch with the golden ringed fingers and grinned nodding his glistening head. The students loved to watch his thin moustache dance like cat's whiskers and his round face redden whenever their naughtiness enraged him.

Sreedharan was always full of self-doubt and so relied on his cousin Suresh Chandran for wise answers. He stumbled over words printed in English and often sat with an air of assumed seriousness whenever the office staff passed files containing important documents to be signed.

"What's this?" Sreedharan asked arrogantly, looking through the golden framed glasses with a frown at the documents as if that was the most obnoxious thing he had ever seen.

Once he sends everybody out of his room, he would ring his cousin and ask for help, "Suresh, what should I do?"

It was Sreedhara Menon, who introduced Suresh Chandran to the other management committee members of the school. Sixty-year-old Suresh Chandran looked younger for his age. The grand-looking old man smiled with a special charm that attracted many women teachers working in the school. His fair skin glistened with a radiant glow. He could speak five languages and a walk around the corridors of the school was a daily habit.

With a wide wave of his smile, he paused to greet sweet Rehana, the fifty-five-year-old English teacher, and the fair Sunekha, the forty-nine-year-old Social teacher.

"Good morning Rehana. How are you?" he asked with a smile as his breath touched Rehana's neck. Rehana would then stare at him with longing.

Though Suresh would have wished them a thousand times, the middle-aged women with painted faces and painted lips gave him a wide-eyed stare. It might have given an outsider the feeling that the old man had forgotten to don his pants.

Krishnakumar was the funniest among the three. His eyes pooped out like two charred pieces of bread with an indignant "Humph, what did I ever do?" look. His tight smile lined on his huge jaw like blackened bread on the pile of burnt toast in the bin. He took exactly five minutes to answer the simplest question. He would first need to raise his head and stare into infinity before his dark eyes finally lit up with an unsure answer.

When someone asked him, "Where is the Principal's room?" He would stare at the person first and then move his huge body around to think. By then the person would have found the way all by himself.

On certain days, he matched his blue joggers with a frilly white shirt and his sports shoes crushed the black leaves under his weight making the green younger leaves wonder, "Did everyone in the universe need to bear him?"

Krishnakumar couldn't orient himself to his iPhone's touchscreen. It was his wife's sister's old phone. She was not willing to give it to him. She gave it to her sister, and Krishnakumar took it from her later.

The trio did one thing in total concentration: sip mugs of hot tea and never risked dropping any crumbs of biscuit and hot *samosa* in the morning and evening.

~ ~ ~

"I expect you are used to much finer things," Sreedhara Menon told Suresh Chandran with a glimmer of amusement in his eye as he saw Suresh sitting in the small room allotted to him.

Suresh Chandran was the Chairman of Saket school. His room was beside the school office, and it faced the huge playground. There were several files on the glass table before him. His grey hair was a misfit on his creaseless face. It only added to his charm. He carried himself with flawless elegance. His crisp full sleeve shirt was cautiously tucked into a matching pair of trousers. The students, parents, and teachers bowed with a *'namaste'* when he crossed them with an unfailing smile and an air of importance.

Sreedhara Menon was keen on appointing Suresh only because he did not know to run the institution. His desire to be respected by the villagers made him take charge as Director of Saket.

"Arjun is waiting outside. So, what should we tell him?" Sreedhara Menon asked his cousin Suresh.

"Let him in. I'll deal with him. You keep quiet," Suresh replied with a sly smile.

Arjun entered the Chairman's room and Suresh Chandran gestured him to occupy the chair opposite his. They sat facing each other on either side of the table while Sreedhara Menon sat at a distance near the wall peering into a class 5 textbook.

"Ah, Arjun, how are you?" Suresh asked as he rested his elbows on the table and moved his head forward.

"Why did you send me the legal notice, Sir?" Arjun tried hard to hide his anger as he asked the question.

Suresh tossed the round, colorless paperweight and looked at Arjun.

"Well, you left without paying the due amount to us."

"Didn't I explain my situation to you? I told you that I am facing a financial crisis and that I cannot afford to pay. Why did you ever tell me that I can leave without making the payment initially?" Arjun asked with clenched fists.

"Arjun, this is the rule. If any employee has plans to leave the institution, then you should inform three months prior to the date of leaving." Suresh briefed as he took a printed sheet of paper from one of the files and pointed out its lines.

***YOU WILL DRAW CONSOLIDATED AMOUNT OF 25,000/- p.m**

***THIS APPOINTMENT IS TERMINATED EITHER:**

   (i) **BY THE AUTHORITIES OF SAKET HIGHER SECONDARY SCHOOL WITH A**

       NOTICE OF ONE MONTH OR IMMEDIATELY IN LIEU OF PAYMENT OF AN

       AMOUNT EQUAL TO ONE MONTH'S EMOLUMENTS i.e. Rs.25,000/- IN LIEU

       THEREOF

OR

  (ii) **BY YOU, IF YOU DESIRE, WITH A NOTICE OF THREE MONTHS OR**

       IMMEDIATELY ON PAYMENT OF THREE MONTH'S EMOLUMENTS.

"Arjun, you left after one month's notice period. As per the clause, you should pay us your two month's salary, or you should have worked here for the remaining two months," Suresh reasoned with his soft, cool voice.

Arjun banged his fists on the files kept on the table as layers of dust spread, and Suresh coughed and sneezed.

Arjun stomped out of Suresh's room, as the cousins smiled willfully.

~ ~ ~

Arjun threw down the two pieces of rotten logs from the attic as they landed with a massive thud on the ground below. He removed a dead rat that lay under the pile of logs.

"Maybe it's the poison I kept last night," he thought aloud.

When rodents and insects trouble, it is always better to kill them before much damage is caused.

He cleaned the attic floor with a broom and cleared the floor off small, insignificant things. That was when he spotted his father's torn red, *Theyyam* dress and tied it around the waist. The white shirt turned brown, layered with patches of dust.

He remembered his father's unnaturally thick arms as they dug the grave for his mother. There were four other men with shovels. Father, who kept his emotions restrained under his thick pursed lips, did not shed a tear for his wife. The clouds gathered in dark circles and threatened to drop down any moment. Arjun was hardly ten when his mother died. He felt that his mother was better as he stood choking back his tears.

"I still think *amma* is the better one. She coped well with death," he spoke aloud as tears brimmed in his eyes.

They buried her and covered her with heaps of brown sand. The rain killed off the flowers the visitors had kept. Rain washed away everything except memories. The village was flooded, and several people died. When the rain stopped, there was an odd peacefulness: the peace from which the villagers rebuilt their lives with the leftovers.

Suresh Chandran

Suresh Chandran drew his shoulders back, and pushed through the rose bushes, and breathed in as if fresh from a swim. His white hair shimmered in the setting golden sun. He bent down and weeded the grass that grew in the potted orchids and marveled as the purple and blue elegance peeped from the huge square flowerpots that lined the vast patio. Water dripped from the pots that hung on the ceiling. The giant palm trees that guarded the house screened vehicles' noise on the road to a certain extent. Suresh pulled a soft cushioned chair to the wooden coffee table. He sipped steaming coffee as he turned the pages of *The Leader Who Had No Title*.

Suresh considered his cousin Sreedharan as a pumpkin festooned with several golden buttons: a buffoon and a puppet weaved into a goofy frame. Sreedharan's potbelly growled hungrily at frequent intervals. He was keen to fill his stomach while he neglected his brain that gradually forgot to think efficiently.

Sreedharan met Suresh in the latter's house one evening. He asked, "Suresh, I am one of the management committee members in Saket school. People respect me now but I am not educated as you are. When it comes to serious matters, I am not able to make a decision. So, can you join the team as a member?"

Suresh scratched his shaven chin and replied, "How can I not help you Sreedhara? But, there's a condition. I will not be settled for a lesser position."

Sreedhara Menon peered at his cousin's shrewd eyes and said, "I don't follow what you say."

"Well, can I occupy the chair of the Chairman of the school?" Suresh moved to the end of the chair and looked inquiringly at his cousin.

"How can I make a decision? There are many other members in the team," Sreedhara Menon gave a tense reply.

"You can do it, Sreedhara. You are an influential person in Kavampuzha," Suresh struck the right chord.

Sreedhara Menon's shoulders expanded with pride, and he assured Suresh that he'll convince the other committee members.

~ ~ ~

Suresh Chandran, the son of barrister Chandran Menon grew in an affluent family. His mother was a retired teacher. He was their only son. He was handsome, tall and the most distinguishing feature was his cool-headed smile even at the worst of times.

When Suresh was just six, he lost to his neighbor in a game of dice. It was followed by curse and blasphemy, anger and tear. Suresh hit his opponent's head with the small wooden block, and his head bled. When Suresh's father came to know about the incident, he reprimanded Suresh for his arrogant behaviour and lack of sportsmanship. As a punishment, Suresh was sent to bed without food.

Each time, Suresh's father punished him for his misbehaviour it was anger not regret that filled the boy's heart. As he lay on his bed gazing at the stars through the huge window, his grandmother sat beside him and brushed her fingers through his hair. Suresh hugged her and cried aloud in huge sobs. She patted him and said,

"How can you give up so easily? I know that it is difficult to accept failure, but why do you ever allow your opponent to win?"

Suresh wiped his tears and looked at her. She smiled.

This was the lesson he learned and practiced in life. From then, he never allowed anybody to win. He devised ways, planned, and executed them meticulously. He won.

Suresh Chandran had elaborate plans to develop the school. He bought five buses for taking students from their home to school and drop them back safely after school hours and appointed two of his trusted men Manish and Vinu for the overall charge of the buses. Manish was tall and hefty with a rugged smile while Vinu was lean and short. Vinu's brown eyes pierced from his unshaven face. Vinu left two of his shirt buttons open as he walked around the school.

"Why do you spit on the flowerbeds?" Kesu once asked him

"I did it unknowingly. I am sorry Kesu," he answered with a squeaky smile and stared at Kesu.

Kesu walked away briskly without entering into more conversation.

Kesu has often seen him chatting with a few women teachers after school hours. One late evening after 5 p.m. as Kesu was digging the ground to plant a new rose plant, he watched a woman teacher talking to Vinu

"Why don't you shave your beard?" she asked as she ran her fingers through his rough, salt and pepper beard.

Kesu bent his head and continued digging.

~ ~ ~

"So, what should we do with the existing loans?" Sreedhara Menon asked Suresh Chandran when the latter suggested that they buy two more buses for the school.

"We will find some way Sreedhara. Don't worry, I am there. All you need to do is put your signature on the papers I give you," he replied calmly with a smile.

Sreedhara Menon trusted his cousin and that was the bond they shared since childhood.

The next week they bought two more buses for the school. Now there were seven buses.

They increased the school fees and the bus fares the subsequent month and that was the solution Suresh had in his mind.

~ ~ ~

Suresh was Sreedhara Menon's aunt's son (father's eldest sister's son). Like the other cousins, Suresh too used to visit Kombath House during the summer holidays. While everybody else played pranks on Sreedhara Menon, Suresh supported him and held him close. He defended him and played with him. Sreedhara Menon had great love and respect for Suresh.

Suresh knew how to fight a battle. To him, the aim was more important than the means. He loved Parukutty as she was intelligent and beautiful. Once when Parukutty was stealthily walking through the backyard to meet Ravi, Suresh saw her. He clutched her hand and asked,

"Where are you going now?"

He sensed fear in her eyes and looked steadily into them.

"I.. I am just walking around. You see there are many mangoes strewn everywhere, and I was looking for some ripe, juicy ones," Parukutty replied in one breath.

Suresh pulled her closer to him and she could feel his breath on her face and neck. She struggled to free herself from his clutches but he was too strong. Parukutty was about to scream when he planted a kiss on her cheek and said,

"Don't shout. Do you understand? Now, listen, I love you so much."

He freed her hand and kneeled at her feet, holding a red rose.

Parukutty was shocked and stood frozen for a while. She pushed him down and took to her heels as fast as she could. She ran indoors as she felt it was not safe to venture out alone.

To add to his misery, Parukutty laughed at Suresh and made fun of him. She did not leave him with that and went to the extent of sharing the incident with her other cousins. As a result of which everyone teased him for years. When Sreedhara Menon came to know of this, he asked Suresh,

"Did you say that to my Paru?"

Suresh hugged his cousin and replied, "Sreedhara, do you ever think that I will do it to you? How can you ever listen to other's words and distrust me? So this is what you've thought about me. How many times have you shared your feelings for your Paru to me?"

Sreedhara Menon heaved a sigh of relief and said," I know that you'll never do it to me. You can never. When everyone said, I was perturbed. For a while, I distrusted you. I am sorry."

"Sreedhara, Paru is always yours. I consider her as my younger sister. You know that I don't have any younger brothers or sisters. I feel that I have everyone when I am with all of you."

Having earned Sreedhara Menon's trust, Suresh walked away with the satisfaction of having fed his soul with victory.

Vengeance does not have a specific form. It occupies the inner heart and gradually flows through the veins like blood. It rests within for days, weeks, or sometimes years until it surges forth with a mighty blow at the right moment.

It was Suresh who saw Ravi and Parukutty together, and it was he who informed Sreedhara Menon about their secret affair. While Sreedhara Menon concentrated more on filling his huge tummy, Suresh wandered around through the fields and climbed tall trees. Nothing escaped his shrewd eyes. Nothing.

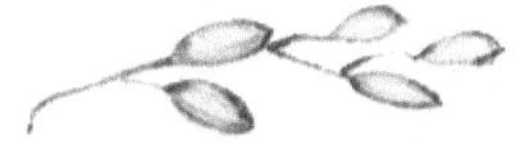

CHAPTER 13

Latha

Latha walked to the river with two huge buckets of clothes and some washing powder from Parukutty's house. She wore a long, thick, cotton nightdress when she worked. She felt that it covered her body from neck to toe. She detested wearing *set mundu* as the two pieces of cloth moved away from her body when she bent down to work in the garden or fields. The other women who worked in the fields wore a shirt above the *lungi* they wound around them.

"You should come here on alternate days to help me. Kaveri and her children are here. There is so much work, and I can't do it alone," Parukutty told Latha.

Latha nodded her head as Parukutty gave her two buckets full of clothes to be washed.

"Wash the children's clothes separately, and don't you know Pankajakshan's shirt? Wash it separately," Parukutty instructed Latha before she left.

Latha obeyed Parukutty and helped her with the odd jobs she assigned. She knew Parukutty since childhood. Parukutty was a few years younger than her, and Latha knew about her affair with Ravi. Parukutty helped Latha financially without the knowledge of Sreedhara Menon. Parukutty gave money to pay Latha's children's fees and a few other times when the girls fell sick.

Latha turned the curve that led to the river, and she felt that she heard a man's voice from the women's bathing ghat. She stood there for a while and looked around. It was late afternoon, and there was no one nearby. The sun was blazing, and sweat trickled down her forehead. She moved slowly, partially because of the heavyweight on both hands and the sudden fear that gripped her. Twigs and leaves cracked under her feet as she walked. She reached the ghat and placed the two buckets down on the first stone step. For a while, she was blinded by the sunlight.

The fleet of steps seemed to be endless as the water in the river retreated to the last step, the twenty-fifth step. The stone steps reflected the heat and burned her sole. She lifted the buckets and walked down the steps breathing heavily. Latha was 50 and felt that she was losing strength and energy. She placed the buckets on the last step and sat there.

"Latha, are you tired so soon?" A fetish voice almost scared her.

Latha turned to her left and saw Sulochana sitting on the farther left end of the burning step. She wore a single cotton cloth wrapped around her chest. The thin cloth covered her glowing, bronze knees. Two golden chains hugged her neck, and her smooth, round shoulders glistened with oil. Her long, black hair flowed down the steps. Two golden anklets loosely hugged her ankles, and they glowed as she stretched her legs. The six golden bangles in each of her hands clanked as she rubbed ground turmeric and green gram flour on her plump arms and legs.

Latha did not reply as she despised her. She had no particular reason for that.

"Maybe it was Sulochana's demeanour or the way she talked," she once told her husband Kesu.

Sometimes Latha thought that it might not be any of these reasons. Aversion need not have a particular reason just as liking. Some people invite attention. They might be people we have never seen or heard before, but we strike a chord the moment we meet. Latha felt that it was always better not to express the hatred or liking the heart develops towards people.

Latha soaked the clothes in water, held one of the clothes by the edge, and slapped it hard on the washing stone. Sulochana looked at Latha with furious eyes as she stood up and sank into the water.

By then, two older women reached the ghat. They saw Sulochana getting out of the water after her bath. She was all drenched, and water dripped from the thin cotton cloth. Her huge, bosom heaved beneath the white cloth and wet black hair hung behind her like serpents.

"Sulochana, how are you now?" One of the women asked her with a soulful tone.

Tears dripped down Sulochana's deep bronze cheeks and her red eyes instantly drooped down.

"How will I forget my daughter? I try hard, but I am unable to. I still don't understand why she did that," Words flowed down like tears with sighs.

"Don't worry. Time will heal everything. When will your husband arrive?" she asked.

"He will reach tomorrow morning. How will I face him? What answer do I have for him?" Sulochana broke down as she spoke in a shattered voice.

Latha washed the clothes and never stopped to listen to the ongoing conversations.

~ ~ ~

Latha reached home and sat beside Kesu outside the hut. She was worried that her daughter had changed a lot. Malu never laughed or talked since the day she returned from Bangalore. All that Malu told her parents was that she did not wish to return to Bangalore.

"Why does she insist that she won't go back? How much money have we borrowed from that devil Kannappan? How will we repay him?" Latha was distressed, and she often asked Kesu.

Kesu was dumb as ever and turned a deaf ear. He had managed to get a seat in one of the private tutorials in the town for his daughter.

"Tomorrow we are going to town. I told you about the tutorial. They have agreed to give her a seat. I've also arranged an auto for her. Again, she need not travel alone," Kesu told Latha.

"Did you borrow more money from someone? Have you gone insane like your grandmother? How can we pay for the autorickshaw?" Latha asked with worried eyes

"No, there is a reservation seat for our caste. They were looking for one student who was eligible to fill the seat. That was when I approached them," Kesu replied, "...and don't bother too much about the decisions I take."

"Then, you could have asked for it much earlier. We could have avoided borrowing money after all," Latha tried to reason out with her husband. Latha knew very little about education and the scope of education.

Kesu sighed and walked through the fields to the river. It was late evening and the sun disappeared behind the tall blue mountains, seizing the blue from the hills and the sky. The sky turned a pale yellow and orange. Kesu immersed his tired body in the cool waters of the Sindoori. He felt that the river knew him well. She soothed him of his wounds as she hugged him into her.

The river flowed with his woes and never returned them to him. Each time his heart was filled with newer sorrow, he dipped them all in her.

"Good relations are like Sindoori. They hug you when you feel so tired of life. They erase all stains caused by worries and absorb you into them as you are," Kesu thought as he dunked his bald head into the river.

PART TWO

Two months later…

"O, what a tangled web we weave;
When first we practice to deceive!"

—Sir Walter Scott

CHAPTER 1

Karkidakam

Thunder crackled in the heavens. An orchestra of alates descended to the ground and shed their wings as they played a hollow sound, a dry rattle, a papery rustling. Two riverboats flowed down the river Sindoori and Kavampuzha became another winged termite rising from the damp soil in protest against the furious rain. Fear pervaded the ensuing silence. All around the village- people, silence, and shadows droned to each other. The banks on either side of the river merged with Sindoori and disappeared into one large body of water.

Karkidakam which falls during the month of July or August is the last month of the Malayalam calendar. The month when the skies tear apart their bosom and pour down incessantly. The *Karkitakam* month gets its name from the constellation of stars shaped like a crab. *Karkitakam* means crab, the crustacean with no backbone. They get their claws at the most advantageous position and angle and inject poison into the body. Treachery, like the poison of the crab, cannot be darker and meaner.

Karkitakam soaks the entire land with monsoon rains spreading epidemic and poverty. It ruins everyday life causing significant loss in cultivation. It is loss and sorrow that makes humans turn to the spiritual and holy, and the dreadful month is rebranded as the holy month, the *Ramayana* month.

Karkitakam drenches the leaves and floods every stream and river. This is the month when Sindoori flows in full spate. The river overflows its banks and swallows the land on either side. Sindoori flows like a fearsome demon spreading her reddish-brown waters like terrible locks of hair. Like those of *Medusa*, the tangled locks gulp down huge barks of trees, rocks, people, and anything that blocks her path.

Sindoori kissed and hugged the land vehemently as she ran her hungry waters over the barren land. The sands sank under her weight and surrendered to her might. Sindoori uncrowned the land and moaned and growled as she tore apart the land's parched skin. The land stood disrobed with contours eroded as the waters pulled the tired trees and plants, forming new lands, greener pastures, and a firmer, mightier world.

~ ~ ~

Kesu looked out from his small hut. The surrounding fields and the stream behind his place were flooded. The dark clouds in serpentine coils seemed to engulf the entire sky. The parched fields gaped wide. The trees and plants could no longer hold their leaves.

"Promise of responsibility falters sometimes. The birds would have deserted their homes. Ah! Only men have boundaries and title deeds," Kesu let out his words like a skilled orator as Latha listened in silence.

Monsoon brought with it the hopes of loan waivers. People like Kesu, who lived on the edges of uncertainty, depended on the cancellation of the recovery of the loan taken from private banks.

"Will I be fortunate enough at least this time? Last monsoon, they did not even write off the loan," Kesu sighed and walked out to Saket school in his brown *lungi*. Droplets of water dripped down his bare shoulders as the tattered umbrella refused to protect him from the heavy rain.

There were times when it rained day in and out until the clouds drained all their woes. The rivers soared, and the seas sucked in everything around them. They reaffirmed that they have no boundaries.

~ ~ ~

Saket school welcomed *Karkitakam* month with holy verses from the *Ramayana*. The huge concrete, three-storied building, painted brown and white, stared nonchalantly at the dark sky in the three acres of land donated by an affluent family in Kavampuzha. Several years ago, the land was a paddy field, and the family donated it for the noble cause of building a school. The swampy land gave away every monsoon season, and the school ground would be flooded with muddy water. Little children played in it, splashing water and floating paper boats on the little pools of muddy water on the ground.

The seven school buses left their rubber tire marks as they dragged along the wet ground. The sixteen-seater bus accommodated twenty to twenty-five students, four teachers, and a cleaner on each bus. It never failed to give the experience of a roller coaster ride as it moved along dangerous winding curves.

Teachers moved around with umbrellas from the main building to the teacher's staffroom. There were three staffrooms in the school: one was in the main building and the other two on either side of the school canteen. The canteen was an open stage covered with low walls, and tin sheets served as a temporary roof. The deafening torrential rain absorbed the sounds of students and teachers and enclosed the entire school within its incessant drumbeat.

The irrigation canal that ran behind the school's rear gate overflowed every year. The fields nearby depended on the water from the canal. Naughty schoolboys climbed the huge stone walls and jumped into the canal. They caught fish from the stream. It was easy to catch fish when the stream was flooded. All they needed to do was to wait patiently. When water carried the fishes, they moved in the direction of the current, and the boys would catch them in their empty water bottles or huge plastic covers. They would then fill the bottles and plastic covers with water sufficient enough for the fish to survive.

Three years back, one rainy season, when the rains poured down their tears, the canal flooded. Hari, an eight-year-old student, stood beside the canal watching his elder brother catch fish.

"There, a black Molly...oh, here comes a goldfish... seize them...quick...," he stood there shouting instructions at his brother.

An unexpected heavy current of water swept away Hari while his brother got out of the water as he was stronger and taller than his younger brother.

After a long search, the villagers found Hari's cold, bruised body lay entangled in reeds, a few miles down the canal.

The boy's parents screamed and howled in grief and accused the school authorities of being so careless.

"Your people killed my son. You were careless. You should have appointed a security guard at the rear gate. You get a huge amount as school fees from us, but...," Hari's father whimpered and sank to the ground. He squatted on the wet ground in front of his small hut and hit his forehead with his palms. Hari's mother and brother were inside the hut hugging each other and moaning. The dead body of the little boy was placed inside the hut for public viewing.

Since the canal did not come under the school property, the parent's claim was dismissed.

Teachers, students, and the managing committee members visited the boy's parents and paid respect to the departed soul before the last rites. The entire school moaned the loss of the student and observed five minutes of silent prayer the next working day.

~ ~ ~

"In a way, isn't the school responsible for the boy's death?" A worried Emmanuel Pereira asked Suresh Chandran the following week.

"How can the school be responsible, Mr. Emmanuel? The gates were closed. The boy jumped over the wall despite numerous warnings. Teachers say that that was not the first time he jumped. Kesu had found him jumping once or twice and caught him red-handed. We punished the boy and informed his parents. Parents are responsible as they did not bring him up properly. You see, they are from the slum, and they do not know how to behave.

How can they teach values and principles to their children? In my opinion, such children should not be admitted to huge schools like ours." Suresh Chandran smiled and assured Emmanuel that the school had no role in the boy's death.

"Hmm…Then, shouldn't we appoint a security guard at the rear gate?" Emmanuel asked as he looked straight into Suresh's eyes.

Suresh felt discomfort and looked up at the dark clouds and said, "Oh, we'll get wet if we stand out on the open ground. Come, let's move to the porch."

They stood on the school porch, which would be soon crammed with students. Rain was a strict timekeeper as it knew when the school hours ended. It came down beating heavily, making thought or movement impossible.

"That simpleton Kesu suggested that we should tighten the security and enforce stricter measures. Who is he to command us? I warned him that a gardener needs to take care of the garden and not to poke his nose into matters related to school administration," Suresh smiled with a mild sneer as the corner of his lips pulled back as Emmanuel listened silently.

Suresh disappeared through the ill-lit corridor that had its exit to the porch. He turned left and vaulted up the stairway that led to the physics lab and a few classrooms.

Emmanuel stared at his impenetrable shadow that stared back with a villainous smile.

Suresh waded in through the clutter of lab equipment and furniture. He looked for the lab assistant. Since no one was there, he took an umbrella he found on the table. As he was about to leave, he saw someone slip into the room annexed to the lab. The old-fangled metal clock on the wall straightened its small hand to four and the larger one to twelve. A hive of activity roared louder than thunder down on the ground.

Suresh walked out of the physics lab and peeped down, holding on to the handrail. He saw students run around with and without umbrellas. They were all scattered and the teachers ran to the Principal's office to sign in the master register before leaving.

"Ugh... It seems like it's been a decade since these students met each other! It's the same every day. The teachers are always in a hurry to leave the school while the students have no intention to go home," Suresh sighed as he thought and climbed down the steps that led to his room downstairs.

~ ~ ~

Every year the water in the canal flowed down fiercely with more fishes, more reeds. Every year naughty boys sneaked around and managed to climb the high stone wall to catch more fish.

~ ~ ~

The rear side of the school faced the fields and a huge pond. The tall trees and creepers enveloped the building into their thick shadows. The backside of the building was devoid of the transparent velvet fold the front view encased. It stared into the empty fields with the paint peeled away and seemed to cough and moan with its rotting skin. As rain tore apart the cobwebs, Kesu felt that it tasted like exile and decay.

"Had I been there at the back gate, this wouldn't have happened. I usually stand there near the gate during lunch breaks. Had the management not called me for asking silly questions about pesticide and manure that was required to grow daisies and lilies in their garden, this could have been averted," Kesu told himself a hundred times over years as he felt guilt and remorse haunt him almost every day.

Kesu's garden bloomed with flowers in all seasons. It knew no summer and winter. His flowers smiled from all corners of the school: besides the main entrance, around the lotus pond, on the sides of the main stage, on the way to the auditorium, and they bloomed in beautiful colors in every available corner.

"Of late, Kesu has developed a strange passion for crimson roses," teachers told each other as they passed the beautiful, red rose plant beside the Biology lab.

Kesu tended to it carefully. He watered and weeded; he put the right amount of pesticide and sang in its ears:

"Sweet little roses, crimson souls,

I see you bleed despite your thorns.

You might droop down into silence

But never fade into your own void."

He touched each petal with fatherly affection. It was in April that he planted the rose, red like the crimson late evening sky. It was an in-between shade, a combination of red and crimson. Strangely it had no odour. Kesu thought that this nature of the flower might protect it from insects and ants that come to suck nectar. Thus, its sweetness can be hidden from the brute world that might trample it and squeeze out its innocence.

A Visitor

Vasudara stood in front of the huge mirror in the hallway on the second floor of the palace. She hesitantly looked at her image, now frail, weak, and coughing. The accident left her with a deserted, bleak look in her eyes.

"Do you earnestly reflect my true self and everybody else's?" She asked the mirror as she wiped her hand through the wooden frame made of medicinal wood. The intricate carvings of elephants on either side of the mirror had accumulated dust over the years. Vasudara's favourite ivory tusks gleamed bright as she dusted and wiped them often. Those were the tusks of Kesavan, her most loved elephant. Among the four tuskers, Vasudara loved Kesavan the most. Kesavan was more like a child and was tame and loving, unlike the other elephants. Kesavan succumbed to old age a few years after Vasudara's marriage. She arranged for the last rites and saw that Kesavan departed as a contended soul. The huge tusks were brought in and fixed to the sides of the mirror in the hallway on the second floor.

She pulled the draw fixed to the sides of the mirror and took a strip of tablet from the red box. She wondered what her grandmother would have said had she been alive to see Vasudara take so many tablets.

"During our times, there were no such doctors. We were all healthy. We never visited the hospital. Even pregnancy and childbirth were managed at home. Now, your parents take you to the hospital even if you sneeze or cough," Vasudara chuckled as she remembered her grandmother's words, and she swallowed three tablets in one gulp.

Vasudara looked at her scoffing image, clad in a saree in the mirror, and crawled up the steep wooden stairway by holding on to the rails. She pulled her aching legs one after the other in a slow, gradual motion, afraid that her feet might get trapped between the steps. She complained to her husband and son about the gaps on the stair treads and the decreasing foot placement space. As both of them did not heed to her, she mumbled worriedly, "One day, you will find me in a pool of blood or hanging midway with a broken ankle."

After the accident, she found it extremely difficult to stand or walk for long hours. The doctor had warned her not to climb the steps.

Vasudara did what she felt was right. This was Vasudara, and people liked her and hated her for the same reason. She listened to all but obeyed only to her little inner voice.

She looked up the staircase that opened up like an unending pathway to heaven. The thin wooden rail had delicate carvings of grapevines: vines that strangled the sides of the stairway like the deadly current of Sindoori during the monsoon. She halted holding on to the rails as she reached the last step that ended on the third-floor hallway. Mural paintings of gods and goddesses stared at her from the high walls.

The dim light faded as she stepped into the worship chamber of the royal household. The vast chamber rested on the weight of six stone pillars. Vasudara raised her head and looked at the stone carving of dragon faces on the top edges of the square stone pillars. The bulging dragon eyes always scared her, and the protruded tongue and sharp teeth whisked her breath away. The four huge wooden windows were open.

She ran her fingers through the almost rusted strings of the *veena* that rested in a corner. The sound from the instrument was mistuned like the tune of her life. She dusted the instrument and covered it with a silk cloth.

Vasudara bowed down to the goddess, who rested peacefully on a high bronze pedestal. The golden idol was draped in red silk and bejeweled with exquisite pearls, diamonds, and other precious stones. Vasudara was the only inheritor of the royal house as the other members received the rightful share of the property and moved to cities and towns. She did not wish to sell the ancestral home and lived there with her husband and son. There were two maids and three manservants in the entire house. She had appointed a priest to perform the daily rituals in the worship chamber. He stayed in a small house behind the palace. It was one of the granaries of the palace and was later converted into a house. The men-servants also stayed in one of the rooms in the three-bedroom tile-roofed house where the priest stayed.

Vasudara sat down on a woolen rug laid on the black marble floor facing the idol. The oil lamps flickered in the wind and threatened to blow out. The only bulb in the corridor outside sighed due to the low voltage current. Streaks of lightning rushed in at frequent intervals, and Vasudara shut her eyes in fear. She saw faces peering at her from the dark corners of the room that were now filled with smudged shades of red.

Memories rushed in mercilessly, and Vasudara saw vague images fade in and out. The fun-filled childhood days and the ritualistic dance of *Kalamezhuthu patu* held during the *Karkidakam* month appeared and disappeared in the form of coloured powder and drawings of goddess.

Rain pelleted harsh drops on the roof, and the noise deafened Vasudara as she shut the huge windows. The wooden doors and windows contracted during the monsoon season and expanded during summer. The wood though lifeless after being slain seemed to know the seasons better than men. It was only 6.30 in the evening, and the sky took a darker grey. While Vasudara struggled with a jammed, creaky, old window, she saw a dark, tall image move into the dark pathway that led to the palace gate. She adjusted her glasses and stretched out to look as far as she could, but old age, fear, and rain smothered her fading vision.

Just then, she heard the huge bronze bell hung on the porch chime thrice. She stood holding to a pillar, heart pounding harder and harder. She had developed a strange sense of fear after the accident. Just then, the intercom in the hallway rang, and Vasudara walked out to the hallway and picked it.

"*Thamburati* (Her Highness) that *madama* (foreigner woman) has come to meet you. She says that you had agreed to meet her. Shall I see her in?" The maid Karthyayini enquired.

"Ah, it might be Evelyn. Show her the way to the stairway and tell her to come to the study on the second floor," Vasudara instructed Karthyayini.

"How will she know where the study is? There are many rooms on the second floor," Karthyayini tried to reason out, hoping that her *thamburati* would have forgotten. Karthyayini had seen everyone remind Vasudara of everything after the accident.

"Don't worry…she knows," Vasudara replied.

Evelyn had spoken about the palace when she spoke to Vasudara over the phone. Evelyn even had a palace map with her, and Vasudara knew that it would not be difficult for Evelyn to find the library in the huge palace.

Vasudara heard Karthyayini chuckle on hearing the name Evelyn before she disconnected the call. Karthyayini found it very difficult to pronounce the foreigner's name, and it was an almost impossible task for her.

"Ma-adam, please come," Karthyayini gestured to Evelyn with a smile. Evelyn grew a sudden liking for the sixty-year-old Karthyayini, who bore a genuine smile that oozed through her small eyes moistened with love and affection.

"I am Karthyayini," Karthyayini smiled as Evelyn took her palm in hers and greeted,

"Hello, I am Evelyn…Kathry…what is your name?" Evelyn asked as she tried to pronounce the maid's name.

Karthyayini pulled out her palm from Evelyn's. With a smile, karthyayini wiped her hands with her saree *pallu*. Karthyayini knew that she shouldn't touch anyone. She knew that she was destined to obey orders and serve her masters.

"Kaarthu. You call me Kaar..thu," Karthyayini opened her mouth widely as she articulated her name loudly.

"Oh, Kaar…thu…nice name," Evelyn smiled as she stood shivering. Evelyn did not take an umbrella, and she got wet by the heavy downpour. Her *salwar kameez* hugged her thin frame as water dripped down from her dress.

"*Aiyoo*, you are all wet. Wait, I'll get you a towel," Karthyayini made Evelyn stand out on the porch while she ran in to fetch a towel.

Karthyayini ran back to Evelyn when she heard a sudden bang on the front door. She was surprised to see Evelyn stand in the living room while she had asked her to stand outside on the porch. There was a pool of water around Evelyn.

Karthyayini handed over the towel and watched the fair foreigner dry her beautiful hair that did not stink of oil. Karthyayini watched the foreigner's wax-like statue shimmer as droplets of water disappeared unwillingly from her face and arms. Karthyayini felt that her dark skin grew darker as she stood beside Evelyn. Karthu's husband always said,

"People like us are leeches of the soil: dark and nauseating filth. We are sinners of the previous birth. The gods cursed us, and we took birth in the lowest, meanest tribes," he also warned their children," Don't go near the upper castes and touch them. Even in your next birth, you'll be born to lower caste parents. Because of you, we'll also incur the curse, and we too will get no *moksha* (freed from the cycle of birth and death)."

Karthyayini never understood why her *thamburati* Vasudara was different from the other people. Vasudara smiled and spoke to her with concern. She always told Karthyayini that every birth in this world is noble and that humanity and love should be the weapon of every human being. She gifted Karthyayini's family with costly dresses and insisted that they enroll their children in Saket school.

"*Thamburati*, how will we pay the fees?" Karthyayini asked Vasudara.

"I will see to that. Don't worry," Vasudara assured her maid and secured seats for the children in Saket school. She did not fail to remit the fees and even met the expenses of buying school uniforms, textbooks, and notebooks for the children.

Karthyayini assumed that Evelyn was afraid of the dark and guessed it as the reason for getting inside the house even before she was ushered in. Karthyayini had heard Vasudara compliment, Evelyn, that she was a good-mannered lass. Evelyn visited Vasudara the previous week to discuss about the palace, the ritual dance of *Kalamezhuthu patu* and to clarify a few other doubts. Since Vasudara had an appointment with her doctor, she sent back Evelyn, assuring her that she would contact her when she was free.

Karthyayini took Evelyn to the guest room and gave her clothes to change. There were a few spare dresses in the cupboard. Vasudara had kept a reserve of dresses for such careless guests. Evelyn kept her bag on a chair and took out the digital voice recorder to check whether it got wet. A bemused Karthyayini crept forward, peering at the strange thing on the chair.

Evelyn smiled, turned on, and played the recorder. Karthu heard the sounds of Ravi, Kesu, and Evelyn in it. Evelyn forwarded the tape a little and pushed the play button to check if it worked. Some conversation rose like whispers from the box. Evelyn was surprised as she listened to the conversation that felt deep and serious. The conversation was in Malayalam, and so Evelyn couldn't make out the subject of discussion, but it was evident that there were only two people, one man and another, a woman.

There was another curious eye who stood dumbfounded in the guest room. It was Karthu. She stood shell-shocked, and Evelyn saw her jaws drop down. There was a visible fear in Karthu's eyes. Evelyn guessed that Karthu knew the people well, and the conversation was both sensitive and important. She turned off the recorder that could record, save, and could be played. Evelyn put the recorder back into her bag and stood up with a forced smile.

A pale-faced Karthu took Evelyn to the living room and gestured her to take the flight of steps to the library. Evelyn was lost in thought, and her eyes didn't take a better view of the grand living and dining rooms she left behind. As Evelyn climbed the steps, Karthu stood staring at the foreigner with bewilderment.

~ ~ ~

The open window gazed helplessly at Vasudara as she failed in her attempts to shut the window door. Thunder shook the old window frame with all its might, and the wind howled louder than the bat-eared reynards in the groves.

Vasudara climbed down the stairs and reached the second floor. The library was on the left side of the long corridor. The rectangular room stood magnificently with six huge glass windows. A wooden table rested at the center of the room, surrounded by cupboards and shelves stacked with books. The warm, familiar air hugged her as she inhaled a lung full of the smell of books, old and new. Silverfish crept within the sea of letters and ruled the kingdom of words. She had a personal collection of a few majestic narratives of Leo Tolstoy, Charles Dickens, William Shakespeare, the Bronte sisters, and Thomas Hardy, and the entire poetry collection of John Keats, P.B. Shelly, William Wordsworth, and Samuel Taylor Coleridge. She had a few of them moved to her room downstairs. A few still stuck to their familiar corners in the cupboard. Her father's and great grandfather's collection of books on philosophy, history, Science, and Agriculture stood with a longing to be touched and caressed from the rest of the cupboards.

Vasudara picked up *The Complete Works of Shakespeare* and flipped through the play, Macbeth. She crushed a silverfish holding it between her thumb and index finger as she read aloud the lines by Macbeth:

"Methought I heard a voice cry "Sleep no more!

Macbeth does murder sleep." (Act 2, Scene 1)

Closing the book and leaving it on the wooden table, she sat beside the huge glass window that overlooked the distant river and fields.

"Don't they have a moral conscience? The ones who did this to me? Maybe they too might be haunted by their thoughts like that of Macbeth: Macbeth who plotted and killed king Duncan, Macbeth who killed everybody. Who is to blame; Macbeth or Lady Macbeth, the soft, pretty hands behind all the crime?" A warm breath escaped Vasudara's lips as thoughts masqueraded in her head.

The mighty, polished wood stood as a grim reminder of a golden era: of kings and queens, soldiers, wars, and power. Raindrops banged their head at the closed glass windows before they shattered into minuscule droplets of pain and memories.

The *kovilakam* (palace) was other historical remains of Kavampuzha like the Sindoori, the *kavu,* and the small village enclosed within the tall blue mountains. The 400-year-old palace, replete with wood carvings and ornate murals, covered 2650 sq. m.

Vasudara was roused from her reverie by a delicate tapping at the door. The door opened and Evelyn stepped in.

"Come in, Evelyn. So pleased to have you here today... please have your seat," she greeted her with an earnest smile.

"Thank you ma'am, hope you are in good health," Evelyn enquired as she pulled out a chair and sat down on the opposite side of the huge table. She ran her fingers through the dimpled table and placed her bag on it. The light from the chandelier glowed with a kind warmth.

Thunder crackled, and the lights went out. Evelyn helped Vasudara light the two brass vintage oil table lamps and the soft light brightened the two faces.

The Flood

Waters screamed behind the hooded night. Kesu rose from the coir cot and felt cold water beneath his feet. He put his cot in the tiny space which Mira called the veranda. The small house could not accommodate all four of them. It had been days since he slept peacefully. He expected the Sindoori to inundate their little village any time. Everyone who lived in the low-lying areas of the village stayed awake during the monsoon season. Every year, water mercilessly deprived them of everything, including self-respect and self-integrity. When their houses and belongings were washed away by water or turned to debris by landslides, they ended up living at the mercy of others. Fear does not have a reason when the mind is psychologically affected.

Kesu was awake until then, but he dozed off owing to tiredness and lack of sleep. He saw people bundling their belonging and snatching whatever they found as they ran, clutching their dear lives. The young and the healthy ones dragged their children and the old and the sick people in their homes. Latha and the girls woke up hearing the loud noises. They were prepared to leave any moment. Kesu had already packed their belongings: a few clothes, some food, blankets, mats, and pillows and left them in the church on the hill. That was the temporary place where the villagers who lived in the low-lying area shifted to.

The water canal behind the slum began to overflow down its stained edges. The black, stinking water lingered around plastic waste before it gradually oozed into the houses nearby. Malu hung a bag on her shoulders and stood outside the hut, reluctant to move.

"Why the hell are you still standing there? Have you decided to kill yourself?" Latha's nose flared with anger and worry as she shouted at her daughter.Kesu stared helplessly at both the mother and daughter.

He hurried to Malu and pleaded with his eyes to go with them.

"Leave me at Evelyn's house. I am not coming with you to the church," Malu told her father.

Kesu did not want to argue with his daughter, so he picked his mobile and dialed Evelyn's number. The severity of the rain had lessened, and it drizzled. Kesu tried thrice, and it showed a poor network. He moved to the road and tried one last time. It went a full ring, but no one picked. As he was about to turn back home, Evelyn returned the call. Kesu handed over the call to Malu, who was standing beside him.

"Hello, Evelyn. I am Malu," Malu spoke into the tiny mobile.

"Ah, Malu, what happened?" Evelyn enquired.

"Eve, the waters are swallowing our houses, and we are moving," Malu's sorrow-filled voice reached Evelyn's ear.

"Umm... you had hinted about it earlier. But... I am... wait, hold on for a while..." Evelyn put Malu's call on hold and spoke something to Vasudara.

After a few minutes, Evelyn returned to Malu, who was waiting at the other end.

"Well, tell your father to leave you at the palace at Mrs. Vasudara's place. I am there with her. She is happy to have you here. Wait, she will talk to your father," Evelyn told Malu and she handed over her mobile to Vasudara.

A surprised Kesu pressed the mobile close to his ears as he listened to Vasudara speak, "Kesu, I am Vasudara. Bring your daughter here to the palace. Don't worry." The call got disconnected, and rain poured down furiously.

Kesu stared at the mobile in his hand and then at his daughter's rain-washed face. Malu watched his jaw slacken and his eyes widen as he stroked his bearded chin, almost grey with age and burden of life. As the rain intensified, Latha and Mira came running to Kesu, holding an umbrella each. They had only two usable umbrellas, both stitched and mended like their lives. Kesu held his younger daughter's hand while Latha and Malu followed him. Malu held her bag closer to her to prevent the dresses from getting wet.

~ ~ ~

The church was crowded, and the statue of Jesus Christ watched the displaced people with tear-filled eyes from the wooden crucifix. Torches and candles lit the main entrance and the altar. The believers kneeled in prayer for redemption from sins that were never theirs while the others secured a place for their family to rest. Some children and a few elderly had already slept, spreading their mats on the floor. A few men gathered outside smoking and discussing the previous year's fatalities caused by rain. They expected a landslide, and so they kept watch outside. Fatalities were significantly less compared to the previous year as the people reached the church on time. The church was located on a quiet cul-de-sac hidden from nature's fury and abysmal human thoughts. Some people brought their cows and goats with them and tethered the animals to the pillars outside. A few others locked their hens in a temporary cage built at the entrance.

The heavy wind shook the huge trees, and thunder echoed in the blue mountains. A few young men collected the meat, grains, vegetables, and provisions from everyone gathered there and locked the grains including perishables in a separate room adjacent to the main building. They formed a community kitchen and cooked food for all the people there. They shared whatever food they cooked and fed the animals too.

Kesu, Latha, and Mira walked up the hill after leaving Malu at the palace. On the way, Kesu saw the toddy shop all lighted up and a few men gulping cheap white toddy. Two men were quarreling while two others lay unconscious. There was a rumor that Kannapan's liquor shop distilled liquor with old batteries and snake venom. Whenever insects and lizards crawled over the houses in the slums, the women mocked their men by telling,

"Go catch them in sacks and give it to Kannapan. He might be running out of ingredients to brew your liquor."

Kesu bumped over a tall, lean man, Kannapan's aide and supplier of liquor and *Taste of Heaven*, marijuana.

"You've only one daughter? Where is the other one? Threw her into the water?" he asked with roaring laughter as he bent down to cup Mira's face with his palm.

Latha pulled aside Mira and walked fast to join a family who walked ahead of them. Kesu stared at the man and tried to walk past him.

"I'll find her out. Wherever on earth you hide your moon, I'll find her," the tall man smelled his index finger and inhaled deeply.

Rain washed Kesu's tears as he pulled his shaky, tired legs up the hill.

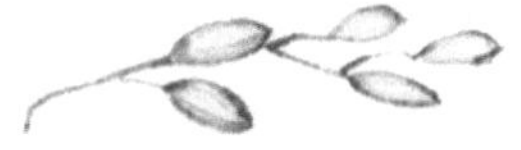

Malu

Malu stood on the porch hugging her bag of clothes when Karthyayini opened the main door of the palace holding a lantern in her left hand.

"Come in," Karthu led Malu into the living room and kept the lamp down on the floor. She then closed the main door and bolted it.

"These days I hear some noises at night. The others don't believe that I hear some strange sounds like someone walking outside in the garden. Some days I feel that someone is hiding inside the house and is watching all of us. *Thamburati* says that I don't get sleep at night as I take an afternoon *siesta*. Maybe she is right," Karthu told Malu.

Karthu and Kesu were neighbours and distant relatives but they never found time to meet each other. Karthu, had been staying in the palace as she was a permanent employee there. Her husband and two children lived in a house near the palace. On some days, the children stayed with her in the palace.

"It's been a long time since I saw you. *Thamburati* told me to stay here in the palace. Her son and husband are busy, and they won't be here with her on all days…," Karthu continued to speak while Malu looked around the huge living room with awe. It breathed of fine polished wood. The ornately carved royal blue sofa set stared at the gold glass chandelier hung from the wooden ceiling. A TV unit in walnut finish adorned the side wall facing the central courtyard. Malu's hands felt the chill of the cold water inside the wall aquarium. Her eyes traced the lines of fishes moving around water ferns and aquarium lilies.

"You can see everything tomorrow in broad daylight. The power supply is cut because of the heavy rain and wind," Karthu's face filled with pride as she watched the girl marvel at the majestic wonder.

Karthu took Malu to the guest room that was dimly lit by a dim light of a table lamp.

"Change your clothes and take rest. I shall get you some tea," Karthu told Malu as she stumped into the kitchen with her short, thick legs.

Malu put her bag down on the floor in a corner and locked the door. She then walked around to check if all the windows in the room were shut and pulled the curtains over the windows. Malu then picked a dress from her bag and changed her wet *salwar kameez*. She looked into the full-length mirror on the wall and watched the low-neck olive green, lengthy nightdress that hugged her slender frame. She got the dress from the town when she got admission to a college in Bangalore. Malu bought two pairs of jeans and tops too along with the nightwear. She dreamt of a new life in a free world. The light in the room dimmed, and her image faded in the mirror.

Malu had always wanted to wear a comfortable dress that gave her more freedom to breathe, but her mother never allowed her to wear such dresses that revealed her femininity. According to Latha, girls should wear a *salwar kameez* or a long skirt with a sleeved blouse. Latha always insisted Malu to cover herself with a shawl over the *salwar kameez*.

"A women's dress should be the reflection of her modesty. Why do you invite attention from men by wearing dresses that reveal all your body parts? It's all women's fault. Girl's like you should cover up properly else men will tease you. Can the men be blamed for touching you? You are tempting them to seek you," Latha once told Malu when the latter stepped out of the house in a full-length *salwar kameez* without a shawl.

"*Amma*, girls of my age wear jeans and short dresses. I look so funny in this attire. Please, why don't you allow me to wear something I like to wear?" Malu pleaded to her mother whenever her mother got her a new dress.

Latha shut her daughter's mouth with a stern look and a firm reply, "No is a no. I am not somebody's mother, and you are not somebody's daughter. As long as you are in my care, you will never wear any such kind of whore's dresses."

All conversations on dresses always ended with that.

Malu sighed and sat on the chair beside the window. She saw potted white and pink flowers outside the window. Rain flooded the ground, and thunder boomed loudly.

The guest room was a bath attached room with a bedroom, a small living, a balcony, and a small study. There were two beds in the bedroom, and a table stood near the window that faced the garden. Malu felt that it was a room that extended out towards the garden as all the four windows in the bedroom overlooked the garden on both sides. There was a lamp on the table beside the window and a painting of a woman holding her child hung on the wall above the table. A round Quartz clock ticked on the opposite wall. The fan churned noisily above her head. She felt sleepy as she sank into the bed and rested her head on the soft pillow. She felt the luxury of sleep overcome her. She had never slept on a mattress before. Her family spread a mat on the cement floor and slept on it.

Karthu woke Malu with a cup of steaming tea. Malu tied her long hair in a knot and opened her large black eyes. Her eyes blinked as her long eyelashes swept the edges of her eyes like ebbing waves. Karthu saw a red sea of tides dissolve into her beautiful black eyes.

"Did you fall asleep so fast? You look very tired," Karthu let out a concerned sigh as she sat beside Malu and stroked her head.

"Ah, I dozed off. It's very cold, and I felt sleepy," Malu replied with a smile as she sipped the hot tea.

Malu bent down to place the empty cup on the table beside the window. Her low, deep neckline lowered more to reveal her soft blossom that glistened in the dim light. Karthu's eyes peered through Malu's low necked top as fear rimmed the maid's eyes and her jaws opened wide.

"Malu...," Karthu screamed as she ran her fingers through the healing crimson scars below the neck.

Malu slumped over with her neck and curved her shoulders as she hugged her knees and bent her head down.

Karthu held Malu's tender frame in a warm, consoling hug as Malu lay down on the warm comfort of the bed like a light, broken blood feather. "I know...I heard something in Evelyn's recorder...," Karthu stopped abruptly sensing fear in Malu's face.

"Did they reach the church safely? *Amma*, *appa* (father) and my little Mira," thoughts swirled around her head, and she finally fell asleep.

Karthu turned off the light, closed the door, and left the room, thinking that the girl needed a good sleep.

CHAPTER 5

Shadows of the Night

Evelyn and Vasudara sat across the huge wooden table facing each other. Evelyn's voice recorder rested attentively on the table, bridging the gap between the two women. The crickets chirped and scissored the wings of silence after the rain. Lingering raindrops hesitantly fell, measuring the distance between the roof and the ground. Most of the books in the library snored peacefully over years of untouched chastity.

Evelyn picked a little, white round pebble from one of the flower pots and felt its smooth edges between her fingers. Two black porcelain teacups with coffee stains hugging the golden lines across the bottom seemed to still savor the sweetness of lips around their mouths.

"So, Evelyn, what was the urgency in calling Malu to the palace?" Vasudara asked Evelyn as her eyes peered through the spectacled, grim face.

Evelyn shuffled her feet restlessly under the table and pressed the pebble hard with her fingers. She had known Vasudara only for the past two months, but she grew a sudden affection for her because of the motherly love Vasudara showered. Vasudara was the first person in the village whom Ravi, the face painting artist, introduced to Evelyn.

~ ~ ~

It was almost 5:30 p.m. when Ravi took Evelyn to Vasudara's house. It had been just a couple of days since she arrived at Kavampuzha. Ravi arranged for Evelyn's accommodation through Kesu. Ravi tried to avoid conversations with Sreedhara Menon after Parukutty's marriage. The entire village knew that Sreedhara Menon was money-minded and would seize every opportunity to pocket as much money as possible without shedding a drop of sweat.

Sreedhara Menon never allowed anyone inside his compound wall. He sat for hours watching the canopy of mangoes that blanketed the garden in yellow, green, and brown. Parukutty would sometimes give a few mangoes to her neighbours without her husband's knowledge. If ever Sreedhara Menon came to know of it, he would bark at Parukutty for being so generous. Sreedhara Menon saw that the branches of the mango trees never stretched beyond his premises. He cut the protruding branches or carefully picked all the mangoes that fell on the other side of his compound wall.

Initially, the villagers were hesitant to speak to the foreigner. Evelyn watched them peer at her when she went out with Ravi. The black mini portable voice recorder accompanied the foreigner wherever she went. The recorder faithfully listened and captured every sound whenever Evelyn pressed a small button on its side. Evelyn recorded the sound of birds during the day and the sound of crickets at night. Later, she listened to all the voices trapped in her recorder.

"*Tamburati* (Her highness), she is Evelyn," Ravi waved his hand and introduced Evelyn to Vasudara. " I had told you about Evelyn when I met you a couple of days back," Ravi reminded Vasudara.

"Oh, yes, nice to meet you, Evelyn," Vasudara welcomed the foreigner with folded hands as a sign of respect.

"It's a pleasure meeting you madam Vasudara,' Evelyn acknowledged Vasudara's hospitality by bringing her hands together, imitating Vasudara's gesture, and bowed her head as a mark of respect.

They were seated in the huge living that spoke of ancient charm and aristocracy. There was no one else in the palace, and so Vasudara excused herself to get something to drink and left for the kitchen. The maid Karthyayini went to her house as it was her mother's death anniversary.

Evelyn followed her through the huge dining hall that could fit in a hundred people all at a time. She marveled at the three-legged, glass-top dining table that stood firmly at the center of the dining hall. Evelyn bent down and closely watched the carving of three dancing women finely carved in wood on the three legs. It seemed that the women faced each other, but when one looked from the corners of the room, it seemed that the women looked at them. Vasudara reached the dining hall with two glasses of lemonade, and she watched Evelyn sketching the legs of the wooden dining table with her left hand. Evelyn's left-hand fingers moved deftly with artistic ease sketching the intricate carving.

"That is a hundred-year-old table," Vasudara smiled and told Evelyn as she placed the glasses of lemonade on the dining table.

"Ah, this is unbelievable. The carving is a marvelous piece of craftsmanship," Evelyn exclaimed as her sea-green eyes glistened under the warm light that shone from the incandescent bulb on the wall.

Their conversation was interrupted when Ravi's mobile rang, humming a famous Malayalam song,

Kalpantha kalatholam kathare neeyen munnil

Kalhara haravumay nilkkum…

Vasudara translated the meaning of the song to Evelyn as she narrated Ravi's sad love story. Evelyn recorded Ravi's story in the voice recorder as Vasudara narrated to her and she loved the lines of the song that meant,

Oh, my darling, you will remain in me holding a garland of white lotus, until the last flood, until the creation ends. like Radha who stole the heart of her beloved Krishna.

"I am sorry. Ravi must be in a hurry. He had told me that he had some urgent work in the temple. Well, I am afraid I have to leave soon," Evelyn apologized for leaving early.

"That's alright, Evelyn. You can visit me anytime," Vasudara assured as she served a glass of lemonade.

"Thank you," Evelyn replied as she held the blue prism, flat-bottomed glass with her left-hand fingers.

"How long will you be here?" Vasudara asked Evelyn.

"Well, I will be here for two or three months," Evelyn replied as she sipped the refreshing cold liquid.

It was 6:00 in the evening, and the sun had not yet set. Evelyn felt the heat burn her as sweat dripped down her forehead. The fans in the rooms let down hot air as it whirled noisily. Through the dining room windows, Evelyn could see the dry fields stretching endlessly in search of a drop of water.

Evelyn and Vasudara went to the living room. Vasudara handed over the glass of lemonade to Ravi, who had by then ended the call.

Ravi got the glass from Vasudara with a smile. He visited Vasudara once in a while, especially after his foreign trips. Vasudara waited for the stories from distant lands which the youngster carried with him.

Evelyn hugged Vasudara before she left, and Vasudara patted her on the shoulder affectionately.

~ ~ ~

The wind howled in through the open windows of the library and blew off the candle with a roar. The scented woodwick wax candle listened to Evelyn and Vasudara as it crackled from the large jar kept in the corner of the table beside the wooden bookshelf. The window behind the shelf remained shut as the bookshelf occupied a large area covering the window. Evelyn inhaled a lungful of the cold air, but her pink lips spread into a thin line as she stared at the sobbing dark sky

Evelyn chose a folder in her recorder and pressed the play button.

~ ~ ~

On the 12th of April when darkness gathered over Kavampuzha like the hundred-headed *Ladon*, the villagers had gathered in the *kavu* to pray. Kesu had transformed into the *koladari*, the holy performer, and his wife Latha too accompanied him to the temple with their youngest daughter.

Malu had been waiting at the village bus stop since 5:45 p.m., but the last bus to town did not arrive even after 7:30 p.m. Malu decided to return home as it was getting dark. Even if she caught a bus to the town, she knew that she would miss the bus to Bangalore.

Malu decided to take the shortest route to her house, which was almost an hour's walk from the bus stop. She thought about whether she should go to the *kavu* but she didn't want to hear her mother shout at her for entering the temple wearing a salwar kameez. Even though Malu had worn a shawl to cover her youthful bosom, her mother detested girls stepping inside the holy *kavu* wearing the pant-like costume that hugged the legs.

"Wear a skirt or *set mundu* to the *kavu*," Latha insisted and the girls obeyed.

Kesu once told Malu, "Often it's fear and not devotion that rules the devotees. All the religions teach the necessity to 'know thyself' and the importance of the realization of oneness with the creator and the universe. Can't change the ones like your mother. Listen to her for the sake of peaceful coexistence in the house," Kesu and his daughter roared with laughter and Malu agreed to listen to Latha.

The faint light from the stars lit the narrow pathway that ended in the fields. Twenty-one-year-old Malu was not thin and delicate like her sister Mira. Malu looked plump and chubby and a pleasant smile radiated from her warm beige face. She hung the huge brown bag on her left shoulder and lit a small plastic torch using her right hand. The faint light from the torch flickered in the dark. Since childhood, she had walked through the path, but her father never permitted her to walk through the narrow lane at night. The lane was frequented by drunkards and Kesu was afraid that someone might harm the girls in the dark.

Malu tried to walk fast, but she slowed down at times because of the heavy bag hung on her shoulders. After a few steps, she put the bag down with a thud and stood panting for breath, drank some water from the plastic bottle, and continued her journey. She walked past the Mexican lilac fences that peered at her in the darkness. She felt relieved when she saw some faint lights from the houses. The doors of all the houses were closed but the walls echoed with conversations. Malu opened the fence gate that led to Sreedhara Menon's backyard. Once inside the backyard, Malu put her bag down and closed the fence gate. She hastened to the house where Evelyn stayed and rang the bell twice. There were no lights, and Malu guessed that Evelyn would have gone to the *kavu*.

Malu took her water bottle from the bag to drink a little more water, but only a few drops were left. She drained them on her tongue, lifted her heavy bag, and hung it on her shoulder. She walked through the thick trees and reached the other end of the yard that had an exit gate to the left. Malu opened the fence gate and stepped out. Once again, she put her bag down and closed the gate. She had to cross three more houses, and she would reach the open fields. From there, it was just a matter of 15 minutes to her slum.

Malu felt tired, weak, and unsteady. Her legs trembled as she leaned against the wall. She saw the window of Sulochana's house open with a thud. The girl felt that her feet sank into the ground, and darkness covered her eyes.

~ ~ ~

Evelyn reached home the next day, on the 13th morning from the *kavu*. She had recorded and took videos of the fiery, spectacular event that would help her in her research work on *Theyyam*. Tired and sleepy, Evelyn slept for eight long hours.

That night Evelyn expected Angela's call. Kavampuzha was a remote village and the network connections were poor. It was almost 11:30 in the night and Evelyn held her mobile in her hand and walked around the yard, searching for a spot that boosted the mobile signal. This was a problem she faced in the small village. The village and the villagers stood detached from the world and sidestepped whenever development tried to saunter in with baby steps. Evelyn felt that the villagers were rooted in their beliefs and preferred to remain crunched under the heavy boots of stagnation. Kavampuzha is enthralled in remaining enclosed within its epochs of retrogression.

Angelina appeared on the flickering screen as her blonde curls fell down her light cheeks. Evelyn moved towards the thick enclosure of trees and pressed her ears hard at the mobile screen as the voice at the other end seemed to be unsteady. The call got disconnected. Evelyn tried dialing twice but failed.

"Why is it always like this here? *J'en ai marre* (I am fed up)," Evelyn clenched her fists in anger.

Only then she realized that she was standing all alone amidst the tall trees in the dead of night. Gripped by fear, Evelyn shivered in the dark. As she turned to leave, she felt she heard a scream from the house nearby and ambled to the fence gate at the other end of the yard with the help of the faint light from her mobile. She did not turn on the torch as she felt that it would invite attention.

The two-storied house rose like a haunted building. Tall trees surrounded it, and Evelyn could not make out anything else. The windows looked like mirrors in the night, and bluish fluorescent lights in the porch flickered.

The fence gate opened with a creak when Evelyn pulled the piece of bamboo and slid across the gate. The window that faced the fence opened and from it peered a mustached, grinning face complemented by a rakish light in soft brown eyes and a tumble of curly black hair.

"That might be the wind," A coarse voice spoke after finding nothing in the wilderness and disappeared into the room as it pulled back the ringed fingers that clutched the window doors.

Evelyn hid behind the wall and tall trees. Sulochana's husband left a few days after Remya's funeral and Evelyn had heard the villagers say that Sulochana lived alone in the huge house. The foreigner sensed danger and decided not to venture into the dark alone.

~ ~ ~

Malu tried to wake up and sit. She felt heaviness in her throat as if she lumped her esophagus and her head swirled. Her legs were stiff, and she felt soreness between her thighs. The eyelids fell heavily as she forced it open.

The young girl did not know whether it was day or night when she opened her eyes. She was lying in a dim-lit room with just a chair in a corner. There was a small room beside the bedroom, and she guessed it to be a bathroom. The only window was partially open. As she pulled off the blanket that covered her, she felt the air rush through her naked breasts. Alarmed, she screamed and slid under the blanket. She touched her body and was shocked and frightened to know that she was stark naked.

Loud footsteps approached the room. Malu tried to get up and rush to the open door to latch it. She stepped out of the bed, wrapped the blanket around her naked body, and dragged her legs towards the door, only to learn that the door had no bolt. Horrified, she rushed to the bed and hid under the covers. She searched for her clothes but could not find any.

A tall, middle-aged man barged into the room.

"Ah, so you are awake, dear?" he asked Malu as his colossal frame seemed to tremble with anger as he pulled out a cigar from his shirt pocket. Malu watched him light the cigar and stared at him as he burned his sixth dangling finger with rage.

"Who are you? Please let me go…," Malu whimpered in soft screams.

"Shut up, you daughter of a whore!" The man slapped across Malu's tired face as the girl shrieked in pain.

"You can call me *mama* (uncle) if a name is all that you need to know," The man spoke as he pushed Malu's tender frame to the bed. He pressed the burning cigar bud to her thighs and let out a burst of beastly laughter as he watched the girl scream in pain.

"Cry! No one is going to hear you. Stop! You bitch! Do you know how much your father owes me? I am tired of asking him. Now, I know how to make my money. You'll be here only for this week. I've already sold you. You worth a million darling!" The man whistled and blew a narrow stream of warm, nauseating air on Malu's neck. The girl felt that the air whisked the moisture from her skin and made her dehydrated.

"Why do you punish me? It's my father who got money from you and I am sure that he will repay you. He's not a cheat," Malu groped for words as thoughts escaped her wounded lips.

"Slut! Shut up and don't dare open your mouth," the beast threatened as he brought the lit cigar to her thighs once again.

Malu sobbed and swallowed her screams.

"That's my good girl," the man smiled and sat beside the frightened girl as he slid his hands through the bed cover and squeezed her breasts hard. Malu screamed and tried to push him away, but the giant overpowered her and slid some powder down her throat.

"Sleep baby," the hapless girl heard a monstrous voice speak as the huge fingers tugged and tore through her soft skin. She felt his coarse lips trace her curves as he thrust himself into her violently.

Tears dripped down her eyes before they closed painfully. The owls hooted in the trees, and the tall blue mountains echoed the wolves' howl that tore through the silent night.

CHAPTER 6

Encounter with God

High up the hills, amidst the dark shadows on the pinnacle, I felt I saw a faint blue light flicker in the rain. The dense trees swayed furiously. I looked around and found everyone asleep. I tried waking up Latha and Mira, but my hands were numb, and my voice choked within. I rose, walked out through the enormous wooden doors of the church, and headed towards the flickering blue light. I could feel the rain pour down all around me.

I walked through the darkness towards the light. The swaying trees closed upon me as I climbed up the hill. Streams of water edged down through the corners of my eyes and slid down my bare shoulders. Lightning lit my path, and thunder echoed to the hills about the strange light. I gasped for breath as I reached the pinnacle and sat down under the umbrella of furious rain. Did I close my eyes for a while? I do not remember, but I know that I saw God. God was a '**He.**' I am sure. He held no divine light around his head and had hands and legs like me. He wasn't an inch taller than me, but his large black eyes stared at me with unfamiliarity. He said he had no name.

God: Why are you here?

Kesu: You seem to be God.

God: Yes, I am God.

Kesu: You're supposed to be fair-skinned, but you are brown like me, like the dirt in which I live.

God: You did not answer my question.

Kesu: You are all-knowing. Then, why do you ask?

God smiled radiantly and said," For every beginning, there is an end."

Kesu looked at God with baffled eyes.

God: Move aside, I am leaving.

Kesu was startled and he jumped up to move three feet aside and paved the way for God.

God smiled contentedly and replied," See you soon."

Kesu saw God walk past the pinnacle of the hill and disappear into the night as the forest resounded to the jingle of the golden *chilambu* (anklet) around his ankles.

Thunder crackled and a fireball lit the other side of the tall blue mountains. Kesu woke up with a sudden jerk and looked around. He was shell shocked to realize that he was sitting on the peak of the hill. He felt his head whirl as he peeped down from the tip of the cliff. He saw the whole village stretch below him as a speck beside the river Sindoori.

"Maybe the Gods might also have the same vision from the heavens. How tinier we humans might appear from there! We who are mere portraits of enlarged insignificance!

Maybe that is why the Gods keep watching all the time while we suffer," Kesu let his words as rain washed his dark frame only to glisten darker.

Kesu tried hard to remember how he climbed the steep, slippery hill bare feet but couldn't recollect anything except the faint blue light. He looked around and saw nothing except darkness. The path down was slippery, and as Kesu put his right foot forward to check for loose rocks, a small piece of rock slid 700 m down the hill. The short plants gave a firmer grip, and Kesu's slender body slithered down carefully. Fear thumped in his chest louder than the thunder as he struggled to keep step after step. His white cotton *mundu* was covered in mud as he had to bend down at times to climb down the steep rocks.

Heavy rain had subsided, and it was drizzling. Kesu covered half the distance. He was afraid to sit down as the hills were the home to foxes, boars, and wild elephants. He had heard stories of *yakshi*, the she-ghost, the beautiful vampire woman dressed alluringly to charm young men to her den. The village folk believed that young men who ventured out to the hills alone at midnight never returned. They were found dead somewhere in the forests with their hearts and brain ripped apart mercilessly.

Kesu climbed down a few more kilometers grabbing his courage that was torn apart by fear. As he climbed down, he felt he heard the sound of flowing water. Kesu guessed it to be a water stream, and he knew that he had to walk just five more kilometers to reach the foot of the hill. He rested his tired body beside the stream and bent down to wash his face, arms, and legs that were scathed by fatigue and thorny bushes.

"I am unafraid of dying but afraid of living with my two daughters," Kesu said as he stood up to remove the *dhothi* draped around him and wash it in the clear water.

Suddenly, Kesu felt the bushes move in the dark. He moved aside carefully, wrapped his *dhothi* around his waist, and turned around slowly. He felt he saw red blood ooze down his direction towards the stream of water. His eyes were by now familiar with the dark. His heart screamed aloud as he moved forward. The darkness echoed the jingle of the *chilambu*.

"So, is it God who…?" Doubt and fear beat the walls of his palpitating heart.

Transfixed with horror, Kesu's heart beat faster, and the muscles around his eyes began to twitch as he spotted a severed hand near the thorny bush. Gold rings gleaned from all five fingers while the sixth one stood apart drenched in blood. Kesu pressed his eyes shut for a few minutes and took a deep breath.

He then turned around, swallowed his fear, and ran as fast as he could. Within two hours, he reached the foot of the hill. He sat down for a while as he gasped for breath. Rain poured down heavily, and he gaped up to heaven with his mouth wide open and gulped down nature's bounty. The church lights sparkled from a distance as they lit the dense trees. Kesu reached the church, and the vast clock struck four times. He realized that it was 4 a.m. Kesu took a quick bath, washed his soiled *dhothi*, and cuddled beside his daughter and wife like a small child, wrapped in the comfort of home.

CHAPTER 7

The Decision

Vasudara wiped the tears that fell inconsolably down her wrinkled cheeks as she listened to Evelyn narrate Malu's story. It was almost midnight when Evelyn finished narrating the incident that happened in Malu's life.

"I can't take in anymore," Vasudara sobbed as she held the edges of the big wooden table in the library with her trembling hands.

Evelyn wrapped her arms around Vasudara in a gentle hug as she tried to console the old lady.

"Well, I wouldn't have told this to you, but the situation demanded it," Evelyn tried to explain.

Vasudara wiped her face with the saree *pallu* and stood up with the help of Evelyn.

The skies groaned and gathered like dark leeches emerging like hundred-headed giants. Fear and sorrow gripped Vasudara's fragile frame as she staggered forward with the help of Evelyn. Night wished to filter the sound of humanity and compassion with practiced ease, but traditional patterns of human life threatened to scald honour and justice.

~ ~ ~

The next day, when Vasudara woke up, she found Malu helping Karthu in the kitchen. It was 8:30 in the morning.

"*Thambrati*, you look very tired. Did you wake up till late night yesterday?" Karthu asked Vasudara with concerned eyes.

"Don't ask too many questions. Give me a cup of tea," Vasudara ordered Karthu with a friendly smile.

Malu poured steaming hot tea flavoured with ginger and basil leaves into Vasudara's white teacup. The smell was invigorating as Vasudara brought the cup to her faint lips.

"So, today Karthu did not prepare the tea," Vasudara said as she looked at Karthu.

"I told the girl that you will like it only if I prepare, but she insisted...," Karthu flashed her teeth angrily at Malu.

"Karthu, I never said that the tea tasted bad. I only said that this is super tasty, unlike the watery mess you give me every morning and evening," Vasudara chuckled as she winked at Malu.

Karthu stomped out of the kitchen, banging at the door on her way out to the extended working kitchen. The working kitchen was where Karthu cooked non-vegetarian food for the menservants, and the two dogs. It was a spacious room that opened to the garden outside. Karthu grew a small vegetable garden and felt proud whenever Vasudara praised her for her efforts.

Vasudara sat alone on a bench in the garden. The rain-washed trees looked fresh and joyous as droplets of water dripped down the leaves. The evening sun appeared with a faint smile and Vasudara watched the rainbow stretch across the grey sky. Butterflies fluttered around flowers and the scent of damp earth filled the air. Vasudara inhaled the fresh air and decided to get an admission for Malu in a college run by one of her former students. She had already discussed the same with Kesu.

CHAPTER 8

Mystery on the Hills

Kesu woke up and stretched his arms and legs as he leaned against the wall.

"Seems like your father was running all night," Latha laughed derisively.

Kesu felt that his muscles ached and watched Latha gaze at his bruised skin.

"My dear husband, will anyone scratch his body so badly when mosquitoes bite?" Latha spoke as she covered her mouth and faked a cough to suppress her laughter.

Kesu rubbed his eye with the index finger and looked at the ceiling turning his gaze away from Latha and smiled. He stood up, rubbing his chin, and walked to the bath area behind the church.

Kesu sat on the small wall under the huge banyan tree with his brown leathery face, pale with fear and self-doubt. He pressed his tired feet on the wet ground and felt the warmth of the soil seep in through his soles. His sunken eyes caught his soiled *dhothi* swaying in the wind, and all of a sudden, he felt his head throb in pain.

"Am I losing my sanity?" he wondered.

Kesu walked in and prepared a glass of peppermint coffee. He was one of the volunteers who helped in the running of the community kitchen. Latha and Mira too, helped chop vegetables and wash the dishes since the day they arrived.

"Kesu, you look so tired. You take rest today," Mani, the tea shop owner, advised as he touched Kesu's forehead and neck with the back of the hand to measure the body temperature.

"You seem to be sick, and you're running a temperature," Mani told Kesu.

Kesu nodded as he sipped the steaming coffee, and he felt better. He decided to climb the hill once again to investigate the truth of last night's incident.

He wished to see the demon dead, but he also wished that it should be a dream as his kind self couldn't bear too much of reality shrouded in mysterious philosophy.

~ ~ ~

"Latha might be still talking to her friends or helping the older people, and Mira might be still studying," Kesu thought as he reached the foot of the hill.

Kesu gazed up the huge hill from the green meadow that shimmered in the faint sunlight. Water droplets covered the entire foothill like a golden sheen mocking at the sun's fragile strength that could never dissipate the momentary bubbles with its furious eyes. His jaws dropped down as he wondered,

"Did I climb 2296.59 feet overnight and get down the slippery hill before dawn?"

Kesu gathered the courage and stepped up the steep hill cautiously. He climbed up and walked for nearly two hours, turned right, and headed towards the stream. He heard voices near the stream and suddenly hid behind the thick enclosure of trees. He moved forward, pressing his foot carefully one after the other so that he avoided stepping on twigs and snakes that might lay hidden beneath the fallen leaves.

"Search there behind the bushes," Kesu heard someone shout orders as he neared the spot where he saw the severed hand the previous night.

Two men jumped into the stream and the search party was frantically looking for something. Kesu guessed that there might be more than five men. He peered from the thick bark of a tree and saw a tall frame squatted down on the clearing as his open palm hit the forehead in exasperation and dejection.

"Why did *anna* ever come here alone at midnight? He could have called any one of us," the huge figure moaned.

Kesu could see only his back from where he stood. A twig fell on the man from the branches that swayed and he quickly turned behind and shot a flurry of insults to the wind.

Kesu's eyes widened with alarm as he caught sight of Kannapan's aide Muthu. He was Kannapan's trusted executioner. He had guessed the severed hand to be that of

Kannapan, but now his doubt was cleared. Kesu's slender frame contorted into a numb scream as terror tightened its grip on him and sweat poured down his forehead.

"We couldn't find the body anywhere," the men screamed as they gathered near the stream.

It was late afternoon, and the skies gathered their dark robes to soak the land in misery. Kesu decided to walk back to the church. His stomach contract into a tight ball as small hairs across his chest, arms, and legs stood on the end. Sudden nausea clamoured to his throat as his eyes caught Muthu hug the bloody severed hand.

Kesu closed his mouth swallowing an urge to retch and held on to a firm bark as the blood drained from his head leaving him dizzy. He halted and took a few deep breaths before he slinked past the shadows of the huge trees before Kannapan's men slit his throat and threw him down the hill. Once far away from their presence, Kesu ran down the hill at full speed within two hours, crossed the foot of the hill, and headed towards the cover of the tall trees on the way to the church. Gasping for breath, he squatted under a mango tree and gazed at the skies as several questions barged into his mind.

"Where did you disappear," Latha asked Kesu worriedly.

"I …I went to meet Malu…," Kesu wiped his face to hide his lying eyes from his wife.

"What! Did you go to see Malu? How is she? Had you told us we too would have accompanied you…Why did you go alone?" Latha poured a sea of questions and complaints.

Kesu was lost in thought that he did not hear most of what Latha uttered.

"Are you deaf? How many times have I been asking you about our daughter?" Latha pinched Kesu's arm savagely as she yelled on top of her voice.

The people around turned and gave anxious looks to the fighting couple.

"Don't you all quarrel with your spouse at home? Mind your business," Latha snapped at them, biting her teeth.

Everyone laughed and they continued with their mundane tasks.

"Latha, she is fine and happy," Kesu replied, pulling his wife closer to him," and don't shout like this again," He warned her.

Kesu had a bath, had his lunch, and stretched his body on a creaky wooden bench in the corner of the church hall near the huge window. Sleep blanketed over his exhausted body, and he closed his eyes.

CHAPTER 9

The Strange Noise

Evelyn walked through the slippery narrow pathway to the rented house where she stayed. It had stopped raining, and it was noon. The sun peeped from the veiled curtains of black clouds as if afraid that it might lose its light. The trees drooped down with the weight of heavy water droplets. The sun-kissed droplets glistened with rainbow colours atop the trees. A few trees lay uprooted, disrupting easy passage through the pathway. Evelyn jumped over the fallen branches and counted 1,2,…5. Five trees fell in the previous night's rain. She clicked a photo of the devastation that canopied the pathway like a painting.

Evelyn had assured Vasudara that she would return before dusk with her dresses and a few other things. Vasundara had warned her that the entire village would be flooded and Evelyn would be stranded in the rented house all alone. Also, she would not have access to food and water, for it would take almost a week for the rescue team to reach the village if ever the rain continued pouring down at the same pace.

Sreedhara Menon's land was far away from the flood plains, and there was no threat of water entering the land, but Evelyn knew that she could expect some wild visitors like elephants or boars at night. Moreover, she wanted to learn more about the palace history from Vasudara. Evelyn searched for the keys in her bag only to realize that she had left them at the palace. As she stood there thinking of getting the spare key from Parukutty, her eyes caught sight of a beautiful mural painting on the wall adjacent to the door. It was not there when she left.

Evelyn ran her fingers through the painting of Radha and Krishna held in a warm embrace. It seemed like they emerged from a glistening blue-green peacock feather in the background that shimmered with a golden light. Evelyn felt something strange about the picture despite its perfection. She peered at it once again and realized that Krishna was bald, unlike the other paintings of Krishna, the Hindu mythological God, she had come across. It was a bust-size painting in which the colours merged with love, longing, and desertion in Radha's eyes. Strangely, the edges of the painting were marked with deep red lines as if blood oozed from the corners. Evelyn clicked a picture of the painting with her mobile and walked towards Sreedhara Menon's house to get the key.

Evelyn rang the bell, and Parukutty opened the wooden door.

"Evelyn, where did you disappear yesterday night?" Parukutty enquired with eager eyes.

"Well, I went to meet Mrs. Vasudara. I never expected such heavy rain. I got drenched in the rain and felt it would be safe to stay there," Evelyn smiled as she answered.

"Good that you stayed there at night. It's not safe for young and pretty women like you to venture out alone in the dark," Parukutty said with a tremulous smile.

"Sure, I'll be careful," Evelyn assured her, "I left the keys in the palace. I remembered about that only after reaching here. Can I get the spare key?" Evelyn asked hesitantly.

"You are so fortunate that my husband does not understand English. If ever he gets to know of this, he would have thrown your bags out by now," Parukutty spoke softly with her usual contemptuous little laugh whenever she mocked at Sreedhara Menon.

Evelyn smiled and nodded her head.

"Who painted the mural on the wall in the house where I stay?" Evelyn asked curiously, pointing her finger to the house where she stayed.

Parukutty seemed to be lost in thought for a while before she answered, "Ah, my artist sister Kaveri painted that. Isn't it beautiful?"

"What a beautiful piece of painting! I love those warm colours. She is indeed a great artist," Evelyn praised and enquired," Is she there inside? Can I have a word with her?"

Parukutty gulped down her saliva and stared at Evelyn, and a smirk expanded on the corners of her mouth as she replied, "Kaveri is not well. She has a headache, and she's sleeping. You can talk to her later."

"That's fine. Let her rest. I just wanted to appreciate her for her great art," Evelyn replied.

Parukutty disappeared into the dark corridors and returned with a bunch of keys fastened to a conch keychain.

"Don't lose it. Return it safely," Parukutty hissed in Evelyn's ears, afraid that her husband might get to know of it.

"Don't worry I will not lose it. I will return it to you safely," Evelyn hugged Parukutty as she replied in assurance.

"Stay safe wherever you are, Evelyn," Parukutty patted Evelyn's shoulder.

"Thank you for being so kind and loving," Evelyn replied as she wiped the tears that streamed down her cheeks.

Parukutty watched Evelyn walk carefully towards the house. The ground was slippery, and Parukutty herself had slipped and fallen twice.

Everything beautiful carries with it the luggage of consequences.

The rain is beautiful, but it is not easy to live in a land that is inundated every year. The flowers, the trees, the river- are all beautiful, but they all carry their burden. Everything is gorgeous only for a short while unless you learn how to see and accept life with your heart.

~ ~ ~

Parykutty watched Evelyn's slender frame disappear as she turned around the corner towards the rented house. With a deep sigh Parukutty, shut the door and walked into the living room. Sreedhara Menon's pot belly spread across the huge sofa, growled in tune with the snoring sound that escaped through his open mouth.

"At least these sounds trapped within him are lucky. They escape from his clutches every time he sleeps," Parukutty sighed as she sat down on a chair.

She flipped through the channels lazily and almost dozed off when a scream woke her. She turned to her left and looked at Sreedhara Menon.

"Did he scream in his sleep?" Parukutty brought her face closer to his," No, it's not him. He doesn't have such a good voice after all," She confirmed.

Parukutty stood up and walked to the dining hall. She found her daughter and Kaveri's children playing in the courtyard.

"Maybe it's the children," Parukutty assumed, and she turned to go to the living room. That was when she heard the faint scream from one of the rooms.

Parukutty felt a chill run down her spine, and she stood frozen for a while. Gathering strength, she slowly walked towards Kaveri's bedroom. The children were still playing unmindful of the strange noise.

Parukutty tapped the door of Kaveri's bedroom. There was no response. She tried hard to push against the jammed door.

"Maybe the door is jammed because of the rain," she assumed.

Parukutty was confused whether the sound that she heard was a howl, a moan, or a scream. The jammed door flung open with a thud when she pushed it hard, and Parukutty looked into the room. For a moment she thought that her mind was playing games as she couldn't find her sister anywhere. She walked a few paces inside the room to look once again.

She noticed that the cupboard doors were left open and clothes were strewn everywhere on the floor. Red, blue, green, and black paint lay splattered on the marble floor. Sketches of demonic faces lay scattered all over the bed and a few on the floor. The pillow covers and bedspreads lay in a corner as a crumbled pile. Kaveri's medicines lay scattered on the floor.

"Kaveri... Where are you?" Parukutty screamed and moved behind the huge cot pushing the things on the way with her feet.

She found Kaveri huddled in a corner beneath the open window. Her long hair was untied and it hid her face like violent, untamed strands. Red paint lined her fingers and window bars. The wind howled and rain shattered the silence into pieces.

Parukutty stood trembling from head to toe. Her shoulders hunched, and she felt that she was shrinking as she wrapped her arms around her own body. She moved forward cautiously with wobbly steps, and terror mounted with every step. The scream filled the room once again. This time she knew it was her sister Kaveri.

CHAPTER 10

The Intruder

Evelyn opened the door and stepped inside the small front room. That was where she left her footwear and umbrella. It was a small dingy room that accommodated a small chair and a cupboard. The front room had a wooden door that led to the living cum dining room. Evelyn turned the key to the door that opened to the living. She picked up her bag of wet clothes and was almost about to step in when she found the room in utter chaos. The file she had left on the table was lying down on the floor with the documents strewn all over the sofa. Evelyn stood rooted to the floor as her jaws dropped down in disbelief.

She stepped inside carefully and decided to take a look at the other rooms. A porcelain plate and a stained coffee mug were on the dining table. A packet of bread she had bought a couple of days back lay open, and several crumbs were missing. It was a new packet, and it was sealed when she left. The bedroom door was left ajar and the cupboard doors were wide open. Her lingerie lay crumpled on the bed, and all the other clothes lay down on the floor. Evelyn stood there transfixed, not knowing what to do. She sat there for a while and then decided to take photographs of the chaotic state of the house. She clicked snaps of the living, dining, and bedroom using her mobile shot a video of the same, and saved everything on her laptop. She had luckily carried the laptop with her safe from the intruder.

Evelyn then walked around, looking for any open window or door. There was only one back door that opened from the kitchen. She was always careful that she bolted all the windows and doors. She even double-checked them before she left. She prepared herself a cup of tea and decided to ring Ravi.

~ ~ ~

Ravi arrived within ten minutes. He was as swift as the wind, and he knew the land like the backside of his hand. Evelyn narrated what she saw when she entered, and Ravi saw for himself the miserable state of the house.

"Shouldn't we call the police?" Evelyn enquired.

"We need not inform the police now. So many people are stranded. The water level in the river is alarmingly rising, and everybody is busy preparing for rescue operations. Even if you inform the police, the procedures are lengthy, and moreover, you are a foreigner. Things will get complicated," Ravi suggested as he looked at the mess stretched in front of him.

Evelyn nodded in acknowledgment. She had to listen to Ravi as he was the only reliable person to discuss such sensitive matters.

"Pick up all the paper and check for any missing document," Ravi told Evelyn.

Evelyn picked up each paper and checked for missing sheets.

"All documents are there. Nothing is missing," Evelyn told Ravi, bewildered.

Ravi rubbed his chin and nodded his head.

Evelyn and Ravi walked to the bedroom. Ravi inspected the room and asked Evelyn to fold the clothes and place them in the cupboard. In the meanwhile, Ravi walked around the house and checked the place thoroughly.

Evelyn folded the clothes, placed them on the shelves, and closed the door of the cupboard. She found something unusual in the cupboard mirror.

"Raavi…Raavi…come fast," Evelyn shouted.

She found it difficult to pronounce Ravi's name and stressed the 'a' like in diphthong *aa*.

Ravi rushed to the room, and Evelyn pointed at something written in the mirror. He edged closer to the mirror and strained his eye.

"Which language is this?" Evelyn let out her words as her head whorled in a state of confusion.

Ravi peered at it for more than five minutes when it struck to him that it was written in a mirror image.

"Evelyn, look it's a mirror image. Now try to read," Ravi beamed with pride when he deciphered the code language.

"It's all smudged and seems to be strenuous to read," Evelyn replied as she strained her eyes to make out each letter.

"The letters are written using charcoal, and it appears to be smudged. Whoever has written this has done this deliberately to confuse the reader," Ravi bit his lower lip as he stared at the black letters.

"Bring me a pen and a piece of paper," Ravi told Evelyn.

Evelyn ran back with a pen and a small notebook.

"Now takedown.

"You stole my voice. Return it or die."

Now, someone is going to reward you generously," Ravi laughed as he winked at Evelyn mockingly.

Evelyn went pale with fear, and she struggled hard to stop herself from trembling.

"Has he left any name?" Evelyn's pale voice rang through the room.

Ravi could feel Evelyn's heart jump to her mouth and her pale face became paler.

"Unfortunately, the intruder hasn't revealed any name. What a coward! Else *madame* fearless *Maid of Lorraine* would have marched to his den and stabbed him straight in the heart," Ravi laughed hysterically, looking at Evelyn.

Evelyn's fear transformed to anger as she clutched her fists and hit Ravi on his chest.

"*Madame…s'il vous plait, pardonnez-moi*, madam, please forgive me," Ravi responded jokingly.

"*menteur*, you liar! Admit that you did this intentionally to scare me," Evelyn shook Ravi's body with all her strength in anger.

Ravi stopped laughing and held Evelyn's hand.

"Eve, it was not me. How can I ever do this to anyone? Be careful. Someone's there behind you. I didn't want to see you annoyed, so I tried to put it more lightly," Ravi spoke in a low controlled voice, with an expressionless face.

Evelyn sank into the bed and hid her face with her palms in rejection of the entire situation.

"Come on, get up. Take a bath and get ready. I will wait in the living room. There is no time to waste. You should leave the house before it gets dark. I will leave you at the palace and remember not to go out anywhere for a few weeks. Let the rain subside, and then we will decide the next action. Until then, I think that the palace is the safest place for you to hide," Ravi ran his palm affectionately through Evelyn's golden hair.

Evelyn wiped her tear-filled eyes and looked at Ravi. She stood up and hugged him.

"Thank you, Ravi. Thank you so much. It means a lot, and I wish I had a brother like you," Evelyn spoke through her sorrow-filled eyes.

"I am always there with you Eve. You are safe as long as I am there with you," Ravi patted her as she cuddled to him like a little girl.

Ravi waited for Evelyn in the living room. He walked around looking for clues the intruder might have left behind.

He moved the chairs and sofa but found nothing. He then walked to the kitchen to drink some water. As he put the empty glass on the glass holder, his eyes caught something under the kitchen sink. His eyebrows twisted and lowering his body he bent down to get a closer look.

A half-burned cigar and a few pieces of red glass bangles laid down in the corner.

"Evelyn didn't smoke...," Ravi thought as he picked up the cigar buds and pieces of broken bangles. He wrapped the only shreds of evidence in a piece of paper and squeezed them into his trouser pocket.

He then locked the kitchen door and waited out on the porch for Evelyn.

The Suspect

Ravi left Evelyn at the palace and walked back to his house near the church. He decided to take the path through the fields to watch if anyone lurked near the house where Evelyn stayed. It began to rain heavily, and Ravi had to slow down his pace as he walked through the narrow pathway that led to Sreedhara Menon's property.

He turned around the corner and was about to open the fence gate that led to Sreedhara Menon's backyard near the house where Evelyn stayed. He saw a shadow sneak onto the porch. He stood his ground waiting for a while, his eyes desperately searching for a human figure. He couldn't find anyone, so he opened the fence gate and slowly, walked towards the porch. Hiding behind the huge square pillar, he observed the surrounding. There wasn't anyone and the door was locked.

Ravi crept to the rear side of the house and tried to peep in through the glass window. He could see no one, and when he turned to leave, he felt he heard the sound of glass crashing to pieces from the house. Ravi wiped the mist in the glass caused by rain and pressed his face closer to the window. A black figure brushed past his feet, he could sense a fleshy body against his legs. With his heartbeat racing, he jumped aside with a howl.

It was the domestic black cat that brushed its fur against his feet. Controlling his fear, his eyes caught the shadow approaching the window. He quickly edged to the wall and hid his slender frame. As soon as the shadow turned to leave, Ravi moved closer to the window to look at it.

Ravi was shocked to see a woman in the house, and he stood perplexed, wondering how she got the key to the house and how many of them would be inside the house. He saw the figure move towards the front door. There was no time to think as he knew that if he lingered there for even a minute, he would be spotted and the intruder might escape or even attack. So, he conveniently disappeared behind the safety of the trees. Innumerable doubts and thousands of rain droplets forged a curtain preventing Ravi from getting a clearer glimpse of the intruder.

The woman locked the door and walked towards the fence at the right that led to the pathway, the way that led to the palace.

Ravi abandoned the thought of following the woman. He knew that it was not easy for anyone to enter the palace with the two fierce dogs and security guards. He opened the fence to the left and walked past Sulochana's house to a narrow street that led to his house near the church.

~ ~ ~

As Ravi walked through the slippery road that led to his house, he watched his childhood friend and neighbor Sebastian sitting on the porch with his head drooped down and staring at the heavy downpour. Ravi opened the gate to Sebastian's house and walked towards the verandah where his friend sat.

"Are you counting the raindrops Sebastian?" Ravi asked mockingly.

There was no reply from Sebastian.

Ravi peered at his friend's face and saw tears rolling down his cheeks.

"Is anyone sick? What's the problem?" Ravi asked as he pulled a chair and sat beside his friend.

Sebastian washed his face in rainwater and wiped it with a towel. He ran his fingers through his hair and lit a cigarette. He took a long puff as Ravi watched the smoke whirl out in a circular loop before them. He didn't offer smoke to Ravi as he was a teetotaler and a nonsmoker.

Sebastian and Ravi knew each other well. Sebastian could never hide anything from Ravi, and Ravi, in turn, helped Sebastian in every possible way. Looking at his facial expression, Ravi understood his friend wanted some time for himself, so he decided to leave him alone.

Ravi walked into the house to talk to Sebastian's wife and daughter. He did it every time he visited the family. It was a small house with minimal furniture that once echoed with love and laughter.

Ravi walked into the small living room that served as a dining room as well. Since he did not find anyone there, he walked to the kitchen.

"When did you come? I didn't see you," Amy's mother Dhanya, said, forcing a smile on her face.

"That is not the matter now. Why do you all look so gloomy?" Ravi looked Dhanya in the eye and asked with a concerned voice.

Dhanya turned her gaze away from Ravi as she stood tracing the edges of the chair in the kitchen.

"Here, have some coffee. We'll move to the dining room," Dhanya forced a cup of coffee into Ravi's hand and walked to the dining table.

Ravi stared at the steaming coffee and walked to the dining room. He placed the coffee cup on the table, pulled out a chair, and sat down on the opposite side facing Dhanya.

Ravi heard a few sobs from the bedroom to his right. There were only two bedrooms in the house. Without further thought, Ravi walked to the bedroom and pushed the door open. To his surprise, he saw Mayukhi sit beside Amy and wipe her tears.

"Madam, why are you here?" Ravi interrupted all of a sudden.

Mayukhi stared at Ravi and warned him to leave the room. Ravi saw Amy hug Mayukhi as soon as she saw him. He saw the little girl cringe and sob when she caught sight of him.

Ravi sensed something unusual, walked out of the room, and closed the door behind him. He walked out to the veranda without speaking a word to Dhanya. Sebastian was still seated on the chair. He had finished taking the last puff as he sat there, lost in thought. Ravi touched his friend's shoulder and gently pressed it. Sebastian touched his friend's hand with that of his and spoke nothing.

Ravi took his umbrella and walked home in the heavy rain.

CHAPTER 12

Pinky

Silence occupied the liminal space between the day and night in Amy Sebastian's home for the past two weeks. There was a time when Amy felt like a dazzling little star when she stood in front of the mirror to take off her uniform, inspecting the new curves and humps in her slender frame as she metamorphosed into a little woman. Her face shined brightly, and her eyes gleamed with a new shyness.

Amy was proud to have her 'pinky' in her pocket and showed it to her friends Riya and Shifana. She shied away from the others, though. She was ashamed to show her pink sanitary napkin to the teachers and other classmates. *Pinky* was her new friend and told her friends that they too would soon get their *Pinky*.

"You are a girl, and from now on, be careful. Don't go near the boys. Take care," Dhanya her mother advised her everyday before she left for school.

Amy nodded her head, but like every other eleven-year-old, she could not fully comprehend what her mother said. She did not understand the reason why she shouldn't go near the boys, especially the grown-up boys who had developed a sudden fascination for her.

Every month Amy cried as her little stomach ached and the pain got down to her slender legs. She wriggled and writhed like the worm Rosa caught once to slit open. Those were the days when she felt that she never wanted to grow into a woman.

"Women should learn to bear the pain. If you cannot bear this pain, then how can you bear the pain when you deliver a child?" Her grandmother once asked her when she saw Amy cry in pain.

Amy stared at her grandmother's wrinkled face through the tears and was even more worried that she might give birth to a child soon. The more she thought, the more she despised being a woman.

Amy hid the first love letter she received from a sixteen-year-old boy in her school. She read and re-read the letter and showed it to her friends. That was when her friends wished to get their *Pinkys* soon. Amy exchanged glances with the boy during the recess hours when he waited for her outside the classroom.

"Amy, come let us play," her friend Rachael pulled.

Rachael was not in Amy's class. Each class had four divisions and students were segregated according to the grades they acquired. That was the new system implemented by the new Principal Zacharias Thomas. While Rachael studied in the B division, Amy was put in the D division. D was considered the weakest among the four. The D division clutched on to the taboo of bearing all 'good for nothings' and slow learners. The teachers propounded the 'useless category' theory as the students' of the 'D' division never scored well in the exams.

Amy stood up from her seat, bent her head, and walked shyly towards the door.

"My mother has warned me that I should not run and play with you," Amy whispered in Rachael's ears with a shy smile.

"Come, let us play. Why does your mother say such things?" Rachael shouted impatiently.

"Don't shout," Amy hushed her with panic in her eyes.

Rachael ran to the ground, leaving Amy alone. Amy watched her nameless admirer smile at her from the ground, and she ran to hide her face behind the books.

~ ~ ~

Amy was a slow learner and found it tough with her lessons. It was a prestige issue for her parents to send her to an English medium school. Since they were not fortunate enough to go to such schools taught in English, they wanted their children to work hard and master the knowledge in the foreign tongue.

Sebastian and Dhanya shared a secret pride when they spoke about their children's education to their less-educated friends and relatives. Dhanya was a good dancer, and Sebastian was a famous theatre artist, and they expected their daughter Amy to become a doctor. They always felt that life was wretched as their profession never earned them sufficient income to run the family. They wanted their children to lead a happy life unlike them, and they believed that only a professional degree could earn them a decent job.

Amy was a dreamer, a thinker, and a dancer who could never comprehend the nuances of mathematics or science. She was always lost in thought and failed to pass the examinations. The teachers tried every way to drive in the multiplication tables, the wonder of science, the beauty of languages, and the history and geography of the earth. The girl stood completely nonplussed whenever she was asked a question.

The tired teachers resorted to punishments and advice.

"I think there is nothing wrong with the girl. She is adamant, and she is determined that she will never study. Look at her face. It says it all," the Psychology teacher finally concluded after four months of observation.

The teachers found it extremely difficult to teach in front of a silent girl who tried hard to listen and understand what they taught, so they decided to send her out when they taught.

"Get out of my class!" Most of the teachers shouted as if they saw a wretched thing in front of them.

Certain other teachers made her sit down on the floor, assuming that the earthly connection could bring in some change to the girl. To them, she was possessed, and they devised every way to get rid of the ghost that had possessed her.

Amy found it extremely difficult to stand out and sit down on the floor during her monthly periods when she used her *Pinky*.

"Amma please, don't send me to school today," she begged every month.

"You're so lazy. You can't skip classes as you wish, and there is no talking about this again," Dhanya shouted at her daughter and forced her to walk to school carrying her heavy bag on her weak shoulders.

There were days when she feared that her *Pinky* might cheat her. There were days when she was reluctant to come out of the toilet. Her mother and teachers blamed her and termed it as an excuse for her laziness to attend the classes.

Dhanya had taught her daughter to hold her tears and not to weep in front of others. Amy did not know whether she was right in asking what she did not know, and she was afraid whether everyone would scold her if ever she asked anything. She grew holding on to others' opinions and decisions.

Life seemed to change when the new Principal, Zacharias Thomas, began to notice her being sent outside the classroom on all days.

"Why are you made to stand outside the classroom?" Zacharias asked Amy as he stroked her hair with his fair, plump hand.

Amy was initially reluctant to speak, worried about the next punishment from the Principal.

Zacharias Thomas had a different method of dealing with students. He helped the students learn better and encouraged the students to bring out their hidden talents. The students loved the new Principal as he played with them, taught them, and punished them whenever they failed to obey the school's rules.

"Never send any of the students outside the classroom, and this is not the way to treat a child," Zacharias warned the teachers in a meeting.

The teachers looked at the new Principal with contempt, fear, and adoration. Since the meeting, none of the students were made to stand outside the classrooms as part of the punishment.

Students like Amy were happy, and they began to adore their new Principal.

"You may come to my room anytime. I will clear all your doubts. Even if some teacher sends you out of the classroom, you may report it to me," Zacharias smiled as he cupped Amy's tender face in his palms.

Amy's face bloomed in joy, and she danced and jumped all way home, happy that at last there was someone who spoke to her softly and even promised that he would never scold or punish her. Amy began to show improvement in her studies as she began to like the subjects. The Principal called her to his room every day and enquired about her studies, difficulties in learning, and likes and dislikes. The Principal became her best friend that she gradually forgot about the nameless boy who stared at her from a distance.

"Amma, today the Principal gave me a chocolate," Amy told her mother once when she returned home.

Dhanya and Sebastian were happy to watch their daughter pay more attention to her studies. Amy's grades improved, and her parents were expectant that the teachers might shift her to a better division the following year.

~ ~ ~

Rain poured down with all its might and had no intention to slow down. The trees swayed in the wind shaking off the excess water. Anything in excess overflows. Amy looked out through the window as she sat hugging her knees. It was getting darker, and fear crept into the little girl, and her heart hurt like the torn, abandoned toy in her attic.

CHAPTER 13

Sulochana

Sulochana waited in the slippery pathway hidden behind the fallen trees until Ravi left. She had seen Ravi following her before she broke into Evelyn's house. But she was not sure if Ravi had spotted her.

Sulochana walked past Sreedhara Menon's garden towards her house. She sank into the chair on the veranda and clutched onto the arms of the bamboo rocking chair as the chair rocked her through her memories. She heard that Kannapan was dead and with it her all-consuming desires were also burned.

~ ~ ~

Kannapan reached Kavampuzha as a rubber tapper from a small, nameless village in Tamil Nadu. A lean, tall, skeleton wrapped in a lungi was how he was when Sulochana met him for the first time in her husband's rubber estate. There were two more workers, but each one was scattered in different parts of the estate that looked like a forest. The tall rubber trees seemed to touch the skies blocking the sunlight. There was a small tiled roof hut in the middle of the estate. The small building housed three workers and a rubber cutting machine. The workers cut and dried the rubber sheets that were sold in the town market.

"*Amma*, where is your husband? He is always sending you to look after all these," Kannapan once asked Sulochana as he caught her standing alone amidst the tall rubber forest.

Sulochana spread her full lips into a smile, and Kannapan razed his eyes through her buxom hourglass figure that seemed to throb with a longing to be caressed.

Kannapan counted the golden bangles to twelve in each of her hands and a gold chain around her neck that he felt would weigh almost ten pounds.

"My husband is working in the Gulf, and his parents are too old. So, I have to take care of everything all alone," Sulochana replied as her lips twitched and her kohled eyelids fluttered.

It had been only two years since Sulochana got married, and marital bliss lasted only six months, after which her husband couldn't extend the available leave. Her life revolved around her husband's aging parents and the rubber estate. Kannapan and Sulochana met every day, and Sulochana loved his company as he cracked jokes and told stories from Tamil movies. The rubber forest wrapped them in its darkness as their hands slightly rubbed against each other when they walked. Sulochana found it extremely difficult to stop looking into his eyes. She knew that Kannapan sensed her feelings for him. One evening, she waited for him under a tree in the rubber estate. The sun was about to set, and fear and guilt wrapped her like darkness.

What are you doing here, Sulochana with this servant, penniless beggar in the middle of this forest? What will happen if anyone comes to know of this? It's always the woman who will be blamed. Don't forget that. Kannapan had told you that he has a family back in his village. His wife, Kanaki, and two small children will be waiting for him. There is nobody else to take care of them. Haven't you heard about Kanaki's curse: the curse of an innocent woman that burned an entire kingdom? A drop of tear from her eyes is sufficient to char you to death. When did you turn to be so heartless? What binds you to him: love or lust?

Sulochana heard her little inner voice in her head speak as she rolled the edges of her saree *pallu* around her tense fingers.

"Have you been waiting here for long?" Kannapan's husky voice roared from behind the tree. Sulochana felt his warm breath mixed with pan and fresh toddy on her neck.

"I am leaving. I just came to inspect today's work. Where are the other two workers?" Sulochana stood up from where she sat and pretended not to be aware of his advances.

Kannapan smiled as he rubbed his lips and pushed her towards a thick tree. He locked her movement with his firm body and kissed her fiercely first on her neck and then on lips, giving her no time to think. She gasped for breath as she stood speechless and numb. She watched Kannapan light a *beedi* with a matchstick. That was when Sulochana noticed his dangling sixth finger. Tears ran down her confused eyes as she ran home as fast as her legs could carry.

Sulochana did not know whether what Kannapan did to her was right or wrong. But she knew that she longed for a touch and a hug every day when she retired to bed after a long tiring day. She longed for someone to sit beside her and listen to her when she had so many thoughts within her.

Sulochana's mother taught her to cook rice and pickle tender mangoes in huge clay storage jars. When she expressed her wish to go to college like her other friends, her *amma* dismissed it with an insignificant wave of her hand.

"Young women of your age should learn to cook and clean. What are you going to do after studying? Anyway, you will get married and what is the use of a certificate to take care of your husband's family? You can study as long as we find a suitable alliance for you. You have two younger sisters. We should see that they too get married," Sulochana's mother told her as she ran the comb through her long, thick hair.

Sulochana's father was a government employee, and his meager income could not afford to get his children new dresses every year. Sulochana was lucky to get a new dress once in two years. When she outgrew the dress, it would be given to her younger sister and then to the youngest.

"Girls should learn to adjust with whatever they have," their mother reminded them whenever they demanded anything new.

Sulochana insisted that she would agree to marry only if the groom promised to send her to college. When her parents found her the groom, she asked him, "Will you send me to college? I want to study."

"Of course, I will. Our family gives great importance to the education of girls. Within one month, I will get you enrolled in a college," the groom promised, and Sulochana agreed to the marriage.

Life went on happily for a month, and Sulochana waited for her husband to enroll her in a college. There was no talk for another week about that as they were busy visiting friends and relatives. The next month too passed by, and one day, Sulochana reminded her husband,

"If we don't get admissions now, it will be difficult later."

"*Muthe* (my precious pearl), I will get the admission for you. I assure you, don't worry," her husband consoled her each time she worried about the admission, and Sulochana smiled coyly each time her husband addressed her '*muthe*'. She left a million dazzling pearls in her heartburn bright with passion.

After five months, when her husband was about to leave, he hugged Sulochana and said, "*Muthe*, my parents are not willing to send you to college. They say that they are old and they want someone to be with them always. I feel that what they say is true. I am not insisting on you. You can make your own decision, but this is my suggestion. Don't worry if you insist; I will make arrangements and see that you get admission to the nearby college."

For the first time, Sulochana felt the pearls sting all over her. She cringed as the pearls stung her dreams.

"So, did you marry me to take care of your parents? Why did you cheat me? You could have told that earlier,"

Sulochana broke down into inconsolable sobs when she thought about her bleak future.

"Sulu… listen, I didn't intend to… but my parents…," her husband tried to explain.

"I don't want to hear an explanation from you. You take advantage of me since you know that I have nowhere else to go. You may please leave now," Sulochana wiped her tears and cleared her throat

She always felt coldness in the nearness, numbness in his kisses, and suffocation in his embrace.

Sulochana did not know that she could dream and desire for herself. For the first time, she felt that her life was like sliced mangoes in huge, dark, clay storage jars waiting to be salted and mixed with red, hot chili powder kept safely away from light and fresh air. Sulochana felt her desires peeled, and it rankled down her throat as she lay wide awake in her bed, watching the moon trapped behind the smoky clouds, and gradually fell asleep.

Sulochana excused herself from going to the rubber estate for the next two days. She busied herself with cleaning, washing, cooking, and gardening so that she had little time to think about the incident. The third night, she heard a knock at her window. She was reluctant to open it, but after subsequent heavy knocks, she opened the window, afraid that it might wake up her in-laws.

"Why didn't you come for two days? Are you sick? Believe me, I am sorry for what happened," Kannapan pleaded in heavy whispers through the vertical window bars.

Sulochana felt her heart beat faster and felt sudden warmth towards the penniless servant who was concerned about her. Nobody in the house, not even her husband, enquired about her health or wellbeing. Everyone assumed that she was alright and happy. Sulochana felt that she was a maid, an unpaid worker trapped in the concrete house. Tears lined her eyes as she touched his hard hands that were clutched to the window bars before she opened the door of her room and let him in.

Sulochana smelled of Jasmine and Rose perfumes her husband had bought for her. She cooked tasty and spicy food for Kannapan as she knew that would feed his starving heart.

"Tomorrow shall I cook fish curry for rice?" Sulochana asked as she watched him smack his symmetrical upper lip half-hidden with his thick black mustache curved at the ends.

She then allowed Kannapan to do whatever he wished to do to her body. Kannapan grazed through her luscious curves and filled her hollows with the smell of half-chewed *paan* and cheap toddy. Every evening, the leaves closed as they watched him drain his hunger into her, and she scratched him down his spine with her long nails and contented moans.

Kannapan visited his family twice a year when Sulochana's husband paid his yearly visits to Kavampuzha. Sulochana was very particular that he sent them sufficient money every month. Kannapan's children were admitted to a good school, and Sulochana paid their fees. She got his wife costly sarees and jewellery once a year.

"From where do you get so much money?" Kanaki once asked Kannapan, to which he replied," I have got a good job as a caretaker in an affluent family. They pay me very well."

"If you are well off, why don't you take us with you?" Kanaki asked.

"I will take you later. Now let me earn as much as possible," Kannapan lied every time his children or wife insisted on taking them with him, at least during the school vacation.

Sulochana got the land where the rubber estate was situated, transferred it to her name when her husband visited her. She then sold a portion of the land and gave the money to Kannapan to start a new business. The weak atoms in Kannapan's body seemed to transmute into dense elements holding superpowers. His biceps, chest, and well-defined curves were visible through his shirt's fabric and he came across as a robust, beefy, and powerful man. He did odd jobs in the town and earned a little money. He stopped working as a labourer in Sulochana's estate and instead became the caretaker of it.

"So, what business should I do, darling?" Kannapan once asked Sulochana as he lay on her lap after lunch.

"Let me think. You are not educated, so how about the money lending business?" Sulochana suggested as her fingers combed through his thick black hair.

Kannapan got up, sat straight, and asked her," so, do you think that will be profitable?"

"Of course, our villagers always want money. Nobody is rich here except one or two like Sreedhara Menon. Your profit depends on the interest rate you set," she replied.

Kannapan thought for a while and kissed her on the cheek," So when is the auspicious day? Tell me my fortune," he asked.

"Anytime is auspicious as long as you are determined and ready to work," Sulochana replied with a smile as she squeezed in a sweet *paan* into her mouth.

Sulochana looked into the mirror that night and wondered at the transformation she had undergone. Her curves straightened, and she looked like a round, beefy ball. That was when she realized that she never took care of herself.

She quarreled with her husband's parents and forced her husband to build a new house for her when the older people began questioning Kannapan's presence in their house. When Sulochana delivered Kannapan's baby girl, Kannapan visited her every day. He bought toys and dresses for his baby girl. When the frequency of his visits increased, Sulochana's father-in-law informed her husband over the phone.

"Are you not ashamed to ask me such a question? I have told you several times that Kannapan is here to help me. I am a woman, and how can you expect me to manage everything without a helper? Once in a while, I have to take your parents to the hospital, get the medicines, take care of **our** baby, cook, clean, and wash. I don't have ten hands. Please try to understand my situation," Sulochana cried over the phone.

~ ~ ~

Sulochana stood up from the rocking chair and went inside the house. The clouds gathered their wrath, circumambulated the sky in thick sheets of vengeance, and squeezed their pain that drenched the earth in screams.

A framed photo of her daughter Remya stood on a table in a living room corner. Sulochana ran her palm through the photo and lit the lamp kept in front of it.

Why didn't you listen to me? Had you listened, you would have been alive. How many times have I told you that Kannapan is your father. You always hated him. When he tried to hug you, you were afraid that he would harm you. You raked his anger, your father's anger when he was drunk. Why did you run away screaming at night? Your father had to pull you all way from Sreedhara Menon's backyard to our house. I saw blood ooze through your soft hands when the glass bangles pierced through your skin. When you screamed aloud that night, your father closed your mouth with his heavy fists and didn't know that you were suffocated to death. Do you know how much he cried? He cursed himself for the first time. He didn't want to go to jail, so he lifted you and tied you on the ceiling fan to make it seem like suicide. Your father was never a coward. He was not afraid of getting arrested by the police, but he didn't want the world to know that you were his daughter, daughter of a thug, a drunkard, a demon. He loved you so much.

Sulochana cried loudly as she sank to the floor beside her daughter's framed photograph.

Lightning struck the distant trees on the tall blue mountains, and Sulochana watched the trees catch fire, and felt that the orange flames danced like an enraged woman, like the woman who burned down an entire kingdom.

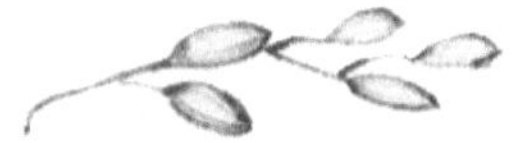

PART THREE

"When the remedy you have offered only increases the disease, then leave him who will not be cured, and tell your story to someone who seeks the truth."

—Rumi

CHAPTER 1

Chingam

Sebastian took a leisurely stroll in his garden and basked in the warmth of the sunshine that washed the trees and flowers in its alluring charm. The freshness of the day whisked him away from the pain and filled his heart with ecstasy.

Sebastian whistled and walked to his room, pulled out his writing pad and pen. Words poured in like a clear stream of water, "Should I name this season 'Spring' when hope blooms in each flower bed? The season when the sun doesn't scathe the skin but lifts each tender leaf and smiles at the peeping paddy crops paints each tendril with brighter green and kisses the waters that flow down the calm river. This is Chingam, the month that soothes and calms. It is mid-August, the calm after the storm when the birds brush their wings against the warm blue sky and seek solace in the faraway laughter of the clouds. The evening sky isn't starkly red but faint like a maiden's lips that part like pink half-moons.

This is the season when the starlit sky stretches across like the folds of a satin dress; bright, smooth, silky, and the moon slides through the sky's honeyed tones. The trees sway with a moonbow glimmer as the moon with its pearl light spreads its shimmer wiping the sins of yesteryears.

Chingam, the month that awaits the arrival of the demon king Mahabali from the inner core of the nether world: the world of the sinners and the cursed. Fate can hurl its scythe at a humane demon and offer heaven to the heartless saint."

"So why was Mahabali punished?" Amy once asked her father

"He had the softest heart and the kindest smile," Sebastian replied.

"Why should you kill someone soft and kind?" Amy's eyes opened wide in disbelief as she climbed onto her father's lap.

"Mahabali was the immortal king, but he was a demon. Since he was too kind and loving, people loved him a lot. The *devas* or the benevolent gods were afraid that the demon king might usurp their kingdom in heaven. So, they approached Lord Vishnu for help. God appeared as a young brahman and asked Mahabali for three feet of land. When Mahabali agreed, God grew in stature and measured one foot by stretching his feet across the entire earth and then the second that covered the entire sky. As God stood there looking at Mahabali not knowing how to measure the third feet of land, the humble king kneeled before the lord and bent his head at his feet. He told God that the holy feet can be placed on his head. So, God placed his foot on the king's head and gently pushed him down to hell," Sebastian lifted his curious daughter and kissed her on the cheek.

"So, did the king know that it was the god who visited him?" Amy peered hard at her father, trying to gauge the meaning of his words.

"Yes, he knew that it was the god who visited him," Sebastian replied, stroking the six-year-old's hair.

Amy did not understand why the kind-hearted king was punished. She cried for the loving king as she said," I hate God. Why does my *amma* pray to this God?"

Sebastian thought that true knowledge is concealed within the hidden universe, and the young, growing minds are ill-fed. Succulent truth lay shrouded in layers of entangled human hearts. Like Trojan soldiers, we spoon the young minds with sediments of half-known truths, thus making them insufficient and inefficient.

"I am no different. Even though I have not scrapped and colored my daughter's little mind with dingy shades of religion, I have not filled her with knowledge and truth."

Sebastian was an actor and a writer. He had played the role of Mahabali several times. On the stage, before the curtains fell, a false floor opened below his feet as he knelt before Lord Vishnu, and Sebastian had to fall into the space beneath to make the audience believe that he was pushed to hell. It so happened once that he got trapped beneath the confined space and had to remain there for almost an hour. That was when he thought about life and death, good and bad, virtue and vice.

How often do we die in our life! Humanity dies, hope dies, love dies. What is dead is reborn, and what is reborn dies. We frail humans are caught between this endless cycle of birth and death. It's all in the human mind, a conglomeration of ideas and beliefs appropriated to cater to individual needs. Virtue and vice terms were coined and manipulated for society's convenience, for the powerful to become more powerful. In reality, there are only two sections: the rich and the poor, the haves and the have-nots.

~ ~ ~

Amy Sebastian stretched her soft hands and yawned as she pulled the pink floral sheet that covered her insecurities at night. Her mother had bought new bed covers and sheets but not her favorite pink. Amy felt that the new covers carried all the hues of the rainbow, so splendid and bright. A butterfly emerged, flapping its wings from its chrysalis, discarding its silken house. Amy felt that its wings were small.

Her friend Rosa had known the secret place of the cocoon much earlier. The girls were only eight then. Amy was afraid to have a closer look at the pupa suspended under a thick branch of the mulberry tree, hidden between the cover of green leaves. When Rosa wished to break the cocoon, Amy prevented her from touching it.

"There are many moths inside, and look how protected they are. They are babies," Amy hugged her giant Barbie doll with one hand and pointed at the cocoon with her other hand.

Rosa laughed at the bulging eyes of Amy's doll and hated the glittering pink and blue dresses wrapped around the toy. Screwdrivers, blades, a hammer, and small pieces of wire always lay scattered around in Rosa's room.

As the young girls stood talking, they witnessed a butterfly emerge out of the cocoon. Rosa ran towards it and watched the tiny wings flap.

"Look Amy, the wings are small and wet too. The wings seem to be folded," Rosa shouted excitedly.

Amy was hesitant and afraid. She did not go near the pupa and ran indoors when she heard her mother call them.

Until now, Amy never knew that emerging out of the cocoon was beautiful. She stood up from the bed, walked towards the window, and lifted a twirled, green leaf that was reluctant to straighten its veins towards the dazzling sun. She saw a red liquid drip down from the butterfly as it emerged from its chrysalis. Her lips parted in a smile as she felt the soft rays of the sun on her face.

Amy watched her father reading the newspaper in the verandah of the house. She walked slowly and sat beside him on the floor.

"What is the red liquid that comes out of the butterfly daddy?" Amy asked as she touched her father's lap with her tender palm.

Sebastian stared at his daughter in disbelief as tears smudged his vision behind the glasses he wore. It had been several weeks since his daughter spoke to him.

"It is a natural occurrence. The red liquid is called meconium. That is a leftover part of the caterpillar, and the butterfly no longer needs it. The liquid is stored in the intestine, and when the butterfly emerges out from the chrysalis, it expels the liquid. Transformation is vital for every being on this earth, and it is essential to shedding down whatever hinders you from growth and emergence," Sebastian replied as he pressed his daughter's hands with a smile and a tear.

Amy hugged her father and laid her head on his lap. Tears ran down her cheeks and wetted Sebastian's thighs through the *lungi*. The father ran his fingers through his daughter's long, black, unkempt hair. He no longer insisted her to oil and tame her long tresses. Amy had longed to cut them like Rosa's, but Sebastian always insisted that girls should grow long hair. That evening, he took a pair of scissors and cut Amy's long tresses. Amy saw her tangled locks fall in heaps. Sebastian held a mirror in front of her face, and Amy could see the contours of her ears and neck hidden until then by the thick locks.

Sebastian watched his daughter smile as she admired her new form in the mirror.

"She'll turn thirteen this month," Sebastian sighed as he told his wife. The latter nodded, folding each cloth with utmost care.

The school reopened after the summer vacation, and Amy's parents decided not to send her to school immediately.

"Did she tell you anything?" Sebastian asked his wife, Dhanya.

"No, but I think her teacher Mayukhi knows something about her silence," Dhanya's eyes moistened as she replied.

"Is the teacher coming today?" Sebastian asked.

"No, she will visit her after two days. The counseling sessions have been going on for quite a while and the teacher has assured me that everything will be sorted out within a few days", Dhanya exhaled trying to gather herself.

~ ~ ~

That night Sebastian had a theatre performance in the town. He decided to take Dhanya and his children with him.

"*Amma*, do you want me to wear this long frock?" Amy asked as she picked the lengthy green frock with laced neck and full sleeves and smelled it.

"Ah! Not necessary. You wear whatever you wish to wear," Dhanya smiled and winked at her daughter.

Amy felt that her long frock smelled of the quaint mixture of boric acid, flour, and sugar that her father made to get rid of cockroaches.

Sebastian had arranged for a taxi from the town. The white, old ambassador car never broke down as it moved along the winding lanes of Kavampuzha. Moreover, Sebastian found the fare affordable. Amy wore a knee-length red skirt and a fitting sleeveless white top. It was a gift from one of her aunts who lived in Cochin. Dhanya never allowed her to wear it as she felt that the dress was too revealing. It was almost six-thirty in the evening, and the sky began to replenish the fading sunlight with bright stars and suspended the argent silver, and the village was awash with the moon's diamond flame.

It had been almost a month since Sebastian watched the moon in all her glory. Heavy rains and sorrow seized his mellifluous poetry from his heart. His daughter's smile pinched the splinter and pulled out the pain that had been residing within him for the past few weeks.

"Tonight, I am too much drunk of poetry. Hold my hand and press your ears against the walls of my heart; then you'll feel the magnificence of this moonlit night," Sebastian pulled Dhanya by her hand and kissed her gently on her lips.

"The children might watch. What's wrong with you today?" Dhanya blushed as she pushed her husband away.

Sebastian sat beside the driver in the car's front seat while Dhanya and the children occupied the back seat. The car drove past the grooves and fields. As the wind brushed through Sebastian's hair, he asked the driver,

"Would you mind if I recite a poem?"

"No problem, sir. I have watched your plays, and I have heard that you are a poet and writer. I am a great fan of yours. I would love to hear you," the driver replied enthusiastically.

Sebastian turned behind to look at his wife and children, all three cuddled together like a furry cat, and cleared his throat:

Shed your light and step into my darkness /To feel the warmth of my moonbeams

Across your numerous nerves. / Douse my yearning with poetry and prose,

Ignite the warmth with couplets from your soul,/ a healing ode, a blank verse,/a beautiful melody with sweet refrains.

Laughter and joy filled the limited space within the car until they reached the town. Kavampuzha slipped into a deep reverie as tranquil peace sailed down the Sindoori.

CHAPTER 2

The Encounter

Sebastian parked his motorbike outside the school office. Amy Sebastian stepped down, clutching her school bag close to her pounding heart. She held on to her father's arm as fear swept across her face. It had been a week since the school reopened after the monsoon flood. Amy missed a week's portions at school. Sebastian had informed the class teacher about Amy's inconvenience to attend the classes.

"Don't worry. I will take care of everything, and nobody is going to question you. I can assure you that," Sebastian held Amy's palm and assured her with a smile.

Sweat dripped down Amy's forehead as she hobbled up the stairs to her classroom. Her teacher Mayukhi had told her not to bend her head down. "Always hold your head high. Why should you be afraid when you have not committed any sin? Be brave." Mayukhi told her once. Amy gathered the courage to hold her head high and look around the school. For the first time, she felt that all the students looked the same. Everyone was happy around her, and their faces shone bright with hope.

Sebastian stepped inside Suresh Chandran's office. He had fixed an appointment with him the previous day.

"Good morning Mr. Sebastian. Please take your seat," Suresh gestured to Sebastian with his fixed smile on the ever-youthful face.

Sebastian was reminded of *Shakuni*, the brilliant, crafty, and devious character in Mahabharatha. He had once played *Shakuni's* role.

He once told Ravi, "If *Shakuni* was the mastermind behind the *Kurukshethra* war, Suresh Chandran is behind every untoward happening in the school that hindered the educational institution's growth and is responsible for the gradual deterioration of the school."

"Well, so what is the important matter you need to discuss, sir?" Suresh frowned as he crossed his legs and tilted his head with an air of authority.

Sebastian gulped down his anger at the unnecessary arrogance and took a deep breath before he spoke.

"Sir, I am Amy Sebastian's father. My daughter is in class 7. It is with utmost disappointment that I bring to your notice the misbehavior of the Principal Mr. Zacharias Thomas to my daughter."

Sebastian could feel the wave of fear scream through Suresh Chandran's body. His glowing skin cringed under the truth of Sebastian's words. Silence besieged the torn edges of the plastered walls of the room that was painted the previous year. Every year the school management plastered and painted the school building. The management committee relied on 'spade' Raju, the contractor who undertook the painting job earnestly.

He was called 'spade' Raju for many reasons, and he was famous for two main reasons. Firstly, his father was a gardener, and as a boy, Raju grew up watching his father dig deep trenches in other people's houses for planting saplings and traveling safely at night with the stolen coconuts, nutmegs, and bronze vessels. Raju learned the art of digging trenches in the soil and in the human mind. He was capable of searching through the secrets of people. Secondly, he always won the card games played by a group of men who were always preoccupied with almost nothing else to do.

Raju worked as a school bus driver for two years. That was thirty years back, and Raju was twenty-five. Raju wished that everyone stopped calling him with the prefix 'spade', so he decided to become the school bus driver. He wiped the front glass of the bus with a clean cloth every morning so that the villagers saw his face.

"Is he not Raju, 'spade' Raju?" "When did 'spade' Raju become the bus driver?" Though Raju became famous in the village, people never forgot to add 'spade' before his name whenever they addressed him. So, finally, Raju decided to carry the spade before him throughout his life.

After two years of service as a bus driver, 'spade' Raju stopped working. After several years, Raju surfaced again as a contractor 'spade' Raju. The new management liked Raju for his charismatic smile that gleamed with the heavy gold chain and appointed his son Sachin as the new bus driver for one of the school buses. Raju believed that his son would one day become a great cricket player like Sachin Tendulkar.

The teachers of Saket school assured Raju that his son was a promising cricketer as the little boy's hands were always restless. Sachin occupied his hands by stealing pencils and snacks at an early age. As he grew up, he nurtured the passion for mobile phones, money, and girls. He stopped studying after he failed in tenth grade for the second time. Moreover, the young talent felt that the school had nothing interesting to offer him anymore.

Every time he sat on the driver's seat, Sachin imagined that he was sitting on an elephant and that he was a prince. He winked at the girls and chatted with them. He befriended young boys by sharing with them porn videos, books, and sometimes drinks. After a year, Sachin went missing under mysterious circumstances. People discussed different possibilities, but no one could trace the mystery behind the disappearance except Principal Vasudara. Whenever someone enquired 'spade' Raju about Sachin, he convinced them that he got a job in the U.A.E.

"So, Mr. Sebastian, what exactly happened to your daughter?" Suresh Chandran leaned forward as he asked.

Sebastian felt a nail being hammered through his chest, and he closed his eyes for a while.

"Call the Principal!" Sebastian clenched his fists, and Suresh saw his blood-red eyes shoot through the bulging sockets.

Suresh Chandran rushed some cold water down his throat and wiped his forehead with the towel from his pocket.

"Well, let us move to the Principal's office then," Suresh stood up, looking pleadingly at Sebastian.

Sebastian followed Suresh Chandran to the Principal's room.

Zacharias Thomas closed the last file and browsed through the e-mails and other correspondences. It was challenging to learn about the school and the various procedures of administration. It had been only a couple of months since he joined the school. The management and Parents Association members were impressed by his qualification and experience in the field of teaching. The title of 'Principal' gave him more authority and respect.

Zacharias adjusted his posture when he heard a knock at the door. He quickly put on his grey coat that he hung on the chair. The door opened, and Suresh Chandran and Sebastian entered the room. Zacharias could not recognize Sebastian. He guessed him to be a parent with some complaint about the infrastructure or teaching. Complaints usually varied from the poor canteen food to lack of proper toilet facilities for the girl students of the school. Zacharias expanded his lips, and his eyes narrowed with an experienced tinge of courtesy as he greeted the parent who accompanied Suresh Chandran.

"Please take your seat," Zacharias gestured to Sebastian.

Sebastian pulled out a chair and sat beside Suresh Chandran facing Zacharias.

"How can I help you?" Zacharias beamed as he asked.

"Zacharias, this is Amy Sebastian's father," Suresh Chandran spoke hurriedly before Sebastian could spill out his anger.

Sebastian saw blood vanish from the fair, clean-shaven face of the Principal when he heard the name 'Amy Sebastian'. Zacharias' fingers fumbled and his legs shivered under the table.

Suresh Chandran stared at the Principal whose face expressed no emotion after a while. Only then Suresh realized something he had missed out on whenever he spoke to the new principal. The non-verbal behavior of the Principal was so convincing to be normal, and he sometimes used powerful hand gestures whenever he tried to defend himself. Zacharias sounded charming and used more expressive words to attract people. He never emphasized inspirational words and carried an intentional calm demeanor throughout the conversations. Some senior teachers, too, had shared their opinion of the Principal being far too normal.

Once during lunch, when Suresh discussed about the students from poorer backgrounds, Zacharias just licked his fingers, saying, "um… the food was great today."

Most sentences he spoke were in the past tense, and he was a great storyteller who could charm anyone easily. Suresh remembered the psychology lessons he learned at college, and a chill ran down his spine as he looked at the quivering Principal who stared hard at them.

Suresh had doubted the grandiose sense of self-worth, and the superficial charm Zacharias exhibited, but he dismissed his doubts when everyone else accepted the new Principal happily. More than once, Suresh had witnessed the Principal's lack of empathy. He never showed his emotions of anxiety, fear, or sadness.

"Amy Sebastian… of which class?" Zacharias smiled as he asked.

Sebastian banged his fists on the table, toppling the files down as he shouted, "Don't you know Amy Sebastian?"

"No, I don't know. Please relax. You seem to be short-tempered," Zacharias smiled as he handed over a bottle of water to Sebastian.

Sebastian pushed down the water bottle and caught Zacharias by his collar.

"I will chop your head if you don't answer me," Sebastian squeezed the Principal's neck with the firm hand, picked up a pair of scissors from the Principal's table, and shoved it down his throat.

Suresh shouted for help, and the office staff came running. They pulled back Sebastian, and Zacharias was saved from his clutches.

"This man is mad. Call the police. Take him away!" Zacharias shouted long after they moved Sebastian out of his room.

Suresh stared at the Principal and asked, "Shall we call the police?"

Zacharias went pale and sat down in his chair. He emptied a bottle of water and gave a stern look at Suresh.

The Witness

Evelyn got her return ticket to France. She waited for the monsoon season to be over. The quaint village and the villagers lived with her through the rest of her life. She had taken a slice of fresh air, the naïve thoughts of the villagers, memories, and fear with her. Evelyn felt that Kavampuzha smiled at her as she turned to bid farewell to the villagers. Ravi accompanied her to the airport.

"Please hand this over to Mrs. Vasudara," Evelyn told Ravi as she took out the voice recorder from her hand luggage.

Ravi looked at her with puzzlement in his eyes.

"Well, there is something important in it, and Mrs. Vasudara knows about it. Please," Evelyn spoke with a tone of urgency and importance.

Ravi got the recorder from Evelyn's hand and hugged her goodbye.

"Thank you for everything, Raavi. I mean it. Hope to see you in France someday," Evelyn felt her green eyes brim with tears as she waved her hand and bid adieu.

Ravi tried to smile through his heavy heart as he held on to the grey voice recorder.

~ ~ ~

It was midnight when Ravi reached home. He sat down with a cup of hot tea and stared at the voice recorder that stood on the small three-legged wooden teapoy in the dingy living room. Everything other than tea was kept on the small table with a tripod base. Ranging from toothbrushes to newspaper and folded clothes to knives and vegetables. Besides Ravi, the teapoy was the other creature in the house that earnestly wished to be a helium balloon with its string cut from the weight of gruesome secrets of the universe. The restless legs of the tripod jittered when it bore Ravi's legs on the old wooden surface.

Ravi lifted the voice recorder and placed it on his lap. He thought for a while before pressing the play button. The chirping sound of crickets in the backyard blended well with the silence of the night.

~ ~ ~

My name is Evelyn. I am a 26-year-old French woman. I am a researcher, and I reached this quaint village in the far end of Kerala to learn more about the art form of Theyyam. Hidden from the outside world, Kavampuzha exists with its laws and customs. I learned about the magnificent dance and ritual of the dying art. My short stay in this village has gifted me with vast knowledge and the key to the secrets of the unknown and mysterious life beyond this earth. I am now free from the shadows of the past. This village is like a stack of books dense with stories and knowledge, and the key to that lay in each person's mind.

This is the place where I learned more about Ravi, my friend, philosopher, and guide, or rather he taught me the secret of unlearning whatever I assumed myself to be. Mrs. Vasudara was the other person who taught me to be a good listener as she listened patiently with her small, weary smile tugged at the curves of her lips.

Ravi paused the recorder as a strange feeling emerged from within when he heard Evelyn's affection towards him. He took a deep breath before he resumed the audio.

Evelyn : *I will forever carry the memories of Kesu, Latha, and their two angels. I no more feel sorry for Malu as she has learned to cope with whatever transpired in her life. The echoes of the good life might reach Malu's ears like a siren's song for the next few years, but I can assure her that a whole new world will unfurl for her as years pass by.*

That destined night when I heard a faint cry from Sulochana's house, I decided not to venture out alone without Ravi's help. I came back to the house and tried to sleep, but the cry pricked through me like sharp needles. The night was dark and threatening. Still, the call was more remarkable and I felt that the entire nature desired that I helped. So, I walked to Sulochana's house. The light from the torch seemed to flood the front yard, and I decided to switch it off and turn on the torch in my mobile phone. I saw fresh tyre marks on the ground and assumed that the visitor had left.

Ravi's eyes widened and he leaned forward as he continued to listen.

Evelyn: *I tiptoed to the rear side of the house and was lucky to open a partially closed window. I peered through the horizontal bars. It was dark inside the room except for a faint light in a corner. I peered hard but saw nothing. That was when I felt I heard a sob, and I strained my eyes until I caught sight of something like a human form cuddled in the corner of the bed. My eyes that got used to the darkness by now, figured out the image of a young woman. I hissed through the window. Initially, there was no response, but after the third time, someone walked to the window. As the figure closed in, I let out a faint howl... It was...well...er..it was our Malu... (voice chokes) Her face bled with scratch marks...(pauses and takes* a deep breath), *and her lips were half bitten...(voice fades gradually) She looked like a starved animal chained, torn, and beaten...(a faint whimper)*

Ravi felt a heavy feeling swell in his stomach and a sudden coldness hit his chest. Tears welled up in his eyes as he swore and screamed in agony, at his helplessness. He emptied a bottle of water, washed his face, and walked out to the verandah to breathe some fresh air.

~ ~ ~

After fifteen minutes, Ravi resumed the audio with shivering hands as he was afraid of further revelation.

Evelyn: *"Malu..." "I tried to touch Malu's face through the window.*

Malu stared at me and did not respond. Her eyes smarted my skin with their stony silence... Wounded cheeks hung down her face like two sagging vermillion hollows... Her tangled hair hid her eyes, and she looked like a weird creature from another world..."

Ravi gulped down his sorrow, pity, anger, and fear.

I took a closer look at Malu and felt a strange, yellow liquid emerge from the pit of my stomach. Though the reflex action was to run, I held on to the window bars and tried not to show my feeling of nausea. Malu stood half-naked... with scratch and bite marks all over her neck and breasts (a frail cry). They have been attempting to put some medicine on the open wounds, but it seemed that they never gave time to heal. She stunk of alcohol and drugs..(a short pause) I heard someone open the door. I hid behind the window door, and I felt safe under the blanket of thick night.

"Malu...," It was a female voice.

I peeped in through the window, curious to know who the person was. I luckily had my voice recorder with me. I recorded the conversation.

Ravi listened attentively.

Malu turned around and moved to the bed. She sat on it with a blank face. I saw the woman sit beside her with a small bottle of red liquid. She poured some from the bottle into a ball of cotton and wiped it over the wounds on Malu's body. She then kneeled on the floor and hugged Malu's knees as she cried loudly.

"Go. Please run away from this wretched place. I can no more watch you die each day," the woman hugged Malu and kissed her on the forehead.

"Wear this dress. I got it for my Remya. It was oversize for her," the woman helped Malu wear the dress.

Ravi was shocked and surprised when he heard the name Remya.

I was surprised to see the woman being kind to Malu and decided to go inside the house. The door was not bolted, and it gave away when I tried pushing it. I ensured that nobody else was in the house. I walked to the room where Malu was held captive and barged in.

The woman jumped to her feet when she saw me and opened her mouth to scream, but I gathered all my strength and closed her mouth him my palm. With my free hand, I squeezed her neck, and luckily I was taller than her. I let her when she began to gasp for breath.

"Take Malu with you. Please," the woman pleaded to me.

I stared at her in disbelief, and without her knowledge, I started recording her words as she spoke.

Ravi realized that it was Sulochana and smiled at Evelyn's bravery and smart thinking that saved Malu. Later when he rang Evelyn, Ravi appreciated her for her wise thought of recording Sulochana's voice in her voice recorder.

Sulochana: *I am Sulochana, Kannapan's mistress. I was too blind with love that I failed to realize the serious crimes Kannapan committed.*

Ravi stared at the recorder when he heard Kannapan's name.

I do not remember how or when Kannapan transformed into a blood-thirsty devil. When Malu was repeatedly raped and beaten brutally in front of my eyes, I felt shattered. I cried and tried driving in sense and humanity into him, but he did not listen. Sometimes it was him and when he was too much drunk, his friends hounded the girl. When I opposed, they threatened to kill me.

The recorder stopped playing. Ravi sat pressing both his hands on his throbbing head that was heavy with secrets and sleep. He glanced at his wristwatch. It showed 4:00 a.m. Ravi latched the door and walked to the bedroom to get some sleep.

~ ~ ~

Sulochana felt the weight of sorrow on her chest increase as she spoke. She fainted, and Evelyn seized the opportunity to escape with Malu. With great effort, she dragged Malu outside. Luckily Malu co-operated with her, and they moved to Evelyn's house in the dead of night.

~ ~ ~

Evelyn wiped Malu's body with warm water and dressed her wounds. That night Evelyn slept with Malu. As she lay beside the young girl, Evelyn saw tears run down Malu's eyes. The next morning, Evelyn decided to get some medicine for Malu. She felt that it wouldn't be safe to inform anyone in the village. As she sat thinking about the various options, she suddenly remembered that she had left her recorder behind at Sulochana's house.

Evelyn ensured that Malu was still sleeping, and she locked the door of the house from outside. She then rushed to Sulochana's house and searched for the voice recorder. She saw it lying on the veranda and rushed to pick it. She felt she heard the sound of a motorbike approaching the narrow road and quickly hid behind a cluster of trees.

"Who's there?" Evelyn heard Sulochana's shout.

Evelyn felt that her heart pounded to her mouth, and was bathed in sweat. Just then, the motorbike screeched to a halt, and a giant of a man got down the huge bike. A cold shiver ran down Evelyn, and she looked around for an exit nearby. She saw Sulochana run towards the man screaming and moaning,

"That bitch escaped yesterday night. I fell asleep. I even bolted the door but didn't know how the wretched girl managed to escape."

Evelyn felt peace within as Sulochana did not mention her name to the man she guessed to be Kannapan.

Evelyn saw a small wicket gate hidden among the bushes. She did not wait to listen to more of their conversation. She quickly disappeared out through the small gate. For the first time in her life, she thanked her ballet teacher, who made her practice the moves every day. Her slender body never put on extra weight because of that, and she could sway and move easily like air.

~ ~ ~

Evelyn returned home and cooked some gruel for Malu. When Malu woke up, Evelyn made her bathe in warm water and dressed her wounds with the medicine she had in her first-aid box. Malu fell asleep after having the gruel. Evelyn thought for long about the next step and decided to inform Kesu.

Evelyn met Kesu in the fields and told him that she had something to say. Kesu understood English but Evelyn needed to slow down when she spoke. Kesu was a fast learner, and he picked up the language from Evelyn and his children with ease.

"Malu is in my house now," Evelyn told Kesu.

Kesu looked at her in disbelief and asked," I sent her to college to study, and how come that she is with you?"

Evelyn narrated the incident to Kesu. She was careful to avoid explaining the entire incident as she knew that it would devastate him. Evelyn held on to Kesu's shoulders tightly with her fist as she narrated the incident briefly. She watched Kesu collapse and gasp for breath. Evelyn took out the water bottle from her bag, sprinkled some water on his face, and watched Kesu drain the entire water from the bottle down his tired throat.

"Kesu, please do not panic. We must now forget the past and think about the next action," Evelyn said, trying to be more practical.

Kesu held Evelyn's hand and thanked her profusely for saving his daughter. Evelyn was reminded of her father when she saw Kesu's eyes stream down with tears.

Evelyn knew that Kesu was a great father who would live and die for his children.

~ ~ ~

Kesu knew the secret herbs and plants that healed any wound. He spoke to nature, and nature returned him with the bountiful wealth of secret knowledge. Evelyn felt that nature opened the hidden doors for those who loved and respected it.

"Please do not tell my daughter that I came to know of the incident. My girl will be shattered," Kesu requested Evelyn with tear-filled eyes.

Evelyn patted Kesu and hugged him.

The herbs and plants healed the external wounds while the internal wounds aggravated with days. Evelyn decided to take Malu for yoga classes. Also, she felt that a change of atmosphere would be better. Kesu arranged a taxi, and Evelyn took Malu to town and rented a house for a week.

"Malu, how do you feel now?" Evelyn asked Malu after a few days.

"I feel better," Malu replied with a faint smile.

Evelyn decided to take her back to the village and felt that Malu should spend more time with her family.

"Please don't tell anything about the incident to my parents," Malu pleaded with tear-filled eyes.

"Sure, I won't. We'll take a bus to Kavampuzha. We both will get down as if nothing has happened and try to believe that **nothing ever happened. It was all a bad dream,**" Evelyn smiled as she hugged Malu.

CHAPTER 4

Retaliation

The sun disappeared with the west wind down the sidewalk surrendering to the approaching dark. Suresh Chandran leaned back on the cushioned armchair and watched the water in the flower pots disappear into the sand with a compelling urge.

Nothing is permanent. One day I'll join you and disappear into the secret depths.

Suresh's voice seemed to emerge from the deep sand clasped tightly by strong rooted beliefs about everything in the universe. He gazed at the fading colours of the sky that seemed to grab the green from the trees. That evening Suresh was expecting Sreedhara Menon.

~ ~ ~

"Come, Sreedhara. Why are you late?" Suresh asked as he welcomed his tired-looking cousin get down from an autorickshaw.

"I don't know. I often feel tired these days," Sreedhara Menon gasped as he talked.

The cousins sat out on the lawn under the stars. Suresh poured some warm water from the kettle and mixed some coffee and milk powder into it.

"How about adding some sugar?" Suresh asked his cousin.

"No. No sugar, please. I am diabetic," Sreedhara Menon heaved and panted.

Suresh smiled and handed over the cup of coffee to Sreedhara Menon.

"So, when did you return from Trivandrum?" Sreedhara Menon asked Suresh.

"I took the night train and reached here by afternoon," Suresh replied.

"Never expected that an ordinary Physical Education teacher like Arjun could file a case against us," Sreedhara Menon spoke, weighing each word as he sipped the coffee.

Suresh rubbed his forehead with the palm and gazed at the starlit sky.

"We forgot that he was at an advantage because of his caste. These degraded tribes can stoop down to any extent to defame respectable people like us in the society," Suresh's lips expanded in a cynical smile as he spoke.

Sreedhara Menon's pumpkin-shaped belly bounced as he chuckled.

"I despise even their shadows. They forget that they were once slaves on our lands, the outcasts, the untouchables. Now, look at the irony. Our fate has led us to work with them and even sit and eat with them. *Shudra is a shudra,*"

Sreedhara Menon's noses flared red, and his body trembled with anger.

Suresh watched his cousin with a sarcastic smile. He had always considered Sreedhara Menon to be a person with poor self-awareness and low cognitive ability.

While Suresh was open to new views and ideas, his cousin always contradicted and debated endlessly. Suresh revised his understanding of the situation and reconsidered every problem.

"Sreedhara… That is not the problem now. We should decide what has to be done next," Suresh reasoned out.

Suresh shoved off Arjun when the latter approached him seeking an explanation for the legal notice sent by the school. That was when Arjun decided to fight for justice. Having worked as a teacher in Saket school for a few years, Arjun never wished to taint the school's reputation, but he had to fight for his right. He approached his lawyer and sought his advice on the case.

"Arjun, you belong to the marginalized section, so you can very well sue the school for mental harassment and abuse. You can file a complaint at the Human Rights Commission and Labour Office. People of your tribe can also approach the committee organized for your welfare. The targeted are always at a disadvantageous position as they are not aware of their rights. People are keen to know the International and national news, but they are lame when it comes to knowing their own rights," Arjun's lawyer stated, looking through his spectacles that rested on his wrinkled nose.

Arjun nodded and made a mental note of things before he left.

A couple of weeks back when Suresh Chandran received a telephone call from the Office of the Commissioner of Police, Trivandrum, he never expected a fatal turn of events. The call was connected to Suresh, and he answered with," Yes, Suresh Chandran speaking."

"I am Venkat Dineswar, Commissioner of Police, Trivandrum. This is concerning your former employee Arjun's case. I want you to visit my office next Thursday. Do see that you reach by 9:00 a.m," the Commissioner disconnected the call with a thud.

Suresh Chandran suppressed a shiver and fear that almost unmanned him when the Commissioner demanded an explanation over the telephone for sending a legal notice to Arjun, who belonged to the socially disadvantaged community. Suresh felt his skin ripped apart with fear and shame as he sank into the chair. He thought for a while and called for a quick meeting with Principal Zacharias and Sreedhara Menon.

"Ensure that not a soul gets to know about this incident," Suresh warned them.

Zacharias and Sreedhara Menon nodded their numb heads that could not still comprehend the matter completely.

Suresh explained the incident in detail as Sreedhara Menon always found it hard to understand clues and codes. Sometimes Suresh had to explain more than twice for his cousin to follow.

"Don't expect to pluck pomegranates from the Neem tree you planted," Parukutty told Sreedhara Menon with a malicious smile when her irate husband used offensive words to curse Arjun, the Physical Education teacher.

"What do you mean Paru?" Sreedhara Menon asked his wife.

"Haven't you heard the saying, 'As you sow so you reap'? When you are responsible for everything, how can you blame master Arjun for that?" Parukutty replied with a contemptuous smile. She knew that her husband considered her as the most obnoxious member of the family.

Suresh Chandran feigned ill health to the Commissioner of Police, sighting his inconvenience to travel long distances.

"Well, make it next Thursday and remember not to give excuses like school children," the Commissioner's rueful voice reached Suresh's ears before the phone got disconnected.

Suresh felt that the whole world was against him and that justice was not meted out to him. He still couldn't perceive the ideology of the biased rules and laws. He couldn't fathom the reason behind the law favouring an ordinary, outcaste like Arjun.

CHAPTER 5

The Compromise

Suresh reached the Police Commissioner's office the following Thursday. Arjun had already reached there. Suresh looked around the Commissioner's cabin that had a huge table that sparkled clean. The case files were arranged neatly on the shelves attached to the walls. Suresh swallowed back the thought of bribing the police officer. Instinct told him not to put himself in trouble by trying to do so. Suresh's entire life was built on bribery.

"Please take your seat, Mr. Suresh Chandran," the Commissioner waved his hand with an air of authority.

Suresh took a seat beside Arjun, who was already seated. A howl and whimper emerged from the deep hollow of Suresh's innards. He felt that the commissioner's eyes could dig through his past, present, and future. His heart cringed with fear, and he found it difficult to look the inspector in the eye.

Suresh looked at the police officer's bold nose that rested intriguingly on his chiseled face. The sharp, tanned, and sunburnt nose seemed to command his 6'3" muscular frame.

"I have thoroughly gone through the rules and law. So, I require no more arguments and explanations from your end. Let us directly come to the point. Mr.Arjun had told you that he was not in a position to pay the two month's salary immediately, and you agreed. Despite that, you sent him a legal notice stating that he failed to obey the school's rules. "Mr. Arjun had not received the salary for the last twenty days he worked in your school, do you agree?" the Commissioner asked Suresh.

"Yes, Sir," Suresh answered with his head bent down.

"Didn't Mr. Arjun work extra hours as you requested? You had promised him to pay for every extra hour he worked, but you never kept your word," The Commissioner continued.

Suresh felt his legs shake in an odd trembling rhythm beneath the table.

"So, if justice has to be meted out, you should pay him the outstanding salary and the payment for the extra work he did," Commissioner Venket Dineswar spoke in his matter-of-fact tone.

Suresh nodded in agreement and replied in his brittle voice," Yes, definitely, Sir."

Venket Dineswar exchanged glances with Arjun as he handed over a neat, white sheet of paper. Arjun saw hope in the vast expanse of the crisp sheet that lay before him. He had had a conversation with the Commissioner the previous week that he would not proceed with the case if the school agreed to his terms. He was concerned about the school's public image that would be tainted if ever he proceeded with the case. So, he decided to give it in writing that he had no complaints against the school.

A week's time was all that Venket Dineswar gave the school to pay the due amount to Arjun.

~ ~ ~

Suresh did not know whether his cousin fully understood the events that had transpired.

"So, are we going to pay him the amount he asked?" Sreedhara Menon asked his cousin.

"Yes. We don't have another option," Suresh sighed.

Sreedhara Menon listened to his cousin in silence and sensed the seriousness in his eyes.

"Sreedhara, now we have a more serious issue with principal Zacharias," Suresh continued.

"I have been telling you since the beginning that you should never appoint a Christian in our school," Sreedhara Menon's nose flared with anger as he spoke.

Suresh decided not to explain any further to his cousin as he would never realize the seriousness of the matter. He was also afraid that his cousin might disclose the matter to his wife or any other person.

"I feel sleepy and tired. We'll talk tomorrow," Sreedhara Menon told his cousin as he yawned.

Suresh watched Sreedhara Menon wobble across the lawn to the house. He knew that Sreedharan would put his signature on any page he showed. His mind calculated ways to make Principal Zacharias resign from the post of Principal.

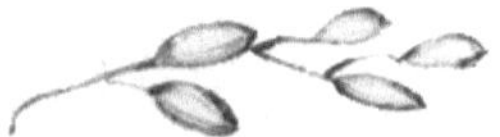

CHAPTER 6

Amy Sebastian

A year after Mayukhi resigned from the teacher's job, she received a phone call from Amy Sebastian's mother Dhanya. Mayukhi was Amy's teacher at school. Amy was not good at studies and she took time to grasp difficult lessons. While some teachers labeled the girl as 'useless' some others decided that the girl was adamant and never co-operated with the teachers. Mayukhi analyzed the student for a month. She spoke to the girl about her interests, likes and dislikes, friends, and family. The girl's long fingers danced effortlessly as she spoke, and her huge black eyes had a certain charm as they spread their eyelashes like peacock feathers. The ten-year-old girl's body swayed to some unheard rhythm as she spoke.

"Do you dance?" Mayukhi asked the girl.

"Yes ma'am I love to dance, and my mother is my dance teacher," the girl blushed and her eyes opened wide with interest.

"What else do you like to do?" Mayukhi started a conversation with her.

"I like to draw, and I dream," the girl smiled innocently.

"Excellent. You are very talented," Mayukhi cupped Amy's face in her palm and appreciated her with a smile.

Mayukhi realized that Amy had a more creative and structurally different brain and possessed an innate artistic talent. Amy visualized everything in the form of pictures, while it was difficult for her to process what she merely heard. Mayukhi had conducted extensive research on the functioning of creative brains and studied the effective teaching methodology that could be applied for such students. Amy required time and special attention, and she picked up more quickly when the lessons were taught with the help of visual aids.

Mayukhi listened patiently as Dhanya's feeble, shivering voice reached her ears like a thunderstorm.

"Hello ma'am, I am Amy's mother Dhanya. I hope you remember Amy. Can I talk to you now?" Mayukhi heard a sorrow-filled voice from the other end.

"Why not? How can I forget Amy Sebastian?" Mayukhi tried to cheer her.

"Well, ma'am, I have to discuss a serious matter with you," Dhanya told with a concerned tone.

"Please carry on. I am listening," Mayukhi replied, trying not to belittle the seriousness of Dhanya's request.

"Madam, I find it difficult to discuss it over the phone. If you don't mind, could you please come to our house sometime this week when you are free?" Dhanya's voice choked as she spoke.

"Sure. That's not a problem. I will give you a call before I come," Mayukhi assured Dhanya as she sensed the underlying seriousness of the matter.

~ ~ ~

It was a rainy evening when Mayukhi decided to visit Dhanya. The villagers of Kavampuzha covered most distances on foot, and they usually enjoyed the long walks. Mayukhi passed the grove and fields and reached Dhanya's house within an hour.

Dhanya welcomed Amy's teacher with a smile as she showed her in.

"Thank you for coming. These days when people are disposed of as out-of-date essentials, I am so relieved that there are at least a few like you who find time to listen to our grievances," Dhanya's mouth cringed like an unhealed wound held by shaggy stitches.

Mayukhi smiled and sipped the coffee as she listened.

~ ~ ~

Amy Sebastian found it challenging to follow the lessons at school, and most of the teachers resorted to strict punishments. Amy's parents felt that things would change with the arrival of the new Principal Zacharias. Amy was impressed by the friendly approach of the Principal. Zacharias gave special attention to Amy and students who were like Amy. He was not hesitant to call each student to his room and counsel each one of them.

As days passed by, Amy showed gradual improvement in her studies. Dhanya and Sebastian were never ashamed to attend parent's meetings. Earlier, they were afraid of the comments passed by various teachers about their daughter.

Sebastian visited the Principal at his office and thanked him for his initiative to encourage his daughter to perform better in her studies.

"You should be proud of your daughter," Zacharias told Sebastian.

"I am so happy to hear such good things about my daughter. For several years she was labeled as a 'good for nothing. We are indebted to you," Sebastian thanked Zacharias with tear-filled eyes.

"It's all God's grace. May God bless you and your family," Zacharias smiled like an archangel.

~ ~ ~

After a few weeks, Amy hesitantly told her mother," I don't want to go to school. I don't want to counsel anymore."

"You are arrogant, Amy. Do you think that you know everything? When teachers are so kind enough to take special care of you, why don't you co-operate with them?" Dhanya scolded her daughter.

"No, it's not that *amma*. I don't like it," Amy tried telling her mother.

"There will be no more talk about this in this house. Do you know that our neighbours and relatives are having fun at your expense? It is only of late they have started to respect us. Do you want to spoil everything?" Dhanya burst out angrily.

Amy walked out silently.

Gradually Amy began to sit aloof even at home. She never played with Rosa or her little sister. Dhanya often found her daughter lost in thought as she sat hugging her knees in the corner of the room.

"She is a grown-up girl. Maybe she might have mood swings, and you can expect hormonal imbalance. It's quite natural. She is a girl, and she knows that she should not play or run as she used to anymore," Dhanya's aunt formulated the theory behind Amy's deep silence.

Nights cast a shadow like mad cats that developed an evil mind on its own. Thoughts swept Amy into the deep pits of fear. She forgot to cry or laugh. Sometimes she gazed into eternity for hours.

"Amy, you lazy girl, did you practice the dance lessons today?" Dhanya pulled Amy by her hand and dragged her to the terrace, where the mother and daughter danced together.

Amy shrugged off and climbed down the stairs without a word.

Dhanya knew that Amy would sacrifice anything for dance and her daughter's present behavior caused doubts in her mind.

"Why isn't Amy talking anything these days? Did you talk to her?" That night Dhanya asked Sebastian.

"No, she doesn't come near me. She doesn't look at my face. My little girl hides from me all the time," Sebastian's voice cracked as he spoke.

Dhanya stared at him in disbelief. Amy was her daddy's favourite, and she wondered what had happened all of a sudden.

Dhanya and Sebastian rushed to Amy's room and pushed the door open. They saw their daughter sitting down on the floor in the corner of the room. Amy sat hugging her knees with her bent head held between the knees.

"Amy," Dhanya went running to her daughter, followed by Sebastian.

Dhanya held Amy's face in her palm and kissed her daughter.

"Speak, what happened to you?"

Amy hugged her mother and shed loud tears that seemed to fill the entire house.

When Sebastian tried to touch his daughter, Amy shivered and pushed her father as she cried.

Sebastian walked out of the room with tear-filled eyes.

Dhanya slept with her daughter the following nights. On some days, she heard her daughter scream and mumble *"white devil"* in her dream.

The couple decided not to send their daughter to school for a few days. They tried talking to her, but it was in vain. That was when they decided to give her a counseling session. They were afraid to share this with everyone as that would affect Amy in the future.

"People would talk different things about our daughter. So, don't tell anyone, especially your aunt. She will come with her remedies," Sebastian told Dhanya.

They thought for a few days and finally decided to seek the help of Amy's teacher Mayukhi.

~ ~ ~

It was a rainy day when Zacharias called Amy Sebastian for the regular counseling session. This time it was not in his office, but he took her to the isolated room on the top floor of the building. Amy watched him bolt the door of the dingy room from the small wooden stool on which she sat.

"Do you practice breathing exercises every day?" Zacharias asked Amy as he pulled a chair close to Amy and held the girl's knees between his.

Amy shuddered as his knees brushed against her fragile knees.

Amy held her breath and felt a strange fear brush through her. She felt tired as it was the day when she befriended her *pinky*: the day when she felt pain in her stomach and legs.

Amy's huge eyes stared innocently at Zacharias as he pressed his enormous white hands against her fragile tummy.

"Breathe in...breathe out...," Zacharias laughed hysterically as he pressed his hands tighter.

Amy didn't know that she could scream and shout, and the sound of rain fell harder on the trees and rooftop, silencing every other sound or cry.

"What happened, Amy? Why are you so silent," Zacharias asked as he pulled the girl forward and peered in through her pinafore shirt.

Amy felt her words stuck in her throat as she sat dumbstruck and shocked. That was all a little girl could do.

Zacharias left the hold off her and asked," Do you have your monthly periods now?"

Amy bent her head down in shame. She sat like a little bud wrapped in disgrace.

"I will teach you the way to stick your sanitary napkin," Zacharias licked his lips as he continued with his definition and procedure to be followed while using sanitary napkins.

Amy felt relieved when the school bell rang and Zacharias opened the door. Amy ran down the stairs as fast as her aching legs could carry.

"Did he counsel you?" Her friend Bindya asked Amy when she saw Amy run to the classroom.

Amy stared at her friend but spoke nothing.

"The Principal counseled me last week. He touched my stomach and thighs. He said that I am fat," Bindya laughed shyly.

"Why didn't you inform your parents?" Amy asked in surprise.

"Do you think that my parents will believe what I say? They trust only the teachers and the Principal. So, I decided not to tell anyone. If ever any such incident has happened to you don't tell your parents. They are not going to trust you," Bindya advised Amy.

Amy did not understand how Bindya could take the incident so lightly and why it was painful and sad only for her.

~ ~ ~

Sebastian consulted his lawyer and discussed the matter with his friend, who was a police officer. Upon their advice, he decided not to file a complaint as it would affect his daughter adversely.

"I do not want them to interrogate my daughter. If we leave it, she will gradually forget it, but if we take the matter to court, she will be questioned, humiliated and the scar will haunt her for a lifetime."

After Sebastian's initial attempt to inform the management committee members failed, he decided to seek the help of his friend, the police officer. The officer warned Zacharias of dire consequences if he further misbehaved with any of the students.

Amy continued to study at Saket school, and gradually, she forgot everything. New friends and new teachers made a new beginning in her life.

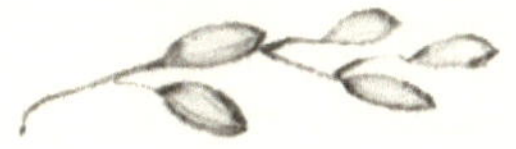

CHAPTER 7

Memories Never Die

The end of the day begins with the roar of the vacuum created by the memories in mind. The pull created by these heavy memories makes the mind older and weaker as it entangles in them all the time.

Vasudara walked through the carpet of red *manjadi* seeds, which Evelyn called *The Red Lucky Seed* that lay spilled all over the walkway in the Palace garden. Every few minutes, a familiar rhythmic sound followed, and Vasudara straightened and looked around. The garden was empty except for her and silence. It was the sound of the falling red seeds. Evelyn had taken a few seeds with her before she left and left a part of her with Vasudara, the voice recorder.

Vasudara listened to the tape thrice and was drowned with the weight of the sorrow. Evelyn had narrated only a fragment of Malu's story when she visited her. She believed that Evelyn left behind the tape as a shred of evidence for the fateful incident that happened in Malu's life. Vasudara got admission for Malu in a college in Cochin and met her education and accommodation expenses. Evelyn taught

Malu that problems cannot be removed from one's life, but one can learn to overcome them.

Vasudara felt much better when the monsoon ended, and the sun shone through the tall trees. Past waited with a watchful eye pacing back and forth across mind's corridors. Vasudara swallowed a tablet without water. The pain in her leg had lessened over months. She looked pale and crusty, having remained indoors for more than a month. She had absorbed the past incidents into her interior monologue as she tried to piece together the stills of her accident.

~ ~~

"So, did you discuss the incident with Suresh Chandran?" Vasudara's husband asked as he plopped down in the chair across the aisle from the dining hall.

"Yes, but he seemed to ignore it. I tried telling him the seriousness of the situation, but he chuckled and brushed it off," Vasudara replied as she hung her cloth bag on her shoulder.

"Then you leave it. They will deal with it," Vasudara's husband told her.

"How can you be so cruel? The girl is hardly six years old, and don't you think that being a Principal, it's my responsibility to report the incident? Do you want me to bend my limbs and bones as if they are made of rubber? If the management members do not listen, then I know what has to be done," words oozed through her sense of duty, piety, and moral consciousness.

"How did the girl's father get to know that it was the school bus driver?" Vasudara's husband asked.

"The girl told him," Vasudara felt her muscle stiffen as she stood frozen.

~ ~~

Effects of certain decisions and social consciousness create ripples through life like a huge stone hitting the water's surface.

The incident happened when Vasudara was the Principal of Saket school. After the school hours, Vasudara sank back into the comfort of hot tea and a sandwich. It was 5:00 in the evening when she had a visitor.

"I am Sofia's father Joshy. My daughter studies in Upper Kindergarten. The day before yesterday, she reached home two hours later than the usual time," the father wetted his dry mouth as he breathed heavily.

"Could you please be more precise in what you say so that I understand what you mean?" Vasudara said as she peered into Joshy's dilated pupils that enlarged with a sense of dread.

"Madam, on that day my daughter reached home late. When we enquired with the bus driver, he told us that the bus broke down on the way. That evening, Sophie did not play or laugh. She said that she felt sick. We thought that she might have caught a cold or fever. She slept the whole evening and did not have food. The next day the temperature soared, and she complained of body pain. So, we took her to the pediatrician. The doctor examined her when she complained of pain in her lower abdomen. The doctor being our family friend spoke to her playfully and came to know about the incident," Joshy paused to drink some water.

Vasudara leaned forward as she listened. She felt his voice choke as he spoke to her.

Sofia's father shuffled his feet and rubbed his palms restlessly as he gulped down his saliva and sorrow. He then narrated the incident to Vasudara.

~ ~~

We took her to the doctor and the doctor asked her why she reached home late on the day the incident occurred. Sophie gave her a toothless smile and replied," driver uncle played with me."

When the doctor asked her what game the driver played with her, Sophie stared at the doctor and hid behind the curtain in the room. The doctor then sent us out and conducted a physical examination of our little girl..., Joshy paused and stared at the ceiling in an attempt to hold his tears.

"The doctor told us that...that our girl was molested...," tears brimmed Joshy's eyes as he narrated the incident.

We got to know the rest of the story from the doctor. The bus driver stopped the school bus at an isolated place and asked Sophia,

"Shall we play hide and seek?"

Sophia was the last student to be dropped home. The driver made friends with Sophie for almost a month and won her trust with chocolates and sweet words. On some days, he made her sit on his lap and let her touch the bus's steering wheel.

"Yesterday, I drove the bus," Sophia once told her mother.

Her mother laughed it off as she thought it to be the girl's imagination.

"Mummy, I am not lying," Sophia insisted.

"And then did the bus move?" Sophia's mother laughed as she asked to pretend to be serious.

"Yes, it moved. The wheels on the bus go round and round…," Sophia ran around the house singing the rhyme.

On the cursed day, when the incident took place, the driver pressed her legs hard and slid his hands through her pinafore. Her fragile body ached and she felt vomit crowd around her mouth when her driver uncle sucked her little lips and forced them open wide with his long, skeletal fingers. Sophie felt dark clouds gather all around and she fell unconscious. After a while, Sophie felt someone sprinkle water on her face and she slowly opened her eyes. The driver forced her to drink some water from her water bottle.

"Don't tell anyone. Do you understand?" The driver brought his narrow face near hers and told her as he put some brownish-black powder between his teeth and laughed like a demon.

Sophie stared at her driver uncle with fear and moved to the corner of the seat.

"You are a good girl. I know that you'll never tell anyone," The driver pinched her cheeks as he pushed a bar of chocolate into her school uniform pocket.

~ ~~

Vasudara's jaws dropped as she listened to the worried father. Her heart pounded and she felt a cold shiver swipe through her spine. There was silence for a while.

"Sir, I am sorry for what happened to your daughter. I know that no words of apology could console you, but still, I apologize on behalf of the school," Vasudara said with folded hands.

Joshy forced a smile on his lips as his fingers fumbled through the bag he kept on his lap. He carefully pulled out a sheet of paper from it and handed it over to Vasudara," Madam, this is a written complaint from our end. Please accept it and I request you to take necessary action."

Vasudara saw a streak of hope in Joshy's tear-filled eyes as she got the sheet of paper from him and raced her eyes through the lengthy letter of complaint signed by the girl's father. She was disgusted and felt a sudden pain on the back of her throbbing head

"I will take necessary action at the earliest," Vasudara promised in a firm voice.

~ ~~

The next morning Vasudara met Suresh Chandran at his office and narrated the incident to him.

"Sir, we should find out who the driver was and inform the police," Vasudara told as her sense of dharma made her believe everyone else to be like her.

Suresh thought for a while and replied," Madam, we will handle it. You need not worry about that anymore."

Vasudara's face turned pale as she tried to drive in the seriousness of the matter," Sir, why don't we inform the police immediately? It is a little girl who is affected and it happened in our school. We should take immediate action."

"Madam, do you know what will happen to the school's reputation if we file a complaint with the police?" Suresh asked Vasudara as he frowned at her.

"Sir, what will happen if we fail to inform? Won't the parents go directly to the police station? Beyond everything, we should do our dharma," Vasudara felt her nerves tighten as she spoke.

"We are not discussing this again. Do you understand, madam?" Suresh Chandran clenched his fists and stood up to leave.

Vasudara stared at the image of Suresh as he left the room.

~ ~~

Vasudara decided to deal with the matter all by herself. She was caught between fear and her sense of dharma.

"So far, the school has not witnessed such incidents. Why do they happen now? Why isn't anybody interested in the welfare of the school?" Vasudara asked Kesu, who overheard the conversation when he entered Suresh's room, to serve him tea.

Suresh and Sreedhara Menon considered Kesu a non-existent being who existed as a lifeless stone or wall in the school. Kesu was a witness to several conversations between the cousins Suresh Chandran and Sreedhara Menon.

"Madam, I am not well versed in Holy Scriptures or philosophy, but life has taught me several things. You worry because you consider it your duty to do justice. You listen to the greater call of the universe but they, on the other hand, are so attached to themselves that they fail to realize that they are a part of this universe. For some, the realization of the *Atman* or the Self comes quite naturally while the others never understand the principles of the cosmos and individual existence. The cosmic guidance that governs not only you and me but the entire universe is a witness to everything that happens around us. I suggest that you try in your way to do what is right to your heart and leave the rest to the mystic powers of the unknown," Kesu, the gardener, Kesu the *koladari*, reasoned out.

"Who is speaking to me now? Is it God or Kesu? Or both?" Vasudara wondered as she stared at Kesu, at the vast knowledge he possessed. She could not fathom the depths of Kesu's words but felt relieved when she had a listener.

The next evening, after a meeting with the teachers, Vasudara decided to meet her lawyer in the town to discuss the matter. It was then that she met with the fateful accident. Vasudara found it difficult to come out of the shock after the accident.

She had to resign from the post as she was found physically and mentally unfit to continue as Principal.

"Madam, you should sign your resignation and leave the school," Suresh locked the room as he pushed a pen into Vasudara's hand.

Panic and grief had overcome Vasudara's fragile frame. She felt that her body and mind were bruised and fractured beyond repair. When she could no longer bear it, she signed in the resignation letter drafted by Suresh Chandran.

Vasudara later learned from Kesu that the girl's father tried to contact Suresh Chandran, but the latter avoided him. The school hurt the father and insulted him by making him walk several times to the school when he demanded his daughter's Transfer Certificate. It is a mandatory rule of the school to hand over the amount collected as a donation from the parents if ever the parents decide to change their ward's school.

"Madam, it was so heartbreaking to watch the father walk for nearly a week to the school requesting for his daughter's Transfer Certificate and the balance amount the school is liable to pay," Kesu told Vasudara when he visited her at the palace.

Vasudara sighed as she listened to Kesu and closed her eyes in an attempt to forget everything.

"Did they give him the Transfer Certificate at last?" Vasudara enquired.

"Yes, after a week, they gave it to him, and I heard that they did not pay him the entire amount," Kesu told.

Vasudara looked out of the living room window and took a deep breath.

"Let me sleep for some time. These tablets make me dizzy," Vasudara excused herself, and Kesu understood that her ill health did not give her the strength to bear anymore.

~ ~~

Kavampuzha witnessed more sunrises, and the antique village stood numb and ageless. 'Spade' Raju's son Sachin resurfaced in Kavampuzha and Suresh Chandran re-appointed him as the bus driver of Upper Kindergarten. Thomas Zacharias continued as the Principal of Saket school as he had an overpowering influence on Suresh Chandran. The accident remained shrouded in mystery.

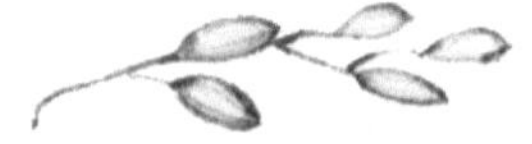

The Interview

The brownish-yellow leaf that dangled from the spider web finally tripped down with the weight of nothingness. Mayukhi considered shutting her eyes for a little longer until the evening sky took a different tone. She disliked the mid-afternoon urgent, bright light that penetrated through her eyelids. The evening light that filled her room was cold and blue. On some days, the blue flared like burning Sulphur.

Emptiness sometimes had the stench of rotten eggs, the disagreeable odour in everything that is in excess. It was like the stench of burning plastic in Remya's house: Remya, the brilliant teenager who committed suicide. It was like the stench of dangerous arching of sullen thoughts. It is not like the little arch on the sullen face of a child, who dropped ice cream on the ground. It takes a more elongated closed curve, an ellipse. It is here where thoughts orbit around you, cutting through your peace, moving on its imaginary axis.

Mayukhi never knew a world outside her village until she was nineteen. Her house was the only house she had seen and memories smelled of sandalwood paste, fresh turmeric powder, herbal oil, and basil leaves. Thoughts did not stink and cringe. They were pure. She borrowed verses from the rain-drenched leaves and flowers and filled the pages of her thoughts.

The dark corridors of her house glistened, and she loved its warm embrace. The carved fine wood peered from the gigantic doors, and they roared when they hauled the wooden bars across to open and close the doors. Huge stonewalls crept above the main building like a fortress. On rainy days, they closed the inner courtyards' drain and waited to watch them brim with water. Water pulled all the children into it. They swam and sank into it as capsized and drooped paper boats that submerged with shrunken insignificance: water, the colourless, tasteless, odourless, wholesome truth.

The emptiness once enveloped her when the management committee members of Saket school called her for a Review meeting, a usual namesake discussion before promotion. Mayukhi was never money-minded and so she never thought about a promotion. Promotion in Saket school only meant an insignificant hike in the salary and a lot of extra work.

It was a hot afternoon and Mayukhi waited outside the Principal's office for more than twenty minutes before she was ushered in. Suresh Chandran and Krishnakumar sat beside each other in separate chairs while Sreedhara Menon sat turning his back to them. Mayukhi took the only seat that was placed opposite Suresh Chandran and Krishnakumar.

Mayukhi noticed a sarcastic smile on Krishnakumar's face since the time she was shown in.

"So, what is your name?" Krishnakumar asked as he laughed aloud.

Mayukhi watched Suresh Chandran sit with his head bent down and look into his mobile.

"Mayukhi," she replied.

Bursts of laughter followed as Krishnakumar said," *Are Suresh suno!" (Hey Suresh listen)*

Suresh laughed silently still peering at his mobile.

Mayukhi felt a discomfort slide through her spine.

"So, where did you do your school?" Krishnakumar rubbed his chin and sat upright as he crossed his legs one over the other as if to enforce authority.

Mayukhi suppressed laughter at Krishnakumar's heightened confidence when he spoke incorrect English. Mayukhi remembered an incident that took place the previous year when the school held an exhibition. The English department too had participated in it. Each department was allotted separate classrooms for the stalls. Mayukhi and two other teachers of the English department wrote a few famous quotes of Shakespeare on the blackboard in the classroom allotted to them.

"Love looks not with eyes, but with the mind; and therefore is winged Cupid painted blind."

"Shall I compare thee to a Summer's day? Thou art more lovely and more temperate."

"To thine own self be true, and it must follow, as the night the day, thou canst not then be false to any man."

Mayukhi and her friends felt immense pleasure when they discussed the great playwright's works. As they stood discussing and relishing Hamlet, Tempest, and Romeo and Juliet, they were interrupted by a deep guttural sound. The teachers stopped their discussion. They were surprised to see Krishnakumar enter the classroom. They never expected any of the management members to visit the classroom as they were never in the habit of doing so. The teachers welcomed Krishnakumar with a faint smile. He repelled everybody with his self-opinionated and egocentric attitude.

Krishnakumar assumed that everybody respected him and that the teachers lived at his mercy.

"Is everything going on well?" he asked with a strained smile.

"Yes, sir," a few teachers replied.

That was when he stared at the blackboard for a few minutes and then turned to the teachers," Well, what language is this? Don't you know that this is an English stall? Rub...rub... write something related to English."

Mayukhi and her friends stood bewildered on hearing that. They stood speechless for a while and exchanged glances.

While Mayukhi and a few other teachers struggled to suppress their laughter at the heightened stupidity of Krishnakumar, one of her colleagues told him, "Sir, these are Shakespeare's lines."

"What! This is not English. Do what I say...," Krishnakumar's nose flared with anger as he commanded the teachers.

The teachers stared back at him as he walked out of the classroom angrily. The teachers never bothered to wipe Shakespeare's golden words instead they all had a good laugh at the expense of Krishnakumar. They even christened Krishnakumar as *Kavampuzha's Shakespeare.*

"St.Mary's," Mayukhi responded after taking a deep breath.

Roars of laughter once again as Krishnakumar passed the comment," Suresh, St.Mary's…ha…ha…"

Mayukhi did not understand the reason behind the laughter. She studied in a girl's convent and that was one of the best schools in her place. A few teachers who taught her were foreigners and the rest were educated from foreign institutions.

The questioning session continued and roars of laughter followed. Mayukhi watched Sreedhara Menon turn behind and join the two when they laughed. She felt her head churn and her heart cringed with strange suffocation. The door and windows of the room were shut and only the wily breath of the three men dawdled within the walls.

Krishnakumar continued,"…so do you say that your father was a temple priest and astrologer?"

Laughter followed. This time it lasted for several more minutes.

Mayukhi felt courage desolate her when they laughed at her father. It had only been three months since her father passed away and she was struggling to come to terms with the loss. She felt that the entire universe plotted against her.

That was when her brother had met with a serious accident and her mother slipped into depression unable to cope up with the loss of her husband.

Death is fierce when it comes to living with memories. Nobody dies when they live in memories. You are forced to live with their presence that exists in the form of things and people. Moments re-emerge in the forms of photographs, teacups, chairs, and walls; in their favourite things that can never be discarded.

Mayukhi felt tears swell up in her eyes as she bit her lips hard to swallow them. She detested projecting herself as a frail, meek being.

The questions continued. "What is your caste?"

Mayukhi did not respond. She was reminded of the manservant Suppaiyan in her house. On certain days Suppaiyan slept in the cowshed. Mayukhi did not know whether he was detested for his dark skin. He was never allowed to enter the house. Mayukhi thought about her grandmother who used to take several baths in the pond each time a maid passed by her. Though the maids stood three feet away from her, she doubted if their shadow fell on her holy, upper-caste body. To her, the cow dung mixed water purified everything. The shadow of caste even fell on Mayukhi's grandfather's mistress' children. A woman's body sought secretly at night did not carry the burden of caste. Mayukh felt she detested herself for the first time.

"You may leave," Krishnakumar's words fell on Mayukhi's ears.

She found it hard to breathe as she stood up from the chair. She saw the three men still laughing at her as she turned to leave the room.

Mayukhi inhaled fresh air as soon as she walked out of the Principal's room. She thought for a while and then decided to meet the Head of the English Department in her cabin.

"Yes, what do you want?" The HOD raised an eyebrow and twisted her mouth as if afraid that the paint on her lips would vanish if she talked.

Mayukhi took a seat opposite the HOD and narrated the unfortunate incident to her. The HOD listened and nodded her head and told her, "Well… Mayukhi… you quit the job. That's it."

Mayukhi stared at her cold face that sneered and mocked. Students commented that her face was a whirlpool of emotions similar to the nine *rasas* (expressions) of the art form *Kathakali*.

As Mayukhi was about to leave, the HOD pushed a sheet of white paper across the table and told, "Sign in this, and then everything will be resolved."

Mayukhi lifted the paper from the table and read it.

Since I do not teach properly in the lower classes, the teachers who are teaching in the higher classes find it extremely difficult to teach.

Mayukhi put the paper down and looked the HOD in the face and asked," Why should I sign in this. I don't acknowledge what you've written. This is fabricated and what is the game you all are playing with me?"

The HOD pulled the paperback before Mayukhi could take a photograph of it.

Mayukhi left the HOD's cabin without speaking another word. She sensed that they were plotting against her and it would be wise to hand over the resignation.

A New Beginning

The next day Mayukhi met Sreedhara Menon in his office room. The moment she stepped inside the room, she saw Sreedhara Menon sit erect pulling an air of authority, and told, "Yes, teacher come in,"

Mayukhi took the chair opposite to Sreedhara Menon even before he offered her. She decided that people like him no more deserved respect.

"Sir, I am here to ask you about yesterday's incident. What was the reason for such high drama? I have been working in this institution for the past 7 years and you people know me very well. Now, what prompted you to ask such irrelevant questions to me?" Mayukhi asked him.

Sreedhara Menon gazed at her for a while trying to decode each word and replied," We men can talk anything. You women should listen and obey."

That was when Mayukhi wished to dunk her head in the blue waters of the pond in her house, in her parents' house. She longed to immerse her body and sink into the rectangular pond in the western end of the huge ancestral house. Water dissolves, purifies, and cleanses the thoughts that stain the body and mind. It binds together fresh thoughts, both dissimilar and identical, into a clear vision. The pond's permeable membrane sieves and separates unwanted dissolved, suspended particles that contaminate the mind. She felt that water absorbed her in her entirety. The caressing cold touch seeped in through her pores.

"She is like a hippo…she remains underwater for such a long time. Do you know why?" Her cousin Diya laughed and told the other cousins once.

Their heads peered at Mayukhi like Scylla, the six-headed monster.

"The problem is with her zodiac sign. She was born in the zodiacal constellation represented by the beautiful youth Ganymede, Aquarius, the water bearer…," she continued with a slight cock of her head and a sly wink," …he was whisked away to the heavens by Zeus". Roars of laughter followed, and Mayukhi too joined them. Mayukhi laughed, imagining each one of the girls as cupbearers, tamed damsels, maids in their future homes.

Mayukhi leaned forward and crossed her legs and replied to Sreedhara Menon," If you want women to obey your orders, bring tamed women from your homes. Moreover, never dare to speak to any other woman like this."

Sreedhara Menon stared at Mayukhi for some time. Mayukhi did not wait for further reply from him as she was determined to hand over the resignation letter within a few days.

The following week, the management members called her for a compromise talk. Mayukhi had expected this turn of events as she knew that the management members would try to save their faces at any cost. They would never wish the world outside to know their faults. When Mayukhi spoke out, everyone came to know of the management's game plan. Several other teachers had to leave the school silently as they did not have the courage to speak, as they believed that they were ordinary women.

"So, Mayukhi you stop pursuing Ph.D." Suresh Chandran told her.

"No, you can't talk like this," Mayukhi retorted.

"Madam, please try to understand our situation. This is a sinking ship…," Krishnakumar left his words incomplete as Suresh Chandran stared at him angrily.

Mayukhi suppressed a smile as Krishnakumar's words conjured the image of one of her favourite Hollywood movies *Titanic*. She picturized the three men in a sinking ship desperately waving for help.

Mayukhi realized that there was no point in compromise talks and so she handed over the resignation letter. She had to work there for three more months as per the school's rule. She felt it inhuman to make someone work even after officially resigning from the job.

Mayukhi knew she had to fight the battle alone like several other battles in her life as she detested to giveup easily. The more they challenged, the more she fought, and to her to give up was to die.

~ ~ ~

Saturday

11:00 p.m.

It's been two years since I resigned from the job. I was busy with the research work and found more time to be with myself. One morning, I woke up with a cheerful smile on seeing a pleasant dream. Birds chirped and the winds whistled melodiously. I felt happy for no reason. In my dream, I saw a distant land where I was always happy, a place where I could always do what I loved the most; a place that transformed me into a writer. I tried to push the dream from my memory but the dream reappeared and when the same dream lasted for a year, I realized that it was not just a dream. So, I decided to embark on a journey in search of the dream, in search of a new beginning. I know that tonight too, the dream will conquer me.

Mayukhi

CHAPTER 10

The Truth

Sulochana stood in front of the huge mirror and hugged her slightly swollen stomach that seemed to feel full and bloated. She neglected the early symptoms and it was after three months she realized that she was carrying a new life within her. Her husband would reach Kavampuzha after two days. He was tired of living all alone for so many years and he had decided to quit his job in the UAE and return to his village. Sulochana did not know what she would tell her husband about her pregnancy when he arrived. The last time he visited her was after Remya's death.

Sulochana peeled an apple, cut it into halves, and deseeded it before she knifed it into two more halves. She felt life slip down her throat and the sweetness spread all over her as she bit into the flesh of the fruit. She munched through her past, present, and future and decided to face life as it presented before her.

Sulochana felt more at peace with herself after Kannapan went missing. The villagers confirmed that he was dead but something within her told that he was alive. Whatever be it, she wished that he never returned. The villagers had begun to sympathize with her and women began to exchange conversations when they met her near the river or in the kavu.

The kavu was all prepared for the yearly festival. Parukutty had invited Sulochana to accompany her to the kavu. Kaveri and her children shifted to the new house in the town with her husband Pankajakshan.

"How is Kaveri now?" Sulochana asked Parukutty.

"Ah, she's fine," Parukutty replied hastily.

Parukutty heaved in silence as they walked through the narrow pathway to the kavu. That rainy night when Kesu saw Kannapan's severed hand, Parukutty found Kaveri lying in their backyard. It would have been almost 3:00 a.m when Parukutty found Kaveri missing in her room. She searched for her everywhere and woke up Sreedhara Menon. With the help of a flashlight, Parukutty searched for her sister everywhere in and around the house. After an hour, she found Kaveri lying numb and senseless amidst the thick enclosure of trees in the backyard. Parukutty felt relieved that she was breathing. She was unconscious and was drenched in rain. She lifted her sister with Sreedhara Menon's help and took her inside the house. Parukutty changed her wet clothes and covered her with a warm rug.

"How did she ever reach there Paru? Is she not taking the medicine regularly?" Sreedhara Menon asked his wife.

"Yes, she takes her medicines regularly. Every night I see that she swallows her tablet before she goes to sleep. But I don't know what happened last night," Parukutty answered as her worried and confused eyes looked at her sister.

"*Chechi*, It is 11 in the morning and I feel so sleepy and tired. I feel like I didn't get a wink of sleep yesterday," Kaveri yawned as she ate steamed rice cake with *chana dal*.

"It's like that on some days. You sleep for a little longer if you still feel sleepy," Parukutty told her as she patted her sister on her shoulder and cleared the table.

Parukutty watched her sister walk into her room and close the door behind her. She decided to lock the door of her sister's room from outside.

That night Parukutty opened the door of her sister's room and peeped in. Hugging a pillow, Kaveri slept like a child on her bed. Parukutty closed the open windows and was about to leave when her eyes fell on a new painting on the easel that stood beside the bed. She stepped towards the painting and looked at it carefully. It was of a hill at night. Water streams and wild animals roamed in the thick enclosure of trees. A bloody severed hand lay beside a stream of water as blood oozed from the hand. The sixth finger was something that caught Parukutty's attention. Bewildered and shocked, Parukutty stared at her sister who was still asleep. That morning when she washed her sister's clothes she had seen some bloodstains on them. Her head throbbed and she rushed out of the room bolting the door from outside

"I know that she is undergoing treatment for depression. Everything will be alright Paru," Sulochana held Parukutty's arm as she spoke and pulled her back to reality.

"That day when it rained heavily, I saw kaveri standing outside the house where Evelyn stayed," Sulochana told Parukutty as the latter stared at her in disbelief.

"It was past six in the evening and I thought that she might be waiting to see Evelyn. When I saw her stand there for more than half an hour, I walked to the porch to get a closer look. Kaveri had almost completed a beautiful painting of Radha and Krishna on the wall. I saw her sink to the floor with a paintbrush in her hand. At first I thought that she saw me but later I realized that she hadn't. She stared infinitely at the trees in the distance as tears cascaded down her cheeks," Sulochana held Parukutty's palm as she spoke.

Parukutty halted and sat down on a stone. "Please continue," she requested when she saw that Sulochana was hesitant to speak further.

Sulochana sat beside her and cleared her throat.

"I was not alone. Kannapan and his assistant were also there...," Sulochana saw fear creep into Parukutty's eyes.

"They feared that Kaveri might tell everyone what she saw and so they dragged her into the house. I felt sorry for her but...I... I...couldn't do anything...," Sulochana wept as she spoke.

Parukutty clasped her knees and closed the eyes as she listened.

"I collected the pieces of broken red bangles and put them in the kitchen. The men pushed her to a corner when they realized that she meant no harm," Sulochana touched her protruded stomach.

"Why did you ever break into my house?" Parukutty asked.

"Hmm… that's a long story. Evelyn saved Malu from Kannapan's clutches. He abused the poor girl and had decided to sell her to a client after getting a huge sum as advance. When the plan got thwarted, Kannapan got furious and he broke in to take revenge on Evelyn but to his dismay Evelyn was not there. He was afraid whether Evelyn had captured everything in her voice recorder… He wanted to destroy the evidence… but before that he went…missing… people say they got his severed hand…," Sulochana shivered and covered her shoulders with her saree *pallu*.

"But isn't he dead? Some animal might have killed him…," Parukutty watched tears in Sulochana's eyes as she spoke.

"I am… sorry… Sulochana…I didn't mean…," Parukutty tried to console her.

"It's alright. Even I wish that he never returned. His child is growing in me… I want a new life… this is my child…my Remya…," Sulochana hugged Parukutty and she did not try to swallow her sorrow.

Parukutty allowed her to break down and cry her heart out. After sometime, Sulochana wiped her tears and sighed heavily as her head drooped down with fatigue.

Parukutty patted her on the back and asked, " So, what happened to Kaveri after that? Did the men…?"

"No… they did not harm her… They lifted her and dropped her amidst the trees… I was the last one to leave the house. Kannapan's assistant was in a hurry to go to the toddy shop and Kannapan told him that he was going to his village to meet his wife and children. When I looked for Kaveri, she was not there. I guessed that she would've reached home, didn't she?" Sulochana asked suspiciously.

Parukutty thought for a while and decided not to tell Sulochana about Kaveri's mysterious painting.

"Yes, she was there in her room," Parukutty replied.

"It's getting late. Shall we move fast to the *kavu*?" Parukutty asked Sulochana who seemed to be lost in thought.

Parukutty held Sulochana's hand and lifted her. They could hear the sound of drum beats as they moved towards the *kavu*.

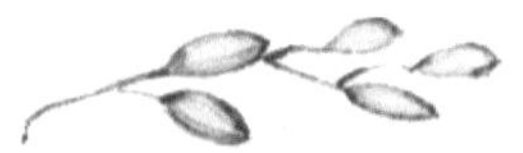

When the Demons Sing

Kaveri looked out through the window of the new house in the town. She watched her small garden awash with moonlight. The crimson rose plant that Kesu gifted her blossomed with an invigourating fragrance. She watched her children sleep peacefully.

"Did you take your medicine?" Pankajakshan asked her as he ran his fingers through her long, greying hair.

"No… I think I should stop the medicines now. I am practicing yoga and meditation and I… I feel peaceful," Kaveri rested her head on his shoulder.

"I want to tell you something… I can't hold this anymore," Kaveri told her husband.

"Yes, speak. I am here to listen," Pankajakshan stroked her hair gently.

"Didn't you see that painting in my sister's house? The painting of the hill and the severed hand? Remember you asked me about it?" Kaveri spoke in a low voice.

"Yes, I remember," Pankajakshan replied.

"I saw that… I saw that with my eyes… I was there on the hills…," Kaveri spoke as she held on to the horizontal window bars.

Pankajakshan stared at her in disbelief.

"It was late evening. When I woke up, I was lying in my sister's backyard amidst the tall trees. I saw two men open the fence gate and I followed them. One was a tall man with six fingers and the other was a short man. The short man disappeared after a while. The tall man walked towards the hill. I lost my way inbetween and sat under a tree for sometime. It was raining heavily and I couldn't see anything in the dark. After a while I continued to climb the hill. I heard a loud… thunderous roar as if someone was in pain and headed towards that direction. I reached beside a water stream and looked all around me…," Kaveri paused and looked out through the window.

Pankajakshan closed his mouth with his palm as his eyes widened and his legs shivered.

""Then I… I saw a…the man…the tall giant…and there was somebody else with him…" Kaveri turned behind and looked thoughtfully at her husband.

"Was that the short man Kaveri?" Pankajakshan shook her to bring her back to reality.

"No… it wasn't him …but…was it a he or …a she…?" Kaveri's eyelids fluttered as she thought.

"What?" Pankajakshan screamed.

"Yes... I don't remember... but I heard the sound of anklets... didn't I Pankaj?" Kaveri hugged her husband as tears rolled down her eyes.

"No, it's alright Kaveri. Relax. Calm down. Let it be anyone. I don't care about that. I am glad that you are safe," Pankajakshan handed over a bottle of water to her and wiped her tears.

"Are you sure that you don't want your sleeping pills?" Pankajakshan asked.

"No. I don't require them anymore. The demons have left me," Kaveri replied as her lips parted with a faint smile.

"Forget everything. It's all over," Pankajakshan smiled as he kissed her on the forehead.

The Festival

The *kavu* was well lit for the ten-day festival. There were sponsors from nearby villages. Ten elephants were draped in caparison and solid gold masks adorned their trunk. Ravi hired more face painting artists as there would be more *Theyyam* performances on all ten days of the festival. Kesu had planned to perform on the tenth day and decided that it would be his last performance. He felt that he was getting older and weaker. He felt that he was not receiving God's call as he used to earlier.

"Only those who receive God's calling can perform. I feel that I will no more be able to perform. This will be my last performance. Let the younger generation take over my place," Kesu announced his decision to the committee of temple trustees a few weeks before the festival commenced.

The committee listened to Kesavan in silence.

"Kesava, if that is God's will, let it happen." The senior committee members proclaimed.

That was when Kesu remembered that his name was Kesavan. The villagers christened him Kesu as it was shorter and easier to call.

Kesavan, Kesavan, Kesavan.

Kesu's father Kolavan whispered the name thrice into Kesu's right ear when he was twenty-eight days old. Kesu's grandmother spread rice grains on the only bronze plate in the family. The plate found its place with the framed photos of gods and goddesses in a corner of the small hut. Children were not allowed to touch it as it was considered holy. Kolavan chanted a prayer and tied a black thread around the baby's hip and lifted the boy carefully in his arms and shouted hilariously, "Kesava… my hope, my dream. You'll be my saviour. You'll save our family from all hardship we are going through now, won't you?"

The baby wetted Kolavan's only white *dhothi* he had saved for such occasions.

"See, Kesavan has promised that he will change all our lives. Look at what he has done!" Kolavan laughed as he handed over the baby to its mother.

He went to work in paddy fields. Kesu was born in the month of Chingam (mid-August), the month of richness and fulfillment. A week after he was born, Kolavan went to work in Thuppan Namboodiri's paddy fields.

"Kolava, I heard that you are blessed with a boy. You are lucky. Meet me before you leave in the evening," Thuppan Namboothiri stood a measured 24 feet away from the workers and shouted through his red teeth that mercilessly bit through thick betel leaves stained with a luscious coat of slaked lime and tobacco.

"What's your son's name?" Thuppan asked as he spit some thick, slimy red mixture on the ground.

"Thambran (highness)…Kesavan…," Kolavan hesitated and swallowed fear as he spoke.

"*Shumban* (nitwit)! Call him Kesu and don't call him Kesavan," Thuppan frowned angrily at Kolavan as his potbelly heaved restlessly.

Kolavan nodded as he stood scratching his bent head.

"It's time for lunch. Let's go," Thuppan told his trusted assistant Gopalan Nair who was his shadow and confidante.

Gopalan Nair accompanied Thuppan Namboodiri. Gopalan carried a bronze metal box in his left hand close to his chest and a palm leaf umbrella in his right hand. The villagers mocked Gopalan and often asked him, "Gopala, are you carrying the names of your master's mistresses in the box? Don't tend to eat the bitter-sweet leaves when your master is not around." Roars of laughter followed as Gopalan shooed them all with the white cotton towel he hung on his wheatish, bare shoulders.

"How dare that Kolavan gives my brother's name to his son!" Thuppan snarled biting his stained teeth and clenched his fists.

"Thambran, don't say anything to them. Heard they are all part of some union. There are doubts that they are Naxalites from the forests. They are teaching these fools to read and write. Knowledge is a serpent that will make them question," Gopalan Nair warned his master.

"It's all fate. Such things will happen as it is *Kali-yuga*," Thuppan heaved as a drop of sweat fell on his nose from the holy ash smeared forehead.

"Shall I take leave Thambran? I will come again in the evening," Gopalan Nair asked as he stood with folded arms.

Thuppan Namboodiri nodded and the knotted bunch of hair on his head danced in approval.

"Be here to give today's wages to the workers. Don't oversleep. When Kolavan comes, give him the extra grains. After all, it's a boy. How long have I been wishing that I had a boy! All five are girls," Thuppan stared at the lonely path that lay barren and stretched in front of the *padipura*, the traditional arched gateway.

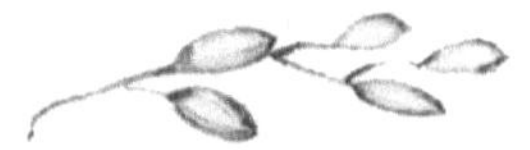

Eravallan

The stage in the kavu was all set for the play. It was a competition held annually and theatre artists from ten villages participated. The winners were declared only after the tenth day when the festival ended.

The makeshift stage stood on a raised platform in the open ground of the kavu. A deep red curtain with black and golden edges held several secret stories that unfolded to those who were ardent lovers of drama. Each troupe had its light and sound providers. The small space evolved as huge mansions, streets, rivers, villages, fields, and anything the scriptwriter dreamt of. The stage brought countries and stories of distant lands the villagers had never seen or heard. People gathered under the star-lit sky willing to be carried away to the land of stories.

Sebastian felt a gentle breeze brush his hair as he gazed out to the open field from the window in the dingy dressing room. He was to enact the role of *Odiyan*.

"Acha, who is *Odiyan*?" Amy asked her father.

"*Odiyan*s are like sorcerers with supernatural abilities. They can see in the dark…," Sebastian stared at Amy as his eyes expanded.

"Like animagus in Harry Potter?" Amy jumped with excitement.

"Yes, something similar to that but more fierce and wild. They come at the darkest hour of midnight and hide in the thick shadows for their prey. They can run on four limbs, jump high, higher than you imagine, climb tall trees by the time you wink your eyes…come closer…they can take any shape," Sebastian metamorphosed into another entity as he described the dark being to his daughter. He covered himself with a black blanket and masqueraded, jumped, and howled like a mad creature.

Amy clapped her hands and gestured him to come closer. "Have you read Harry Potter, Sebastian?" she laughed as she pinched her father's ear with her tender fingers.

Sebastian laughed and ran his palm through his daughter's hair. He was thankful to the whole universe for having healed her of her wounds.

~ ~ ~

Sebastian wore a black sleeveless stitched top that had no opening accompanied by black dhoti lined with red and golden brocade. His eyes were kohled in black and his hair combed behind. The makeup man pasted thick, dark, false eyebrows on his forehead and lined and shaded his lips with deep grey. He fixed shell wristbands on either hand, two enormous bluish-black beaded chains hugged his neck, and black metal rings shone brightly on all fingers. A black metal chilambu fell loose on his ankles and it jingled as he walked.

Sebastian closed his eyes and took a deep breath. He recited his lines and opened his fierce, bloodshot eyes. He had already transformed into the dark entity, *Odiyan*. Theirs was the last play on stage and the people of Kavampuzha were eagerly waiting to watch the team perform.

The red curtain fell like shimmering waves after the ninth play. Sulochana and Parukutty popped peanuts into their mouth from the piece of paper folded like a cone. Amy counted the stars above and tried to chase sleep.

"Will Sreedhara Menon be angry if you go home late?" Sulochana asked Parukutty.

Parukutty laughed. "He would be snoring and would have woken up all the demons of the night. I have decided to live life on my terms. I tried a lot to change him but failed so I have decided to change myself. After years I have connected with my real self, the raw self that I had longed to be," Parukutty popped another peanut into her mouth and chewed unhurriedly as she spoke.

Sulochana squeezed Parukutty's palm and smiled.

Ravi walked around serving the people with water and helped the committee members in organizing the event.

"Isn't it Sebastian's performance next on stage?" Latha asked Kesu.

"Yes. How many times will you ask?" Kesu got irritated by Latha's trivial questions.

A few people from distant villages had already left leaving more space for the others. The little children were awake as they were curious to watch the *Odiyan*.

The lights went out and the wind howled through the trees. The announcer announced the name of the next play, "*Odiyan*". The curtain rose after three bells. The audience who had dozed off woke up startled when they heard the announcement,

"*...and Sebastian as Eravallan, the Odiyan*"

The curtain opened with a calm field in the background where a family lived peacefully. The father Raghavan was a farmer and his wife Rukmini and three children helped him in his work. He had two bullocks and a few acres of land. Life moved on peacefully until a quarry owner encroached on the settlement on the hill near the fields. The villagers were lured to sell their lands as the owner gave them some money and even gold. When Ragavan opposed, the quarry owner killed him and usurped the land. He mercilessly sent Ragavan's wife and children out of their house. While they were wandering on the streets at night, Eravallan saw them and took them to his house. When Eravallan heard their story he was deeply moved.

"Eravalla, don't you possess magical powers?" Rukmini asked wiping her tears.

"Yes, I do," Eravallan had already read her mind.

"Can you help me take revenge?" Rukmini's blood-red eyes peered into Eravallan's eyes.

Eravallan looked at the hapless woman. *Odiyan*s kept their word and they were hired assassins. If he agreed, then he should do it.

"If you cannot then I am not going to beg you. I will do it myself," Rukmini told in a determined tone.

Eravallan's wife lit the lamp kept beside the dark gods to which he prayed and arranged for the ritual. Eravallan exchanged glances with his wife and walked towards the lamp. He sat down and closed his eyes as he awakened the dark forces that guarded him. He cut the vein on his wrist and dripped a few drops of blood before the gods. Strange energy vibrated through Eravallan as he chanted louder and louder as if possessed. He touched the burning flame with his bare hands and made the promise to the dark deity.

Rukmini's children hid behind her in fear. The youngest even cried loudly pleading Eravallan to stop. Heavy rain fell in thick sheets and the wind howled in hunger. Dark smoke filled the entire stage and the children who were watching the play hid their faces with their palms.

The next morning Eravallan transformed into a beautiful woman and met the quarry owner in the village. Lured by the woman's sensuous approach, the quarry owner agreed to visit her on the hill that night.

"I will wait on the hill near the stream," the woman told as she bit her lips and ran her fingers through his spine.

The love-struck quarry owner stood mesmerized as if he had drunk some magic potion.

The curtain fell for a break. The silence was broken with the sound of men, women, and children.

When the curtain was lifted after a few minutes, the stage setting was a thick forest on a hill. It was raining heavily and the sound of water filled the audience's ears that it gave them the presence of a water body nearby.

Eravallan hid on a tall tree at the top of the hill. He had horns on his head and wrapped the tiger's skin like cloth around his waist. His ears were huge and he roared like a tiger. He waited and when he saw the quarry owner pass that way, he pounced on him and came down on all fours. The *odiyan* tore through the quarry owner's huge body with his claws and teeth and dragged him into the thick forest. Thunderous roar echoed from the four speakers. The red curtain lowered down at a measured pace with the scene of a bleeding severed hand lying beside the stream of water.

In the darkness of the night, nobody watched the frightened and bewildered faces of Parukutty and Kesu.

Epilogue

Kesu planted three more crimson roses in Saket school and lovingly touched them with his fingers. All the other rose plants had by now taken deep roots and bloomed brightly. That was his last day in Saket.

The members of the management committee summoned him and told, "Kesu you are too old to work. You have become weak so we appointed a young man for your post. Here, take this money and…"

Kesu stared at them with his sunken eyes and nodded his head as his trembling fingers fumbled to pick the money from the table. He bowed to the three men and walked out of the room wiping his eyes with the towel on his shoulder.

"I thought that I was at last Kesu, the gardener. But, who am I now? Once again 'a nobody', nameless and jobless…," Kesu sighed as he took a last look at the huge building around him. As he was about to leave, Principal Zacharias called him and gave him 500 rupees which he denied accepting. A chill ran down the Principal's spine as he watched Kesu stare back at him.

"Why don't you accept the money Kesu? Isn't this sufficient? Well, I wanted to ask you whether you would send your elder daughter Malu to work as my personal assistant. How much salary do you demand? I leave it to you," Zacharias spoke calmly trying to hide his fear.

Kesu's face hardened and a frown flickered across his forehead. Without further thought, he inched forward and brought his right palm heavily on Zacharia's cheek. There was absolute silence in the room and Kesu walked out before the principal regained consciousness.

When Suresh Chandran entered the principal's office, he saw Zacharias raging with anger.

"Why do you look so tensed?" Suresh enquired.

Zacharias rubbed his cheeks with his palm and Suresh noticed the finger imprint on his fair cheek. His skin took a crimson red like the roses Kesu planted.

"Kesu… that impertinent fool… I just offered him 500 rupees and he slapped me…," Zacharias bit his nails and furiously spit the words. Suresh watched his fuming, eyes turn red.

Suresh ordered Kesu to report to the Principal's room and demanded an explanation letter from him.

"How rude of you! Is this the way you behave when someone offers you money? If you didn't want the money, you could have told him. Will anyone behave like this?" Suresh asked Kesu in his low, monotonous voice.

"I ask you the same question. Will, anybody get angry if he is offered money? Why don't you think? And, I am no more your employee so there is no need to give an explanation letter," Suresh and Zacharias were dumbstruck as they watched Kesu speak out loud and clear. Until then they had never heard him speak anything. Kesu left the room and Suresh watched Zacharias shuffle his feet restlessly under the table.

~ ~ ~

One week later, Kesu sat outside his hut on the creaky cot. The crescent moon lit the night sky and a cold breeze caressed his aging skin. Kesu peered at the flight tickets in his hand and read the names printed on them: Kesavan, Latha Devi. Ravi told that Evelyn arranged for the tickets to France. Kesu didn't know whether he could perform *Theyyam* in an alien land. He agreed as the amount they offered was high, something he could never earn even if he worked for his entire life in Saket.

"Malu is a lawyer and Mira is still studying. I should give Mira good education. She should live happily and nothing unfortunate should happen to her like...," Kesu hugged Ravi and Ravi felt drops of warm tears fall on his neck.

"Evelyn has made all the arrangements. Everything will be fine. See that you take all the *Theyyam* costumes with you. I am accompanying you so you need not worry," Ravi patted him on his shoulders.

"Will I be able to perform Ravi?" Kesu asked with his eyes brimmed with doubt and fear.

"You are Kesavan, the all-knowing. You are the *koladari.* How can you carry such self-doubt in your heart?" Kesu listened in silence as Ravi spoke.

"I should meet madam Vasudara before we leave. I am indebted to her," Kesu sighed deeply.

"Kesu, you told me that you saw madam Vasudara lying in a pool of blood on the day of the accident. Did you see someone or something suspicious there?" Ravi's curious eyes popped out inquisitively.

Kesu thought for a while and scratched his head," Well… let me try to recollect. I was afraid whether I would be blamed if people saw me there. So, I ran fast…but I saw a car pass by… it was a Ford like… er… the one Suresh Chandran has…"

Ravi stared at Kesu and neither of them spoke for some time.

"Malu has bought new dresses for us and you should see Latha in *salwar kameez*, the dress she once detested the most. She looks much younger in that..," Kesu broke the silence and both the men laughed as they walked towards the palace.

Glossary

Maricha	-	mythological demon in the epic Ramayana who had the ability to shape-shift.
Vishu	-	Hindu festival celebrated in the Indian state of Kerala.
Medam	-	corresponds to the English months of April- May
Kavu	-	traditional name given to sacred groves
Mundu	-	garment worn around the waist in the Indian states of Kerala, Tamil Nadu, Lakshadweep and Maldives
Daivam	-	God
Thambran	-	his highness
Set mundu	-	traditional clothing of women in Kerala
Karkitakam	-	corresponds to English months July - August

Kalamezhuthupatu	-	a ritual art form of Kerala wherein the deity's form is drawn on the floor using coloured powders. It is performed as part of the rituals to worship and propitiate certain gods.
Chingam	-	corresponds to English months August - September
Moksha	-	Hindu scriptures describe Moksha as liberation from the endless cycles of birth, death and rebirth.
Kali yuga	-	in Hinduism it is believed to be the last of the four ages. It is believed to be the present age that is full of conflict and sin.

Bibliography

Ritual As Ideology: Text and Context in Teyyam, (New Vistas in Indian Performing Arts, no.5), Chandran T.V, D.K. Printword (P) Ltd., New Delhi, 2006

Puranic Encyclopaedia, Vettam Mani, Motilal Banarsidass Publishers Private Limited, Delhi, 2010